The Vecellio Connection

A Genevieve Lenard Novel
By Estelle Ryan

First published 2016
Copyright © 2016 by Estelle Ryan

Acknowledgements

Writing is fun. It gives me energy. It makes me happy. But my life is rich, nuanced, interesting and filled with love because of the many amazing people surrounding me.

I realise every day just how invaluable your support is to me. Charlene, Linette, Moeks, Julie, Jane, Jola, Ania, Maggie, Krystyna, Kamila, Hubert, Tomek, TJ and Patrick – thank you so much for standing by me and cheering me on. I love and value each one of you.

RJ, you have my undying love for your amazing editing. Anne Victory, for coming through and TJ for your superb help. You are the team that makes my books shine.

Last, but most definitely not least, I want to thank each of you for reading Genevieve's adventures. And for your support. Your messages, posts and comments on Facebook and my blog never fail to make my day brighter and give me even more motivation to get cracking on the next book.

Dedication

To all my readers

Chapter ONE

"Um? Doctor Lenard?"

I looked away from the monitor with my open inbox and glared at one of the other fourteen monitors in front of me. The micro-expressions of Timothée Renaud, personal assistant and general office manager of the exclusive Strasbourg-based insurance company Rousseau & Rousseau, revealed grave concern. It took me a second to analyse Timothée's *depressor anguli oris* muscles pulling the corners of his mouth down and his *corrugator supercilii* muscles drawing his eyebrows downward. This was not his usual discomfort with me displayed on his face. It was something else. "What's wrong?"

"Um... There's a Monsieur Gallo downstairs insisting on seeing you." He leaned away from the screen as if expecting a verbal attack.

I couldn't even manage a small nod. Not when Timothée had just named the man who had been sending me threatening emails for the last eight months.

It had been exactly three hundred and eleven days since I'd been instrumental in making sure Gallo's business partners and best friends had been arrested for numerous white-collar as well as more violent crimes. The kidnapping of a law enforcement officer's family members had brought them to our attention. My team, who were also my friends, had helped me save the two young people who'd been kidnapped. That case had put an end to these men's reign of fear in Rio de Janeiro.

Our success had not been complete. Gallo had escaped and had been moving from country to country, sending me emails every Wednesday, promising to avenge the loss of what he called his family. The last two weeks I had not received any emails from him and had become increasingly discomfited by it. His presence in the foyer of the building next door might explain why.

The shock of Tim's news rendered me speechless. Even though I had many questions, I couldn't utter a sound. I couldn't even move.

"Doctor Lenard?" Timothée cleared his throat and squinted through the glass doors to my left into the team room. "Anyone! Yoo-hoo! I need some help here!"

I wanted to tell him that shouting was unnecessary, but my face felt paralysed. I sat frozen in my chair, darkness entering my peripheral view. Being on the autistic spectrum, fighting shutdowns was one of my biggest challenges. A daily one.

Footsteps entered my viewing room, but I could only focus on taking my next breath. And not giving in to the darkness threatening to claim me.

On the next inhale, I called up Mozart's Symphony No.36 in C and mentally listened to the first two pages of the ingenious work that had only taken Mozart four days to compose. A few deep breaths later, I looked down at the hand resting on my forearm and the darkness receded. I was only comfortable with the physical closeness and touch of one person.

"Jenny?"

It took another two bars before I could pull my eyes away from Colin Frey's hand and look into his face. I swallowed and blinked a few times. "I'm here."

He smiled. I had used his phraseology.

The first time he'd asked me where I went when I shut down, I hadn't understood his question. Physically, I had not gone anywhere. After knowing him for three and a half years and being romantically involved with him for three years, I understood neurotypical communication a bit more every day. Not that it always made sense.

I winced. My mind was veering off to safer ground, avoiding the danger that was downstairs.

"Doc, you have to snap out of your little Mozart bubble." Colonel Manfred Millard knocked on my desk to get my attention. He was standing to my right, glowering at me. "That bloody bastard refuses to speak to anyone but you and I want to know whether you're going to speak to him or whether I'm going to throw his murdering arse in jail so he can rot there."

"Prisons in France are too modern and human rights are generally too well observed for anyone to rot." I moved closer to Colin when Manny's eyebrows lowered and his chin jutted. "You were using an expression."

"Of course I was. Now tell me what you want to do."

The oldest member of our team, Manny was the only law enforcement officer and constantly reminded everyone to stay within the confines of the law. Our IT expert Francine, one of the best hackers in the world, frequently ignored Manny's numerous warnings. Colin's skills as a thief were well-respected in the crime world and used by Interpol to retrieve top-secret documents and data. In the past three years he'd come to greatly respect Manny, but still considered laws and rules to be mere guidelines.

"Daniel is two minutes out." Vinnie, the largest man I'd ever known and also one of my best friends, was leaning against the doorframe separating my viewing room from the team room. Daniel Cassel was a GIPN leader—similar to America's SWAT or Canada's Emergency Response Teams. Vinnie frequently joined Daniel's team for training sessions. "He's bringing the team. This motherfucker is not getting away again."

I turned back to the fifteen monitors in front of me. My viewing room and these monitors were where I used my expert skills when I watched recordings and analysed the nonverbal communication of suspects, witnesses and any other persons of interest. Francine had set up and secured our entire system, which included access to the security videos of Rousseau & Rousseau's foyer in the building next door.

Three clicks later, the video feed came up on three monitors—one for each camera in the foyer. Nine years ago, I had entered through that door to start my job at Rousseau & Rousseau. Then there had been no security guards, cameras or limited access to the insurance company. Those security measures had been brought in when the cases we investigated as a team working directly for the president of France had become increasingly dangerous. We had also moved our investigations into the building next to Rousseau & Rousseau, access from one building to the other limited to a select few people.

The security guard in the foyer was a retired GIPN officer and Daniel's former team leader. He was leaning back in his chair, wearing the bored expression found on most security guards' faces. It was an illusion. He wasn't staring into space. He was looking at Gallo's reflection in the antique mirror hanging above a small eighteenth-century table.

I looked at the man who had tried to intimidate and terrorise me with his threatening emails. He was sitting on one of the two leather chairs across from the security desk, his ankle resting on the knee of his other leg. A position of comfort, indicating that he didn't feel the need to be alert, ready to attack or defend.

He was wearing a bespoke suit, yet it didn't fit him well. I leaned forward. He'd lost weight. The last time I'd seen Marcos Gallo, his face hadn't had the gaunt look it had now. He did, however, have the same over-confident posture and smirk that pulled at one side of his mouth.

Gallo had worked his way up from humble beginnings. He'd grown up in one of the poorest areas in Rio de Janeiro, but through education and hard work had become a very successful businessman. That was the legal side of his life and only part of what had contributed to his wealth. Stealing five paintings in 2010 and getting away with the theft of sixty-three million euros in diamonds three years later had brought him great black-market wealth.

The Brazilian authorities had seized any and all assets they could find, but Gallo had been prepared. In the last six months, Francine and I had found sixteen accounts he'd opened in countries all over the world. Most of these countries' banking laws made them attractive for law-breaking individuals to hide their ill-gotten gains there. Thirteen of the accounts had been drained since his escape. Francine enjoyed speculating what he'd done with the seventy-eight million euro. I didn't enjoy speculating. Since Gallo was waiting to meet with me, I now had the perfect opportunity to receive an answer to that question.

Onscreen, the front door to the foyer swung open and Daniel entered, his gun drawn. Right behind him was Pink, the IT expert of Daniel's GIPN team. Two more team members followed into the foyer, their weapons trained on Gallo as they surrounded him.

Gallo leaned back in his chair and smiled. I narrowed my eyes at his response to having four guns aimed at his head. His ankle still rested on his knee, his hands were not fisted and his arms were a comfortable distance from his torso on the armrests of the chair. He was not feeling threatened. Yet he couldn't hide the micro-expressions revealing distress. Curious.

Daniel took a step closer to Gallo. The GIPN leader was in full combat uniform, his bulletproof vest adding to his muscular chest, his bald head covered with a helmet. "Keep your hands where we can see them. You move and you'll have bullet holes all over that fancy suit of yours."

Daniel Cassel was one of the calmest people I'd met. His astute observations, patience, understanding and smart handling of situations no longer surprised me. Neither did this anomalous behaviour. Even though it was uncharacteristic, I remembered Daniel's rage when he'd helped us save the teenagers. He'd been outraged that anyone could cut the finger off a young woman to ensure his power over the law enforcement officer he'd been blackmailing.

"I wouldn't mind seeing holes in that asswipe's suit," Vinnie said from the door.

"He's more use to us alive, big guy." Manny stared at the monitors, his *levator labii superioris* muscle curling his top lip. "We need to know what he's doing here."

Onscreen, Gallo's smile widened and he turned his arms until his open hands were facing up. He glanced above the door at the camera aimed at the foyer, then looked at the one on the far end of the foyer aimed at the door. He winked. "I want to speak to you, Genevieve. I know you want to speak to me too."

Daniel inhaled to speak, then held his breath for two seconds. He slowly let it out and tilted his head. "Why do you want to speak to Doctor Lenard?"

"Because I don't want to speak to him." Gallo didn't move his eyes from the camera, just nodded towards Daniel. "Neither he nor anyone else will understand me as well as you do."

"There's no way Jen-girl is going to speak to that bastard." Vinnie rested his hands on his hips, his thumbs facing back. Argumentative. "Don't tell me you're going to listen to that killer, old man."

Manny inhaled to respond, but Gallo's voice drew our attention back to the monitors. He was still looking into the camera. "Genevieve, I have information that can save lives. Hundreds of lives. No, thousands of lives. And I'm not going to give this to anyone but you. If you want to know what information I have, you have to speak to me. If you want to know why I'll only speak to you... well, you'll have to speak to me. And just in case your protective entourage is thinking about putting me in some police interrogation room or prison cell, please tell them that I will not say a word if I even sniff transport somewhere. It's either you or nobody, here or nowhere."

Gallo kept one eyebrow raised for a few seconds, then inhaled sharply. He schooled his expression, but not fast enough. I'd seen the micro-expression revealing physical pain.

"What do you see?" Colin rested his hand on my forearm. It had become an unconscious habit on his part, but it had become instrumental in grounding me.

I focused on the strength of his hand lightly touching my skin and analysed the last few minutes. "He's been truthful in everything he's said. But he has ulterior motives."

"Anyone with three functioning brain cells can see that, Doc." Manny narrowed his eyes at the monitor where Gallo was once again lounging in his chair. "I want to know what his bloody motives are."

I tried to keep my mind trained on Gallo and his nonverbal cues. I really did. But the words burst from my lips. "It's impossible to have only three functioning brain cells. Neurons are the basic functional units of our brains. They send electrochemical signals to other neurons and can send signals to specific target cells over long distances. These actions require around one hundred billion neurons and trillions of synapses interconnecting them. Each neuron needs up to fifty glial cells for structural support, protection and more. No one can be alive with only three functioning brain cells. It's a ludicrous statement."

Manny stared at me, his brow lowered, his jaw clenched. "Are you going to speak to him or not?"

I thought about this. Gallo had spent excessive amounts of money to ensure we couldn't trace him, or if we did, we would be too late to find him at the hotel or restaurant where he'd accessed the internet. Like Manny, I was also curious to find out why, after all this time, money and effort, he would appear at my place of work, knowing that he'd be arrested. "I'll speak to him."

"Not without me, you won't." Vinnie took a step into my viewing room. "You said yourself that sick bastard is playing all of us like a chess game."

"Don't get your knickers in a knot, criminal. Of course Doc is not speaking to him alone. He can speak to her, but Daniel, you and I will be there."

"Stop." I got up and looked at Vinnie. "If you're going to quote me, do it correctly. I said Gallo would be good at chess. His actions have shown how good he is at strategizing and thinking ahead." I turned to Manny. "Vinnie isn't a criminal. Not anymore. Your recent use of 'big guy' is more accurate. And he doesn't wear knickers. It's an illogical expression that I do wish you would not use. Now can you please get Daniel to move Gallo to the conference room so I can speak to him?"

"Um, Doctor Lenard?" Timothée waved from the monitor on the far left. "I... um..."

"What Tim has difficulty saying is that I would rather not have that man in my place of business." Phillip Rousseau stepped in behind Tim's chair. As always, he wore a tailored suit, a perfectly folded burgundy handkerchief peeking from his jacket pocket. He was the owner of Rousseau & Rousseau. He was also one of the very few people I held in high regard. When he'd hired me nine years ago to work for his company, I'd never expected him to take on a parental role in my life.

If it hadn't been for my extensive training in nonverbal communication and psychology, my non-neurotypical mind would never have registered Phillip's deep affection and concern for my wellbeing. I saw evidence of that on his face now. "I will be safe. Vinnie, Manny and Daniel will be there."

Colin cleared his throat. "Me too, but I won't be carrying a weapon or fists that could fell a tree." He squeezed my arm. "A silly expression, love."

"I would hope so." I looked back at Phillip. "Is your concern for your business?"

"You know it's not."

"Right then." Manny turned towards the door. "I'll get Daniel to secure Gallo and take him to the conference room."

Phillip glanced at me, then back at Manny. "Use the large conference room."

It took ten minutes for Daniel and Pink to settle Gallo in the conference room. He didn't resist when they handcuffed him and gripped his elbows, leading him to the elevator. Manny and Vinnie were first in the small elevator that took them to the basement where they would take another elevator to Rousseau & Rousseau's reception area. When they'd designed the security of our workspace, the small elevator had been strategic. Three large men would fit uncomfortably in that space, making it hard for a large assault team to reach us at the same time.

By the time Colin and I reached the reception area, Tim had calmed down slightly, his shoulders no longer reaching for his ears. He was, however, still sending concerned glances in the direction of the large conference room. "I haven't heard any shouting or shooting, so I think it's safe for you to enter."

Colin smiled warmly at the young man and walked next to me down the corridor. Timothée had only been working as Phillip's personal assistant for the last two and a half years. It had not been enough time for him to be comfortable around me. Whenever Colin was with me, he only addressed Colin. When he had to speak directly with me, his facial muscles contracted in numerous expressions of worry and discomfort and his skin fluctuated between being pale and flushed.

The door of the conference room was closed. Colin took his hand off the door handle when I slowed down and stared at the door with wide eyes. I took a shaky breath and mentally wrote another two lines of Mozart's Symphony in C. The beauty of the harmonic arrangement of this work brought calm to my erratic thoughts. It had been a trying eight months of weekly being threatened by the man now waiting for me behind this door. I took the time to remind myself that he was not alone in there. I had Colin and three armed men who would protect me with their lives.

I pulled my shoulders back and nodded at Colin. His smile was genuine. And filled with affection. I'd come to accept the irrationality of feeling empowered by the unmistaken evidence of his love. I held onto that as he opened the door and I walked into the room.

Gallo was sitting at the far end of the table, his cuffed hands resting on his lap. Still he maintained the appearance of confidence and comfort. Daniel was to his right, his assault rifle aimed at the floor. His helmet was on the table next to Pink's, his muscle tension revealing his readiness to act at any second. Pink was on Gallo's other side, his body language mirroring Daniel's. Neither looked at me when I entered.

Manny was slumped in a chair to Gallo's right, looking uninterested. This show of indifference and incompetence had often aided Manny in getting suspects to relax their pretence in the face of such lack of a challenge. Vinnie was standing next to the door, his arms crossed. He was an imposing figure, the scar running from his left temple to his chin and under his black t-shirt adding to his intimidating appearance.

"Genevieve." Gallo's initial expression was replaced by a false smile. But I'd seen the genuine pleasure and wondered what he would say next. "Checkmate."

Daniel raised his rifle and aimed it at Gallo's chest. Manny narrowed his eyes, his top lip curling slightly. I took another step closer, my one hand slightly raised to stop Manny from reacting and giving Gallo what he was looking for.

We were dealing with a person who displayed all the signs of a psychopath. Speaking to him like I would to a neurotypical person would not render results. I took my time forming my thoughts and sat down next to Manny, placing him between me and the man who was looking at me with joyful challenge around his eyes and mouth.

"There can be no checkmate without a king." I watched

as his eyes widened slightly and I knew I had correctly connected his presence with his body language. "The game you've been playing with me can no longer be sustained. Someone has taken your king, your power away from you and now you want to use me to take revenge on them. I will not do that. I am not your pawn."

Gallo's body relaxed, his facial muscles losing their tension. The smile he gave me was genuine, lifting his cheeks. The cuffs on his hands rattled when he pointed from his chest to me and back. "This here. This is the reason I wanted to speak to you. No one else would get this. Everyone else would think I was making a threat."

"You are underestimating everyone else." I looked around the room. Colin was standing next to Vinnie. Daniel had lowered his weapon, but didn't take his eyes off Gallo. "All of these men would easily come to the same conclusion. They would 'get this'. Did you underestimate the people who are the reason you came to me? Did your arrogance impair your judgement so severely that you couldn't see how they were manipulating *you*?"

Gallo's lips thinned. "It wasn't my arrogance. It's their lack of true vision. Such idiots. They don't understand what is truly important."

"Yet you do." In the minds of people like Gallo, they alone had true comprehension.

"Of course I do." This time his smile wasn't genuine. "But you're not going to get me to give away my information so easily. You'll have to work a bit harder for it, my dear."

"Work harder for what?"

"Saving all those lives."

"That claim is meaningless without proof that lives are in danger." I got up. "You are looking to feed your need for attention. I will not give that to you. You have nothing of value to offer."

I didn't wait for a response and I didn't look at any of the other men in the room. My hand was already on the door handle when Gallo laughed softly. "You're also going to make me work for it, aren't you?"

I glanced back at him. The joy of playing a game was back on his face. I turned and stared at him for another four seconds. "Give me proof."

His chin lowered in the slightest of acknowledgments. "What's the time?"

I didn't answer.

"I'm asking this to give you proof."

"It's sixteen minutes past ten." Manny's bored tone was convincing.

Gallo's eyes widened. "Fantastic. That means you can see it all in action. At quarter past ten a heist started. It's happening right now and will for the next... oh, I don't know... maybe for the next fifteen minutes. If you hurry, you might just be able to save some poor idiot's life."

Manny shifted in his chair. "This is not enough information. You could be talking about a heist taking place in Brazil."

"But I'm not." Gallo sneered as he looked at Manny. He shook his head and looked back at me. "The longer you stand here, the more time you waste. Go and find the heist I'm talking about. You'll see. It's a very special, very unique type of heist."

"Then what?" I saw only truth in Gallo's revelations, but it was only the beginning of the game he wanted to play.

"Then we negotiate." He leaned back and rested his cuffed hands on his stomach. "Then I tell you what I want and give you something that will make you happy to give in to my demands."

Manny and then Vinnie started pushing him for more information, but I knew he wasn't going to reveal anything beyond what he had already given me. I left the room and the arguing behind me. When I reached the elevator, I was relieved to feel Colin's presence next to me. He took my hand in his and held it until we reached my viewing room. I hoped we wouldn't be too late.

Chapter TWO

"I had no control. No matter what I did, I had no control."
Monsieur Norbert Sartre threw his arms in the air for the
third time since we had arrived in this quiet street in the
north-eastern part of Strasbourg. When he wasn't repeating
himself in his high-pitched voice, he was glancing fearfully at
his car.

I turned from the short man in frustration and looked
around the quiet street. There were not many places that
looked this deserted in a well-developed city with one of the
lowest unemployment rates in France.

We were in the industrial area of Strasbourg. Most car
dealerships and large outlets had their warehouses here, the
main streets carrying much less traffic than in the city centre.
Not one car had passed us in the side street where we had
found Norbert.

As soon as Colin and I had reached my viewing room after
talking to Gallo, I had looked for any reports on heists.
Without Francine's hacking expertise, it had been a much
slower process. I had been annoyed that Francine hadn't
been there to help. I truly didn't understand women's
enjoyment of manicures. On Colin's suggestion, Pink had
joined us, but even his advanced searches hadn't found any
ongoing heists. Not until it had been over.

Pink had received an alert about a driver who'd phoned the emergency services claiming to have been car-hacked. At first I'd thought it had been a mistake in the report, but Pink had insisted that the driver had shouted over and over that he'd been car-hacked. By then Daniel had left the two other GIPN officers to guard Gallo and had joined Vinnie and Manny in the team room. We'd all left for the scene of the car hacking.

I pushed my gloved hands in the pockets of my winter coat and glanced at the sky. This was a most unwelcome cold front. It had snowed early this morning and looked like it was about to start again. The tracks in the snow on the street revealed that Monsieur Sartre's car had been the only one to enter the street after this morning's fall. In front of the green BMW were no other tracks, only two sets of shoe prints leading further into the street.

"Norbert, take a deep breath and tell us what happened. We cannot help you when we don't know what happened and what was taken." Daniel's posture and tone aimed to instil trust. Apart from Phillip, he was the best natural negotiator I'd come across. "Why don't you start with telling us where you were going?"

Norbert looked at Daniel, the muscles in his pale face contracting while he attempted to regain his composure. After a few seconds, he inhaled deeply and let it out loudly. "I was going to Le Pinceau. I'm friends with Olivier Bissette and he agreed to mediate the sale of two of my paintings."

"Your paintings?" The slight hitch in his voice had caught my attention. I was familiar with the art gallery he was talking about. Phillip had insured a few paintings bought from

Le Pinceau. It was a well-respected establishment in the art community in France.

He lifted one shoulder. "My family's paintings."

"Where are those paintings now?"

"Gone!" Fear constricted the muscles in his throat, causing the word to come out at a much higher pitch. "Those two bastards took my paintings. How am I supposed to get out of this mess now?"

I was still trying to prioritise my questions when Colin stepped forward. "What paintings did they take?"

"Two Vecellios."

Colin's eyes widened. "You own two Vecellios?"

"My grandfather collected them. I'm not a big Vecellio fan." He pushed his hands through his dark hair, messing up the careful styling. "I inherited all the paintings as well as my family's failing business when my father died last year. I never really liked the paintings. Selling them was my last attempt to salvage the business. If this cash infusion didn't work, I was going to call it a day."

"What day?" I asked.

Norbert looked at me in confusion. "Pardon?"

"Never mind that." Manny waved his hand around as if to erase my question. "So you were going to sell the paintings. Where were you when you were car-jacked?"

"I wasn't car-jacked." Norbert closed his eyes and shook his head. "Not that I really know what constitutes a car-jacking. Isn't that when some thug puts a gun to your head when you're at a red light, makes you get out and drives off with your car?"

"That's roughly the definition, yes," Daniel said.

Norbert threw his arms in the air, then shook both index fingers at his car. "Well? Does it look like someone drove off with my car?"

"Did you lose control of your car?" Pink had been quietly standing next to Daniel, observing and listening.

"Yes!" Norbert looked up at the sky for a few seconds, shaking his head. "Do you people not listen to me at all? That's what I've been saying from the beginning. It was as if my car became possessed. It just took off all by itself. I couldn't brake, I couldn't slow down, I couldn't turn the steering wheel. Hell, I couldn't even open the door to jump out. I didn't know if this car was going to drive itself into the river and kill me. I've been reading about this, you know. About cars being hacked. This is what happened here, isn't it?"

I swallowed back my frustration. When panicked, neurotypical people seldom relayed information in a rational and chronological manner. Even after everything Norbert had just told us, I still didn't know exactly what happened.

"My apologies, Norbert." Daniel's sincerity was genuine. "Where did you first realise you no longer had control of your car?"

"I was coming down Rue le Fleur, three blocks away from Le Pinceau, when I couldn't slow down to turn right into Rue de Louise. I braked, pulled up the handbrake, but nothing happened. Whoever took over my car even stopped at the red lights and successfully manoeuvred around other cars."

"Why didn't you phone the emergency services?" Manny asked.

"Because my freaking phone didn't work!" Norbert took a

few deep breaths. "I tried. A few times. But my phone had no signal at all. Nothing worked. It was horrifying."

I agreed. Routine and having control over my life brought calm to my non-neurotypical mind. Having that taken away from me even in its smallest form could send me into a shutdown for hours or at the very best bring on a paralysing panic attack.

"Then what happened?" Manny asked. "Where did the car go?"

"It drove around for about ten minutes before it purposely came in this direction." He swallowed and crossed his arms tightly over his chest. "Two men were waiting here when the car rolled to a stop. They had guns aimed at me the whole time. When the car stopped, one man pulled open the door and told me that I'd die if I moved. I didn't move. He opened the boot, took both paintings, thanked me and walked off with his partner."

My eyes narrowed. "They did something else before they thanked you. What?"

"Nothing. They thanked me and walked off."

"You rubbed your neck, then touched your mouth." I pointed at his feet. "And you shifted three times. You are not being truthful. Did you recognise them? No. Did they steal something else? Aha. What else did they take?"

Norbert took a step away from me. "Nothing. They only took the two paintings."

"Don't bother lying to her, dude." Vinnie snorted when Norbert appeared offended at being called 'dude'. "Seriously. She could tell if you say you had one chocolate when you'd actually had two."

"Save us the time and just tell us what else they stole." Manny sighed with boredom. "Or else I might just have to arrest your arse and look through every single item you have in your safe."

Manny's threat had the desired effect. Norbert's eyes widened before he sighed. "They took my diamond ring."

"A diamond ring?" Vinnie's *levator labii superioris* muscle curled his top lip. "Dude, tell me it is not a pinkie ring."

Norbert straightened a bit. "There's nothing wrong with a man wearing a pinkie ring."

"Of course not." Vinnie sniffed. "Not if you're a sleazy salesman or a fat pianist."

Connections started forming in my mind. "How big was the diamond?"

"Half a carat." He sighed when I raised one eyebrow. "Two carats."

"Where did you get this diamond?"

The change in Colin and Manny's muscle tension indicated that they'd come to the same conclusions as I had. Manny pushed his hands deeper into the pockets of his oversized winter coat and lowered his brow. "Answer the question."

Norbert scratched his forehead, then slammed his hands on his hips. "I'm the victim here. I was kidnapped in my own car. Then two thugs stole paintings that have been in my family for generations. Why am I the one being interrogated?"

"Because it will help us find the people who are behind this crime." And confirm how Gallo knew about this heist. I watched as Norbert struggled with his decision.

His shoulders dropped in defeat. "I got this diamond

through somebody who knows somebody."

"Only one diamond?"

"No, dammit. I got three diamonds for an incredibly good price."

"Who is this somebody who knows somebody?" Manny asked.

"Shit." Norbert pushed his hands through his hair again. "What about my Vecellios? Are you even going to look for my paintings?"

"That will be one of our top priorities," Manny said. "You can be sure of that."

"Dammit. Okay, fine. The same gallery owner who was going to broker the sale of the Vecellios got me those diamonds."

"Do you know where he got the diamonds from?" Daniel asked.

Norbert shook his head. "No. I only know that there were quite a lot of diamonds to choose from. I didn't buy these as an investment, you know. I only bought them for myself, for my own jewellery. And for a ring for my wife. I wasn't going to ever sell them."

"Says all the criminals." Manny's disgust was clear on his face. "Can you even see that buying diamonds on the black market is no different than someone buying your bloody stolen paintings on the black market?"

Colour crept up his cheeks, his arms again tightly across his chest. "Of course. Um. Yes."

"Your car will be taken in for evidence and an officer will escort you home." Manny's tone invited no argument. "And you will give the officer the other two diamonds."

Norbert's lips thinned, but he nodded his agreement. Daniel led Norbert to one of his team members standing by the BMW. Pink stepped closer, his *frontalis* muscles raising his eyebrow with excitement. "I'm going to speak to Dan about this, but I really want in on this. Francine cannot be the only one having fun with this car hacking case. As far as I know, this will be the first of its kind in Strasbourg, if not in France, and I'm sure I can help."

"Stop trying to convince me…" Manny broke off before he used Pink's name. Once he'd told Francine it was wrong on many levels to call a man such a feminine colour. I had asked what levels Manny had used as a benchmark to reach such a conclusion. He'd glared at me and stomped off. He was glaring at Pink in a similar manner now. "Just do it. We can't have some pimple-faced kid hacking cars and racing them through our streets."

"How do you know it's a child?" My frown intensified. "And how do you know he or she has acne?"

"Logic, Doctor Face-reader." Manny tapped his index finger against his left temple. "I came to a logical conclusion."

"If you're using the study results that showed the average age of a cybercriminal to be seventeen years, you're still being presumptuous in your deduction. We have far too little evidence to point to the hacker being young. And we have no evidence to the condition of his or her skin."

"Then what… deduction would you come to, Doc?"

"None. You know I don't speculate."

Manny leaned closer and stared at my face. "But you have a running theory, don't you?"

I took a step back and resisted the urge to cross my arms over my chest. "It's merely a theory."

"Share, Doc."

I didn't want to. I loathed hypothesising, yet I knew that my team worked best when they could brainstorm, dismiss and analyse different ideas. I exhaled in defeat and counted off on my fingers. "Firstly, Gallo has a direct connection to stolen diamonds. We never discovered what he did with the diamonds from the 2013 heist. Secondly, hacking a car would fit Gallo's profile. He's shown a consistent interest in the latest technology and using it for his criminal purposes."

"So you're saying Gallo is behind this?" Manny waved at the car being raised to the back of a towing vehicle.

"No, what I'm saying is that your supposedly logical conclusion doesn't have as many tangible connections as mine."

"But why would Gallo steal two paintings?" Vinnie asked.

"Well, he does have a history of art heists." Colin was referring to the Léger, Matisse, Picasso and other paintings recovered from the estate of one of Gallo's best friends. Our investigation into that case had revealed that Gallo and the friends he called his brothers had stolen those artworks from the Paris Museum of Modern Art in 2010. Colin exhaled loudly. "Hmm. But what doesn't make sense is that he would steal these paintings or have them stolen while he is in our custody. After he surrendered himself."

"Exactly what I was thinking." Vinnie crossed his arms and tilted his head. "The dude could be playing some kind of mind-fuck game."

"I'm not familiar with such a game." My lips thinned when

Vinnie's smile turned mischievous. "You're not talking about a real game."

"Nope. I'm talking about those chess-like strategic stunts he likes so much."

I closed my eyes against the distraction Vinnie's latest expression offered and compared what he'd said to what I'd observed in the conference room an hour ago. "Gallo is definitely planning something. There was an element to his demeanour that has me questioning his true purpose for surrendering himself."

"You're talking about the fact that he looks like he's about to land himself in hospital," Manny said. "I also noticed the bastard looks poorly."

Vinnie and Pink suggested a few painful illnesses that they were hoping Gallo was suffering from. I turned away from them and once again scanned the street. Having one of the best hackers in the world as my best friend had made me paranoid about all computerised security. I did not yet know how someone could remotely gain full control over a vehicle, but planned to educate myself on this topic.

I wanted to get back to my viewing room. There were things I needed to research and I hoped Francine had already returned from her frivolous nail appointment.

But something else took priority. "We need to speak to the gallery owner."

"What did you say, Doc?"

I turned around and faced the men. "What is the gallery owner's role in this? Did he know about this heist? If he's the one who sold Norbert Sartre the diamonds, what is his connection to Gallo?"

"Well, let's go and find out then." Manny started walking towards his car. "We're not going to get any more answers here, so we might as well go get a few somewhere else."

Fifteen minutes later, I stood in front of a beautiful building in Strasbourg's historic old town, looking through the window into the art gallery. I loved the old buildings, the Gothic and Roman influences in the architecture, the cobbled streets and the covered bridges.

It was hard to get my feet to move. Manny and Daniel were already in the gallery, asking the young female assistant to call the owner. I didn't want to go inside. The gallery was spacious enough, but whoever had put the paintings up for display had no eye for logic, symmetry or even basic aesthetics. Paintings were haphazardly hung on walls or placed on easels that were at wrong angles while other paintings merely rested against any available vertical surface. Such visual chaos caused my non-neurotypical mind great distress.

"Jenny?" Colin's hand on my forearm was so light, I barely felt it through my thick winter coat. At first, I kept on focusing on his hand until I felt prepared to step into that horrifying disorder. I kept my eyes on the middle-aged man who entered the room from a side door. His was one of those faces that revealed every thought and emotion he experienced.

I stopped close to the door, giving myself some comfort at the easy escape if it became too much for me. Colin stilled next to me, then pulled his knitted cap lower over his brow and hunched into himself. I sighed.

Clearly he knew this gallery owner, but as another persona.

I hated his different disguises. It was unbearably hard for me to be deceptive. Trying to go along with Colin's different identities was most taxing, so I did what I was best at—I studied the man. He had glasses so thick that I wondered how much he could see.

"Gentlemen." He looked at me. "And lady. What can I do for you?"

"You can answer some questions for us, beginning with your name." Manny must have changed from the elegant fitted coat Francine had picked out for him to his old oversized winter coat. It was hanging loose around his frame, his hands disappearing in the large pockets. He fidgeted as if he was nervous or bored. He mixed up his nonverbal cues, but most people wouldn't notice.

"I'm Monsieur Olivier Bissette." He glanced at Daniel and Pink, his eyes narrowing until recognition widened them. "Why are the police visiting me? Did something happen to Mother?"

"We're not here about any family matter, Monsieur Bissette." Manny leaned forward and whispered loudly. "We're here about the illegal sale of forgeries and stolen diamonds."

"Oh, my goodness." Monsieur Bissette clutched the deep purple cravat at his chest and looked at his assistant. "Jeanne, go for lunch."

She looked as if she was about to argue, but then narrowed her eyes and nodded. The calculation that had flashed across her features had me wondering about what she would do. There had been malicious pleasure in the glance she'd given Monsieur Bissette. It was likely that Monsieur Bissette had been treating her badly and she was happy that he was in trouble with the law.

The door closed behind her and Monsieur Bissette clutched his hands together. A sign of self-comfort. "What questions do you have?"

"Did you agree to sell a painting for Norbert Sartre?" Manny asked.

"Um. No?"

Vinnie burst out laughing. "Dude. Seriously. You must be the worst liar I've ever come across."

"I have to agree with the big guy, Monsieur Bissette." Manny pointed his thumb at me. "She's a world expert at catching liars. But looking at you, I don't think we need her here. So why don't you just save us time and come clean?"

Monsieur Bissette stepped back until his thighs hit the desk. His *mentalis* muscle caused his chin to quiver, his eyes shining with tears. Colin sighed next to me and walked to Monsieur Bissette. He waved back the other men and they responded immediately by retreating and appearing less intimidating.

"Monsieur Bissette." Colin stopped in front of the man and held out his right hand. "Isaac Watts. I'm sure you remember me from five years ago?"

It took all my self-control to keep a gasp from escaping. Colin's German accent was strong even though his French was perfect.

"Isaac Watts?" Monsieur Bissette straightened slightly and stared at Colin. Then he leaned forward until it looked like he was about to kiss Colin. His eyebrows shot up and his facial muscles relaxed. "You're with them? Oh, thank all the goddesses. At least now I know I'll be treated well. I have never forgotten how much you helped me when there was that horrid misunderstanding with the Cézanne."

"Tell us about the misunderstanding, Fr... um... Watts." Manny's request was quiet, but strong.

Colin turned to put himself between Monsieur Bissette and the men. That would give the gallery owner more time to compose himself, but would also give him the impression that he was being protected. "Monsieur Bissette's gallery had been open for about three years when one of my clients from Bonn asked me to verify the painting he'd bought here while on a business trip. Within a few seconds I could see it was a forgery."

"Instead of going to the police and ruining my career, Isaac came to me." Monsieur Bissette pulled his shoulders back and faced the men. Either he didn't see me or didn't consider me a threat. "Unlike many other people in this industry, he believed me when I told him that I had no idea it was a forgery. I had all the provenance papers and even authentication certificates from two independent authorities. We'd all been fooled by that forger's expert work."

"It was really great work." Colin nodded and stood next to Monsieur Bissette. "Monsieur Bissette immediately returned my client's money and did everything he could to help me find this forger."

"You found him." I saw the pride on Colin's face.

"We did. We made sure Interpol got some anonymous tip about this man's work and within a week, he was no longer a threat to the art market." Colin looked at Monsieur Bissette. "I remember your outrage at anyone creating and selling art on the black market. Has your position on this changed?"

"No. Yes. No, definitely not." Consternation twisted his face into numerous expressions, fear the most prominent. "I hate these people!"

"Then why are you dealing with them, Monsieur Bissette?" Colin's tone was gentle.

"Because I made one small mistake!" Monsieur Bissette slapped both hands over his face and pressed hard for a few seconds. With a sniff he lowered his hands, his expression tortured. "He was going to destroy me, destroy everything I've worked to build in eight years."

"Who?" Colin asked softly.

"I don't know his name." He grabbed Colin's arm. "You have to believe me, Isaac. I never wanted this, but he didn't give me a choice. This man scared me." He glanced at the other men. "Much more than they do. He's dangerous."

"How did you meet?"

"I… oh, goddess! I sold him a forgery. I swear that I didn't know it was a forgery. It was like the Bonn situation all over again. The difference this time is that he came to me three weeks after I'd sold him the Picasso. Again, I had all the paperwork from the seller and everything had seemed legit. He wouldn't accept that I had no part in cheating him. He was furious, even grabbed a Degas from the wall and threatened to smash it on the ground. That's when I asked him what I could do to fix this."

"He didn't want to accept his money back?"

Monsieur Bissette slumped against the table, one hand pressed against his forehead. "I didn't have the money. I have a lot of stock here, but the market is not that strong at the moment. With all the terrorism happening in the world, people have decided to stop buying art. Or maybe it's global warming. I don't know, but the last eighteen months have been the worst since I started this business. I'm running on fumes these days, Isaac."

"Which means that you met this man within the last year and a half?" Colin gently steered him back.

"It was ten months ago. I was going to borrow the money from my brother to pay this man back, but he wasn't interested. He told me that he knew a way that would help us both. I would make enough money to keep my business afloat and he could get rid of some merchandise."

"What merchandise?" Even though Colin asked the question, I was quite sure I knew the answer.

"Diamonds. And before you shout at me, these were not blood diamonds. They are real, authentic diamonds, but they are stolen. I would never sell blood diamonds."

"Oh, Monsieur Bissette. Don't you think that maybe someone could've died in the acquisition of these illegal diamonds?"

"Oh, please don't make me think about this. I haven't slept one decent night in the last four months. I tell you now, having financial worries is much preferable to having some crazy man threaten me."

"Where did you find clients for the diamonds?" Pink asked.

"Rich people are the most tight-fisted bastards on this planet. I know some of my clients quite well. Not all of them have the highest ethical standards when they're doing business. I used this knowledge and looked for those who were always looking for a bargain. They weren't difficult to find, I tell you."

"How many diamonds have you sold?" Manny asked.

Monsieur Bissette wiped his brow with the back of his hand. "Thirty-four."

"I beg your pardon?" Manny leaned forward. "It sounded like you said thirty-four."

"Oh, dear goddesses." The gallery owner's shoulders hunched as he exhaled in defeat. "You heard right. Most of those diamonds are around two and a half carats, a few larger. I'm guessing that my clients had the larger diamonds cut into smaller diamonds. Even though it diminishes the value of the larger diamond, it does make it easier to… you know… to hide the fact that it was stolen."

"What can you tell me about Norbert Sartre's Vecellios?" Colin asked.

"They've been in the Sartre family for many years. I found out the grandfather was a collector when Norbert brought a small Vermeer to sell last year. He's been trying to keep his family business from going bankrupt. Times are really hard on all of us."

"Have you actually seen the paintings? Or the authentication certificates?"

"No." Monsieur Bissette stared at Colin and for a moment I thought he would cry. "Are you asking me because they're forgeries? I was going to sell more forgeries? Oh, my career is over. My life is over. Everything is over."

Colin patted Monsieur Bissette's shoulder. "I haven't seen those paintings yet and have no reason to believe they are forgeries. We're just asking questions at the moment."

Monsieur Bissette pressed his palm against his forehead and exhaled on a whimper. Vinnie turned away from the drama to look out the front window. Both Pink and Daniel barely succeeded in hiding their mirth.

I didn't understand how they could think this man's distress was humorous. I would ask Colin about this later, but there were far more pressing issues. "Can you describe the man who supplied you with the diamonds?"

"Of course I can. Even when I close my eyes to sleep, I see him. He's everywhere."

"Then describe him." I was growing weary with the man's dramatic reaction to the situation.

"About the same height as Isaac, but with much more muscle. The kind of muscle that the giant over there has. Like he spends hours every day lifting weights. He has light hair, a few freckles on his nose, wears a Tag Heuer wristwatch and has a tattoo on the inside of his left wrist."

Colin took a step back, his eyes wide, his lips tight. "What tattoo?"

"A tattoo of a spider. A black widow spider."

Chapter THREE

"At least tell me you like the colour." Francine pushed her nails in front of my face, successfully taking my attention away from the hostility between Manny and Colin.

I took a step back, glaring at her nails. "It reflects like real silver."

She turned her hand and stared at her fingers. "I know. Isn't this the coolest ever? Personally, I like to think of this colour as liquid mercury. My toes are the same colour. Want to see?"

"No." My tone was harsh, but I didn't even attempt to temper it. If I acquiesced, she would take off her red knee-high boots to show me. Today, Francine was wearing tight black trousers with a shiny finish down the sides and a deep red silk blouse that perfectly matched her boots. The large silver earrings, bracelets and four fine chains around her neck matched her nail polish. Unlike the stereotypical woman who was obsessed with her appearance, Francine had a depth to her emotional intelligence that made her penchant for frivolity tolerable. Despite her unrelenting efforts, I remained uninterested by fashion. "What do you know about hacking the computer systems in vehicles?"

"Ooh!" Her bracelets jingled as she clapped her hands. "I know I shouldn't be excited about crime, but I'm totally stoked about this one. I mean, how often does one get to be the first to work a big case like this?"

"The first we know of." Pink was sitting at the large round table in our team room. He and Daniel were two of a select few people outside of our team who had access to our secure facility. They had wisely stayed out of the argument between Manny and Colin, and had taken their places at the table as soon as we arrived here.

Francine lowered her voice. "I checked. This is the first case in Europe involving crazy out-of-control hacked cars."

"Why are you whispering?" We could all hear her.

"Supermodel!" Manny slapped his hand on the round table. "Start talking about this hacking nonsense before I arrest you."

"Will you use your handcuffs?" She pouted and winked seductively at him. "Like the other night?"

The laughter in the team room drowned out Manny's cursing. I had seen the moment Francine had noticed the tension between Colin and Manny. With her flamboyance, she'd brought some lightness to the atmosphere. I didn't know what to do about the tension and trusted Francine to know the best way to calm Manny.

The two of them were an unlikely couple, but I'd come to the conclusion that it might be their differences that made their romantic relationship work. I'd been sceptical when they'd become romantically involved nine months ago, but so far they'd grown closer. And argued more—an element to their relationship that seemed to bring them both enjoyment and arousal.

Manny turned to Pink, then huffed in disgust at the

merriment on the younger man's face. "Start talking before I handcuff you. And don't even think about talking about anything but car hacking."

Pink pinched his nose, but didn't make any effort to dim his smile. "Right. Car hacking."

"No, I want to." Francine grabbed her tablet and rushed to the round table. She didn't wait for everyone to settle at the table before she started explaining. "So, modern cars are computerised and most are connected to the internet. There are many entry points for hackers to get into the system and take control."

Pink counted off on his fingers. "There's the engine and transmission ECU, the steering and braking ECU—"

"Stop." Manny lifted one hand. "What the bleeding hell is an ECU?"

"It stands for electronic control unit," Francine said. "And they are all over cars, like Pink said. There's also the airbag ECU, the Bluetooth system, the remote key and a bunch of other ways to access the computer system of a car."

"One of the biggest security risks automakers are yet to fix is the lack of an authentication system," Pink added.

"With all these connected computerised units, there needs to be a way to ensure that they are communicating with each other rather than with an unknown, outside source." Francine raised both eyebrows. "That source can be a hacker who wants to steer a car into an alley so he can steal some paintings."

"Holy hell." Manny rubbed one hand over his face. "Suddenly I'm glad that I haven't bought a new car yet."

"As much as I passionately hate that unsexy wagon of

yours, there's something to be said about being old-school."
Francine winked at him. "It's similar to a lot of spy agencies
going back to using typewriters. Russia was the one of the
first to go back to something that cannot be remotely
accessed."

"But that takes the fun out of your job, doesn't it?" Pink
leaned back in his chair. "Of course, I won't hack. I'm bound
by the oath I took as an officer of the law."

I held up my hand to stop him. "You're quite good at
limiting your micro-expressions, but I can see your
deception."

Daniel raised both eyebrows. "I think you better stop
talking, Pink. Unless it's something I can put in a report."

"Sir, yes, sir." Pink's salute and formal address were not in
agreement with the mischievousness around his eyes.

"Another thing to remember"—Francine tapped her silver
nail on the table—"is that every time a car goes in for a
service, it stands a chance of receiving counterfeit parts or
parts that have been embedded with code or with malware.
Even just having one's car cleaned could mean someone
could put a USB drive with a virus in the USB slot and your
car is no longer yours."

Pink leaned forward. "And if someone has access to your
car, they can also access your phone or computer if ever
those are connected to the car system via on-board Wi-Fi or
Bluetooth. They can have full access to your life."

For five seconds nobody spoke. It was a lot to process.
For me, it wasn't as much the information about hacking a
vehicle as it was the loss of control that I found most
perturbing.

Colin shifted next to me and cleared his throat. "We've talked about the car hacking, but we haven't talked about the stolen paintings yet."

"I would rather know what you know about that tattoo, Frey." All the tension that had eased returned to Manny's face. I had not been the only who'd noticed Colin's reaction to Monsieur Bissette's revelation. Once Manny had established that the gallery owner had nothing else of value to tell us, he'd ordered us to the cars. There he had interrogated Colin as if he was a suspect. Colin had refused to share his thoughts about the tattoo.

"And I will repeat myself until your deaf ears hear me: I first need to verify my suspicions. I'm not going to implicate someone who's not involved."

"He's right, old man." Vinnie leaned towards Colin, his loyalty always first with his best friend. "We know that you investigate every name we mention even in passing. Back off and give my man the time he needs. You know he'll come through."

I read the micro-expressions on Manny's face. "Manny trusts Colin. He's just impatient to have pertinent information."

"In other words, he's like a kid wanting to know what he's getting for Christmas even though it's only October." Colin smirked when Manny scowled. "Give me twelve hours. After that, I'll tell you what I know."

Manny slumped deeper into his chair. "Then you might as well bore us with art crap. What do you know about this Velario guy?"

"Vecellio." Colin took a calming breath. "Tiziano Vecellio

was born in the late fourteen hundreds and died in 1576. Most art scholars just refer to him as Titian. He was one of the most versatile painters of his time. He painted everything. Portraits, religious subjects, mythological creatures, landscapes. But most importantly, he led the Italian Renaissance."

Manny looked at Daniel. "Do you know which paintings Norbert had in his car?"

Daniel took a small notebook from a side pocket in his uniform pants. He paged through it and I knew when his eyes widened slightly that he'd reached the page he was looking for. "Norbert said it was *Diana and Venus* and *The Magician*."

"Hmm." Colin's *corrugator supercilii* muscles drew his eyebrows down and together. "That's odd."

"What's odd?" Manny grunted when Colin didn't answer him immediately. "Don't let me bloody wait, Frey. What the hell is odd?"

Colin ignored him and looked at Francine. "Double-check for me, would you? As far as I know, Vecellio never painted anything called *Diana and Venus* or *The Magician*."

Everyone watched Francine as she tapped and swiped her tablet screen. After two minutes, she shook her head. "Can't find those two. I've checked on all three of those websites you trust and did a separate search, but nada. Nothing."

"Hmm." Colin leaned his head back and looked at the ceiling. "I would have to see those works to be sure, but it could be Giordano Donati's work."

"Who the hell is Gigi Donato?" Manny asked.

"Giordano Donati was one of the best forgers of the

twentieth century. Donati died a free man at the age of seventy-three in 1954. By then he had flooded the art market with forgeries of Italian Renaissance artists."

"How is it that he never got caught?" Daniel asked. "Surely someone would've noticed duplicates of important paintings popping up all over the place."

"That's just it. Not all forgeries are copies of original paintings. There are also forgeries that are classified as 'in the style of.'" Colin looked at Manny and spoke slower and louder. "For the rest of the class, that means he painted original paintings, but did it in exactly the same style as, for example, Vecellio."

"Bugger off, Frey. I know what that means. You've explained it before. Or did your feeble mind forget that?"

Colin's smile was genuine. "Not at all. But I do worry about your aging memory."

"Stop digressing." I found this most annoying. "Do you know how many Vecellio paintings Donati created?"

"To date, seventy paintings have been attributed to Donati, of which forty-three are said to be Vecellios." Colin always became more animated when he talked about art and art crimes. "Nowadays, Donati's paintings can also fetch in the millions for each painting. He was a great artist."

"You'll have to explain a bit more for me." Daniel raised both shoulders. "I wasn't there the last time you explained the in-the-style-of forgeries. Why would it be a forgery if the original artist never painted it? Isn't a forgery only a forgery if it is a copy?"

"No," Colin said. "A forgery is also classified as such when the forger uses the same style, brushstrokes, paints and canvasses as the original artist did and then signs the painting as the original artist. I can paint something that looks like it came from Van Gogh's brush, but if I sign my name to it, all is legal and well."

"Huh." Daniel nodded his head slowly. "Didn't know that."

Manny asked Colin again about the tattoo and another argument ensued. I walked to my viewing room and sat down in front of the monitors. A few clicks of my computer mouse later and I was looking at the conference room video feed. Gallo was in the same chair he'd been when we'd left to find the heist.

Whenever we received a new case, I felt conflicted. On the one hand, I loved the new challenge, knowing that I was going to discover many disjointed pieces and connect them in order to find a complete picture of whatever crime was being committed. These were also the reasons I hated the beginning of new cases. The lack of information brought out an obsessive compulsion in me that I had to fight hard so it wouldn't consume my thoughts, my actions, my life.

Hyperfocus was one of my weaknesses. And one of my strengths. It had taken a lot of control and discipline to learn when to step back from a project. Too many times I would lose myself in something that had caught my interest only to resurface a few days later. While lost in my own world, I would forget to eat, drink, bathe and sleep.

That same compulsion was now pushing at my brain to find out why Gallo was looking ill, why he had sent us to discover this car hacking, what his involvement was in the hacking. I also felt compelled to determine why those two paintings were stolen, whether Norbert Sartre's diamonds were of importance and what Gallo's connection to the gallery owner was.

In an odd moment of reflection, I was grateful for the people in the room next to mine. Not only were they my team members, they were also my friends. And they always took it upon themselves to make sure I didn't get lost in my own mind, but also gave me the space and time to focus on finding answers.

"What are you thinking?" Colin sat down next to me and looked at the only monitor that was showing footage. "He's not looking well. Is that what you were thinking about?"

"No." I wasn't comfortable with emotional conversations and didn't want to enter one when we had so many unanswered questions.

It didn't stop Colin. His smile was gentle. "That short answer in that tone tells me that I really want to know what you were thinking before I came in."

I'd read a lot of books on relationships. Most of the advice given was naïve and irrational, but one thing they all emphasised was communication. I sighed and ordered my thoughts. "You make me stronger."

Colin's eyes widened. "Wow. Okay. Care to elaborate?"

"No."

He laughed. "Please?"

"If you insist." I pointed at the team room. "They, but especially you, bring a balance in my life I could not attain on my own. It makes me better at my job, but also stronger as a cognitive being." I swallowed. "Thank you."

Colin looked at me while I studied his expression. I didn't

need to be a world-renowned expert to see the deep affection on his face. He leaned towards me and took my hand in his. "It's because we all love you, Jenny. Although I love you a little more. And a little bit differently."

I didn't know how to respond to that, so I only nodded. After another two seconds, his expression changed. He knew me well enough to know there would be no further discussion. I grabbed the opportunity to change the topic. "I want to speak to Gallo."

"You and me both, Doc." Manny was standing in the doorway. "Giving us a random clue about a heist is not enough. I need to know more about whatever he's involved in. Whatever this thing is that you can save thousands of people from."

"I'm staying right here." Francine tapped a manicured nail on her desk, not taking her eyes off her computer monitor. "Pink and I will be looking for any chatter we can find about hacking cars."

"She's going places on the dark web I didn't know existed." Pink scratched his chin. "It's a good thing she's using her powers for good and not for evil."

Manny's lips thinned in disapproval, but he didn't say anything. He frequently complained about Francine's tendency to completely ignore the legality of what she accessed on the internet and how. She usually responded either by flirting with him or ignoring him.

I got up and walked to Francine's desk. "Don't limit your search to hacking cars. If there's any chatter about hacking any engines or large machinery, it might be worth looking into."

"Ooh!" She started tapping on her keyboard. "Are you

thinking about hacking turbines, power grids, airplanes?"

"Not in particular, but at this moment we can't rule out anything." I closed my eyes for a moment while I considered another question that had been in the back of my mind. I opened my eyes. "Where did Gallo come from?"

Francine's fingers froze above the keyboard and she glanced at me, one perfectly shaped eyebrow lifted. "Is this like an existential question? Or are you talking about his country of origin? Or... are...?"

I saw the moment my question made sense to her. "Yes, I'm talking about the route he followed coming to Rousseau & Rousseau."

"If you want us to backtrack his steps from here to wherever he might be staying, I'll get right on it." Pink looked at Manny. "I have legal access to all the CCTV cameras in Strasbourg's streets."

"Once you've located his accommodation, see if you can trace his steps back to how and when he entered Strasbourg." We could find valuable information in his hotel room or wherever he had been staying. "This is as important as finding any online discussions about the hacking of larger machinery or engines."

"Done, my bestest bestie."

I no longer reacted when Francine called me such ridiculous names. In the last three years, I had spent far too much energy trying to convince her that 'bestie' was not a word and the superlative suffix in 'bestest' was both redundant and superfluous. Even though I'd made the decision not to argue about such things, it was still hard to walk away from this. I did.

Colin followed me to the elevator, Vinnie right behind him. "No way you're speaking to that sicko alone, Jen-girl. We're all going."

"Not me!" Francine's bracelets jingled when she waved one hand without looking from her computer monitor. "Have fun, my lovelies."

I entered the elevator with Colin and Vinnie, knowing that Francine would be monitoring our interview with Gallo from her computer.

Three minutes later, we stopped at the conference door. I was behind Manny and Daniel, Colin at my side and Vinnie at our backs. On each side of the door was a member of Daniel's team. Their relaxed postures were deceptive. Not only did my training in nonverbal communication alert me to their readiness to act at any moment, my experience with this team confirmed it.

Manny turned to look at me. "Ready, Doc?"

"For what?"

Daniel laughed and reached for the door handle. "You should know better than to ask, Manny."

"Don't be too hard on the old man." Vinnie's tone was serious, his expression insincere. "He's a slow learner."

"Bugger off, all of you." Manny pushed past Daniel, opened the door and walked into the conference room.

We followed him in and the team member who was guarding Gallo inside the conference room stepped out after a terse nod. Gallo chuckled. "He doesn't like me."

"Nobody likes you, arsehole." Manny fell into a chair with a loud grunt. "I can't imagine you even like yourself."

Gallo's *buccinator* muscle pulled one corner of his mouth

into a disrespectful smirk. He made a show of slowly turning his head towards me. "Hello, Genevieve. Did you find the heist?"

I considered my answer while I took my seat next to Manny. Everyone else took the same places they had when we'd first spoken to Gallo. I thought about the profile I'd created on him in the last ten months. "We found something."

Just as I had expected, his pupils dilated at my evasive answer. He was enjoying this game. "Something? Was it good?"

"Crime is never good." I shrugged as if I didn't care. "But I have no way to determine whether the crime we found is the one you wanted us to discover."

"Really?" He raised one eyebrow. "Surely you give my intellect a little bit more credit than that. You are far too smart not to put the pieces together and find evidence pointing to me."

Again I shrugged. And waited.

His smile was small, but genuine. "Okay. I'll play. Two Vecellios, one diamond ring as a surprise bonus and a gallery owner who didn't know what he let himself in for when he agreed to sell those diamonds."

His face revealed numerous interesting expressions. I stored most of them for future reference and focused on what Gallo had revealed. I nodded. "What part did you play in that heist?"

"Oh, no, my dearest Genevieve. I'm not going to make it that easy for you." He shifted in his chair and wasn't quick enough to hide his wince. The corners of his mouth turned down and his nostrils flared. "You took away everything that was important to me. The least you owe me is to work for the information you need."

"The flaw in your reasoning is your assumption that I want or need your information. All you've proven so far is that you knew someone was going to steal paintings that were on their way to an art gallery. You have not given me any incentive to believe that there is any imminent threat or danger to anyone."

"You want more?" His tone was hard. "How about I tell you that President Godard is meeting with eleven other European leaders on Saturday afternoon at three o'clock? Or that they are going to discuss the current hostility between the EU and Russia? Or that there will very likely be a successful attempt on all their lives? Or that their spouses and families are all in danger even though seven of the twelve leaders sent their families to places of safety?" He leaned forward and his lips tightened, not from emotion. From physical discomfort. "Check this out if you don't believe me. But you'd do well not to dismiss my gift to you."

I didn't respond. Gallo was revealing so much more than just his words. That was why I relied completely on the interpretation of nonverbal communication to bring clarity to anyone's words. I was grateful that no one else spoke either.

"You want even more?" Gallo was fast losing his composure. Despite the controlled temperature in the conference room, sweat beaded above his lip and on his forehead. His movements had also become much less smooth. He inhaled loudly through his nose. "I'll give you more. I'll give you three sets. Goya and Rubens, Horace and Claude Joseph, and finally Monet and Cassatt."

"What the bloody hell does that mean?" Manny pushed his hands into his trouser pockets.

"I'm not talking to you." Gallo's tone was harsh, but softened marginally when he turned to me. "Verify that meeting. You'll see that I'm telling the truth. Then solve my little riddle. You'll be glad that you did."

I allowed my mind the time it needed to add the information Gallo had given to his past behaviour. "What do you want in return?"

"Ah. Genevieve." He gestured with his palm up towards me. "This is the very reason I came to you. No one else knows me as well."

"You didn't answer my question."

"I know." He slowly leaned back in his chair, his facial muscles held in tight control to portray enjoyment. "I will give you my request when you come back with the solved riddle."

Chapter FOUR

"Where did you get this intel from?" The voice of Lucien Privott, director of public relations for the president of France, boomed through my viewing room. "This is classified information. Highly classified!"

Manny shifted behind me, his breathing louder and increased. I was certain if I turned around I would see the supratrochlear artery raised on his forehead, his face red. Lucien's reaction had been immediate and strong when I'd relayed the information Gallo had shared. I'd insisted we Skype Lucien instead of a normal phone call. I'd wanted to see his reaction to the news. I was not disappointed.

"How many people have access to this information?" I asked before Manny could exacerbate the situation with one of his acerbic responses.

"This meeting was called by the leaders themselves. As far as I know, only a few of their trusted staff know about this." Lucien took a breath and looked up and left—recalling information. "Obviously, their spouses also know there is a meeting, but very few spouses are brought in on the topic. All they know is that they need to be somewhere safe while these discussions are taking place."

"What are they discussing?" Manny asked.

"This is way above your pay grade, Colonel Millard."

Lucien enounced Manny's rank with an unmistakable tone of disdain.

"Seriously, dude." Vinnie stepped away from the door and walked closer until he was within the view of the camera. "Do you really need us to kick your ass again like we did the last time? You know that we're best cronies with the president and his wife. All it's going to take is a phone call and then it will be your ass in a sling."

I twisted towards Vinnie and frowned at him. "Why are you talking like this?"

Vinnie winked at me. "This dude is not as smart as you, Jen-girl. He needs all kinds of metaphors to understand that we have the highest security clearance."

I was about to argue with Vinnie. We didn't have any such clearance. But he winked again and I sucked my lips between my teeth and bit down. I hated deception. It was as if the truth was pushing against my teeth, desperate to burst from my mouth.

"Do you really want to go another round with us, Privott?" Manny sounded bored. "It will be better for all of us if you just give us what we need so we can do our jobs."

"I need to... oh, dammit." Lucien slammed both hands on his desk. "I'm coming to you. If this is involving the president's and his wife's safety, I want... no, I *will* be part of this investigation. I'll see you soon."

"No, you wo—" Manny walked right up to the edge of my desk and shook his fist at the monitor that was now dark. "That bastard put the phone down in my bloody ear."

"It wasn't a phone call." I closed the Skype application. "And the expression 'to put the phone down' is antiquated unless someone is phoning you from a traditional landline. If it is a smartphone, they simply ended the call."

Manny spun to face me. "Do you have any idea how much I miss slamming the phone down in someone's ear? No matter how hard I stab that little red button on my smartphone, it doesn't give me the same satisfaction."

"I don't care how you feel about phones. We should focus on the case." I got used to a lot of things working with the neurotypicals on my team, but the constant digressions were the hardest to accept.

Vinnie chuckled. "She told you good, old man. Our Jen-girl doesn't care about your little prom-queen frustrations."

"Bugger off, cri… big guy." Manny rubbed one hand over his face. "Okay, I suppose we're going to have to deal with Privott nipping at our heels. That means he'll be annoying me, missy."

I held the breath I'd taken to ask about that expression and nodded.

"We can always send him on some random treasure hunt through the city." Vinnie looked at the ceiling and nodded, satisfied. "Yes, that's a really good idea. He'll be running around the whole day looking for stuff and we can do our jobs."

For a moment it looked like Manny would consider this mysterious hunt for treasures. Then he sighed and shook his head. "No, it's better that we keep him included in the investigation. Who knows when we might need his help. Supermodel!"

"I'm right here, handsome." Francine blew Manny a kiss

when he turned to glare at her standing behind him.

"What are you doing sneaking around like that?"

"I'm working on my ninja skills." She leaned closer to him and dropped her voice. "I plan to wear a black catsuit when I practise at home."

Manny took a step away from her and pushed his hands deep into his trouser pockets. "Stop being difficult, woman. I need you to find out anything and everything you can about this leadership meeting. I want to know about this before Privott comes and gives us his watered-down, censored version."

Francine's eyes widened with pleasure as she straightened to her full height—added to by her eight-centimetre heels. "If this is as hush-hush as Privott said, I'll need to practice my ninja hacking skills, handsome. Are you authorising it?" Manny didn't answer her. He merely stood there, glaring at her until Francine clapped her hands in glee. "Ooh, goodie!"

"If you get caught, I will deny any knowledge of this."

I didn't know which one of the many troubling issues to address first. I went with the most outrageous one and looked at Francine. "There is no such thing as ninja hacking skills."

Francine wiggled her fingers in the air. "Oh, there is, my bestest bestie. Just you watch how I find out what tie the president is going to wear to this super-secret meeting."

"Focus, supermodel." Manny snapped his fingers in front of Francine's face. "Do you have any other useful information?"

"Oh, do I ever!" She waved Pink into my viewing room.

Immediately, I leaned away from the growing crowd in my space. Even though my viewing room was designed to easily accommodate the entire team, for some reason, Pink's presence made me feel claustrophobic.

Colin must have noticed the widening of my eyes and my shallow breathing. He put his hand on my forearm and squeezed lightly. "Why don't we take this to the round table? I think we could all do with some coffee and cookies."

Vinnie looked from Colin to me and started pushing everyone out. "I baked a fresh batch of my auntie Helen's ginger-honey cookies yesterday. Three minutes and we'll all have coffee and cookies."

It took five minutes. Once we were settled with steaming mugs of coffee and Manny with his milky tea, Pink laid both his hands flat on the table. He looked around the table until his eyes rested on me. He appeared troubled. "I know I'm the outsider here, so you guys have to clue me in when I'm overstepping the line."

"Oh, honey, you didn't overstep any line." Francine patted his hand. "The viewing room was just getting a bit crowded. That's all."

Pink smiled at her, then looked at me. "They understand you much better than I do. If I do anything that makes you feel uncomfortable, please tell me. I'm a fast learner."

And not fooled by anyone trying to protect me from him seeing my weaknesses. I resisted the urge to cross my arms tightly over my chest. "Francine is right. There were too many people in my viewing room. Now can we please talk about the useful information?"

Francine nodded vigorously, but didn't say anything.

Instead she pointed with her open hand towards Pink. He smiled. "It wasn't just me who got this intel, but Francine insists that I tell you."

"Then bloody tell us." Manny grabbed another cookie and pushed it whole in his mouth.

"Okey-dokey." Pink leaned back from Manny and turned to me. "Well, we followed Gallo back as you asked. I won't bore you with the details, but we got the address of the hotel we think he's staying in."

"From there we tracked him even further back." Francine put her empty coffee mug on the table. "He came to Strasbourg by train."

"From where?" I asked.

"Give me a moment to tell the whole story."

I shook my head. "Don't tell a story. Just give us the final facts."

"You're such a spoilsport." Francine huffed. "Well, fine. We don't know how he got there, but we did trace him back to Amsterdam two days before he left Paris for Strasbourg. Then nothing. We have no idea how he got to Amsterdam."

"He could've hidden on a ship that docked in Rotterdam," Vinnie said. "Enough money can buy you a secret trip anywhere in the world if you're willing to sacrifice some luxuries."

"Anything else?" I put both hands on the armrests of my chair. When Francine and Pink assured me that they'd shared all pertinent information, I pushed up and walked to my viewing room. "I have to decipher this ridiculous code he gave us."

"No, Doc. I think you need to come with us." Manny

also got up and nodded towards the elevator. "You always see something extra wherever we go. We need your eyes at the hotel."

"Take a photo," I said over my shoulder. I didn't want to go into another establishment that challenged my sense of hygiene.

Manny followed me into my room and waited until I sat down. Then he sat on the chair to my right. He rested his elbows on his knees and lowered his head even more to emphasise the look he gave me. It was a look that annoyed me. Every time his *orbicularis oris* muscles caused that specific tightness around his lips and his *frontalis* muscles raised his eyebrows just so, I lost the argument. "Doc. Take supermodel's tablet. Or do your research on your smartphone. Just come with us and be there when we go through Gallo's hotel room. You know as well as I do that photos don't give you the same impression as being there."

He was right. But I really didn't want to go to a hotel with lots of unhygienic people. "I can't use Francine's tablet. It's not clean."

"Of course it's clean." Francine walked into my viewing room, holding her tablet out towards me. "Take this one."

"I'm not taking your tablet."

"It's not mine." She lifted her other hand and shook the empty box. "Brand spanking new. I did clean it up for you. I mean, I uninstalled all unnecessary apps, installed necessary ones and made it look almost like your computer. It's also got my super-duper search engine, so you'll find info here just as quick as on your computer."

"I don't want it." I didn't like change. Using a tablet

irrationally diminished the importance of my computer and therefore my viewing room and all of this meant change. I closed my eyes and took a deep breath. It didn't help. I pressed my little finger to my thumb, hoping to recall all the calm emotions associated with this physical act. It didn't work. I mentally wrote the first two lines of the overture for Mozart's The Marriage of Figaro and found my equilibrium slowly returning. I opened my eyes. Francine was still holding the tablet in her hand. "I really don't want a tablet."

"But you will overcome your fear and take it. You've seen me use mine a million times—"

"It's not possible that I've seen you use it that many times."

"—and you are stronger than your dislike for change and for new things." She was getting good at ignoring me. "I'll be working on Gallo's strange clues on this side. You can do your Mozart thing in the car while your boy toy is driving you there. And who knows? Maybe being in Gallo's hotel room will help you make sense of all those names Gallo gave you."

I stared at her. "I don't have a boy toy. What is that?"

Everyone laughed.

"I'm the boy toy, love." Colin walked into the viewing room and held out his hand. "Come on. Let's go before Millard starts begging."

"As if." Manny got up and stood next to Francine. "Take the bloody tablet, Doc. You'll definitely get more from it than I can."

I got up without taking Colin's hand and stared at the tablet Francine was holding out to me. Manny lied. He pretended to be intimidated by technology, but his skills were far above basic. I reeled my mind back from seeking out safer topics and focused on the tablet.

It had taken me months before I had accepted a smartphone and the change it represented. Now I loved the fast technology that fitted in the palm of my hand. I'd seen Francine use her tablet enough times to know that it was an expedient substitute for my computer, especially when I was mobile. It took another line of the opera overture before I carefully took the tablet. "I don't want this."

"I know, love." Colin stood behind me, his warmth at my back a secure comfort. "Just think of it as a tool that will help you be more efficient."

I didn't pay much attention to his last sentence. Not when I realised that there was no designated space for this tablet in my perfectly organised handbag. Where was I supposed to keep it? How was I supposed to carry it around? My breathing shallowed, my heart rate increased and darkness entered the edges of my peripheral vision.

"Ooh! Wait!" Francine ran to her desk and came back carrying a sealed plastic bag. "I got this antibacterial cover for you. It even has a place for wipes so you can frequently clean the screen. Can I take it out for you?"

"No." I snatched the plastic bag from her and sighed with relief as the smell of some cleaning agent filled the air when I opened it. The dark green tablet cover I took from the bag was not an exact match for my handbag, but it also didn't clash.

"Chop, chop, people!" Manny clapped his hands impatiently. "We don't have all day before Privott is going to start following us around like a little puppy."

I swallowed against the panic rising in my throat at this change coming too fast at me. I hadn't had time to process this new addition to the devices I owned. Or the implications of owning it. I sighed heavily and got my handbag from one of the three antique-looking cabinets at the back of my room.

Only when I reached the elevator did I remember the expression on Francine's face when I'd taken the tablet. I walked back to where she was sitting at her desk. She watched with interest as I clutched my handbag against my chest, the tablet still in my hand. I organised my thoughts. "This was a very thoughtful gift. Thank you."

All the muscles in Francine's face softened, making the affection she felt towards me clear. She blinked slowly, her smile beautiful. "I love giving my bestie something that can make her an even better superwoman."

My shoulders sagged and I gave in. "There is no such word as bestie and no such thing as a superwoman."

"I'm looking at her." Francine was serious. Truthful. I didn't understand why she would say such a thing, but didn't get a chance to ask her. Manny was shouting again that we had to leave. Francine's sincere comment replaced the distress I felt about my new tablet as I followed the men to the SUVs.

The next eighteen minutes I delighted in the smart technology of the paperback-sized tablet in my hand. Francine had indeed made sure it used the same operating system as my computer and that the background and everything else appeared very similar to my computer's desktop. Navigating to what I needed was not difficult at all.

Colin had stopped trying to talk to me after his third attempt was met with silence. I had started with a basic search for Francisco Goya and Peter Paul Rubens. It had rendered an overwhelming number of search results on each. I decided to read condensed versions of their biographies as well as summaries of their professional histories.

By the time Colin parked his SUV in front of the hotel, I was reading about Rubens' final years. I almost insisted on staying in the car to continue the research, but Manny's expression when he got out of Vinnie's SUV made me reconsider. I didn't know if it had been Vinnie's driving or teasing, but Manny looked severely aggravated.

I carefully closed the tablet cover and opened my handbag. Every item in my handbag served a purpose. I could feel a shutdown nearing just thinking about the chaos in Francine's handbag. I didn't understand why anyone would carry around a small spanner, seven different lipsticks, pedicure toe separators for only one foot, three half-empty packets of tissues, cherry-flavoured condoms and a small bag of bluebell flower seeds.

I had my wallet, a full packet of tissues, my smartphone, disinfectant hand cleaner, antibacterial lotion, disposable toilet seat covers, one lipstick, a notepad and a pen in my bag. Each had their own place. I contemplated the interior of my bag and decided that the tablet would fit well next to the notepad in its compartment. It did.

"Missy, get your butt out here right this minute." Manny knocked on my window. "You're not going to find your answers in your handbag."

I pulled my gloves on before opening the car door. Despite the unseasonably warm start to winter, the weather had turned. Today it was minus four degrees Celsius—too cold for naked hands. Another reason I loved my thick fleece gloves was that I didn't have to touch anything. But in case I did, the hand cleaner and lotion were within easy reach.

I put my handbag over my shoulder and Colin and I followed the men into the hotel. I had been so absorbed in Francine's statement and my new tablet that I hadn't seen both Pink and Daniel joining us. I was surrounded by alpha males intent on protecting me.

Daniel took the lead at the reception desk and soon we were being escorted to the fourth floor by the hotel manager. In the large elevator I wrote another line of Mozart's overture to clear my mind of strange statements and devices. The doors pinged and I walked into the hallway, paying full attention to the environment.

I was pleasantly surprised. This was a four-star chain hotel, but looked more like a boutique hotel. The carpets were a thick dark blue, the wallpaper elegant and understated. There was nothing generic about the interior decoration, which made me wonder about the cost of a room in this establishment.

We stopped in front of a beautifully carved door with the usual slot for a hotel keycard above the door handle. The manager handed the keycard to Daniel and stood back. Colin and I were standing against the wall. Manny, Daniel, Vinnie and Pink were in front of us. All four men had their weapons drawn, their postures and facial muscles revealing their focus.

Daniel slipped the keycard in and out of the slot and

opened the door the moment the small green light flashed. He followed the door as it opened to the inside of the room, Vinnie and Pink immediately behind him. Manny took a look down both sides of the hallway before he followed the men into the room.

"Clear." Daniel came out and holstered his weapon. He thanked the manager for his co-operation and gently ordered him to leave us to do our jobs. The portly man looked grateful to return to his office. There had been nothing in his appearance and nonverbal communication to have made me take any notice beyond an initial observation. He was the kind of man people easily forgot.

I stepped closer so I could look into the room. No matter how spacious a hotel room was, when Vinnie, Pink and Manny were in the room, it most likely would be too crowded for me. I was right. The room was beautifully decorated in a style similar to art deco, but not quite. It was a large room for just one occupant, but the three men currently looking around and lifting everything made the room seem smaller.

Manny looked towards the door from where he was opening the desk drawers. "What are you waiting for, Doc? Get in here and do your magic."

"You have to leave the room first." I pressed my lips hard together, but just couldn't let it go. "You know better than to describe my skills as magic. It took many years of studying and practicing to be considered a world expert."

"Oh, don't get your knicke… Oh, bloody hell. Give us five minutes and you can have the room, missy." Manny was irritated with me. I didn't need to see his body language or hear his tone of voice to know this. He only ever called me 'missy' when I'd done something that vexed him.

"So? Want to tell me all the interesting things you discovered while searching on your new tablet?" Colin leaned against the wall and casually crossed his arms.

I studied his expression. "Why are you looking smug?"

"Do you like your tablet?"

My eyes widened with realisation. "You told Francine to get me a tablet. Why?"

"She wanted to do something special for you after you helped her two weeks ago."

"Why would she want to do that?"

"Jenny"—Colin lowered his chin and waited until I saw how serious he was—"you spent three days driving her around and doing her errands."

I still didn't understand. "She hurt her foot and couldn't drive. Manny was in Lyon, meeting with his Interpol superiors. It was the most expedient way to calm her down and get her to work."

Colin tilted his head to the side. "Really? That's the only reason you helped her?"

"Don't sound so sceptical." I swallowed. "Those were not the only reasons. But they were important reasons."

"Tell me the most important reason." His *orbicularis oculi* muscles tugged slightly on the corners of his mouth.

I remembered the uncomfortable emotional state I'd experienced when Francine had called and told me that she'd twisted her ankle. She'd been more outraged that it had happened while she was wearing flat shoes than that she had to rest her foot for a few days. "I was worried about her."

"And you care about her. *And* you're an amazing friend. That's why she wants to thank you."

I never balked at any compliments regarding my skills. But when it came to anything emotional, I found myself highly resistant to praise. I finished the entire overture from Mozart's opera before I could nod tightly. I felt a strong desperation to return to a more neutral topic. "We'll have to look deep into each of these artists to find the connection between them, to find whatever clue Gallo hid there."

"All yours, Doc." Manny walked into the hallway. Vinnie followed him carrying a suitcase and Pink was carrying a laptop, tablet and two smartphones—all in transparent evidence bags. Manny nodded to Gallo's devices. "Pink will get those tested for fingerprints before he and supermodel find out whatever secrets Gallo had on them. Go in and see if we missed anything."

I entered the room, not minding Colin's presence. He was the only person whose physical closeness never caused any panic. I stepped past the washroom on the left and stopped. The room was artfully decorated. Only the foot of the bed had been visible from the door. Similar to the door, the dark wooden bed frame also had intricate carvings that required a skilful hand.

Above the headboard was a painting that I immediately recognised as an Edgar Degas print. The dark wooden frame was not one of the usual cheap frames one found in hotels. It looked like it could've been made by the same carpenter who had made the bed frame and doors. Something about the painting pulled me in. I ignored Colin as he walked around the room, taking everything in.

I stepped closer to the painting, trying to relax my mind so the connection that had formed could reach my cerebral cortex—my thinking brain. I needed to know why my mind was drawn to the connection between the two older men standing behind the man and women in the foreground.

Colin asked me a question and Manny sighed loudly when he realised I was in my 'zone'. I didn't respond. Instead I flooded my mind with another Mozart composition.

The connection came to me just as the violins started the second, and very lyrical, theme. I turned around, my eyes wide. "I need to get to my viewing room."

Chapter FIVE

"This bloody waiting is killing me." Manny's complaint barely registered in my mind as I looked into the last two names Gallo had given me. This was leading exactly where I'd thought it would and was very close to confirming my suspicions. The results of my other searches were on ten of the fifteen monitors in front of me. Manny sighed heavily behind me. "Frey, do you know what she's thinking?"

"Go irritate someone else, Millard." Colin continued tapping on his smartphone, not even raising his head. "Let Jenny work."

"Or maybe you can tell me what you know about this man with the spider tattoo." Manny stopped next to Colin's chair and crossed his arms. "Is that what all your phone chatting has been about the last hour?"

"Back off, Millard. I'll tell you when I'm good and ready to."

"Stop." I lifted both hands, palms out. "I cannot work with your aggression so close to me."

"Our bickering doesn't usually bother you, Doc."

I took a calming breath and turned away from my monitors. I pointed at Manny's posture. "Your clenched fists, your lowered eyebrows and your wide stance reveal your aggression. It's most distracting. If you want the results of what I'm working on, you need to leave my viewing room. And close the door behind you."

Manny's face turned an angry red when Colin looked up from his phone and gave Manny a wide but insincere smile. Without another word, Manny walked out of my room and slammed his hand on the button to allow the soundproof doors to slide closed.

Colin shook his head and returned his attention to his phone. "Thanks, love."

"You're going to have to reveal what you know about that man." I studied his face for a few seconds. "Even if you're not emotionally ready to do that."

"Shit." Colin turned his full attention to me, allowing me to read every expression. "I need your help, Jenny. If this man is who I think he is, it's going... it's going to be bad."

"What can I do?"

"Don't say anything when you see me react. I'm not asking you to lie, just asking you not to comment on my body language."

He didn't ask me to stop studying him, so I did. For a full minute. I saw grave concern, sadness and even regret. "Not even now? When it's just the two of us and no one can hear us?"

"I know you want to ask me about what you're seeing." He leaned closer. "And I promise you I will tell you. But for now I need to keep my shit together... I need to keep myself under control if I want to handle this correctly. Please trust me."

"I trust you."

Some of the tension left his facial muscles. "You have no idea how much it means to me to hear those words."

"Oh." Should I say this more often? I didn't want to start obsessing about my limited relationship skills, so I returned to the topic at hand. "I can see that this is very personal to you. But if your knowledge can help us prevent Gallo from executing whatever plan he has, you will need to overcome your fear of revealing what you know."

"I'm trying to keep everything from falling apart, Jenny. I just need a little bit more time to make sure about what I'm suspecting." He rubbed his palms hard against his thighs. A pacifying gesture we employed to soothe ourselves.

"What does it mean that everything will fall apart? What is everything? And how does this one man have the power to cause that?" I stopped the rest of my questioning when I saw Colin's expression. I tilted my head and studied his face. Then I nodded. "I will try my very best not to mention your nonverbal communication. But you are broadcasting very strongly at the moment. If you want to deceive Manny, you're going to have to lie much better. I suggest you approach this like you do when you're dressed as one of your aliases."

Colin's expression softened as he laughed. He took both my hands in his and pulled me closer and kissed me lightly. "Getting deception advice from the most honest person I've ever met. This does not bode well."

"Please sort out whatever this is as soon as possible."

"I'm trying." He kissed me once more before settling back in his chair with his smartphone in his hand. "Why don't we both get back to work?"

I didn't need any more encouragement. It took me another seventeen minutes to find exactly what I was looking for and confirm the facts in three separate places. I knew that I was going to have to explain this to my neurotypical team, so I took a few minutes to organise the information and my thoughts.

I looked away from my computer and found myself alone in my viewing room, the soundproof doors closed tightly. I got up, but stopped in front of the glass doors to observe my friends. Francine was at her desk, Pink next to her, working on a laptop. She was frowning at the smartphone in her hand, another lying in front of her. Manny and Colin were in a tense discussion, but I didn't observe the same animosity as earlier. Maybe Manny had decided to give Colin the time he'd asked for.

The sounds that greeted me when I opened the doors were familiar and overwhelming at the same time. In the last three years, I'd grown used to noise around me. Yet when I spent any length of time in my soundproof room, I always needed a few seconds to adjust to the constant sound created by other people.

"Doc!" Manny nodded at Colin and walked towards me. "For the love of all that is holy, please tell me you've got something."

I looked around the team room. "Where's Vinnie?"

"Training with Daniel." Colin walked to the round table and took a seat. The sadness and regret I'd noticed earlier were more pronounced. But only for a second. He pulled his shoulders back and smiled at me. "He got bored with the waiting."

"And annoyed with handsome's whining." Francine turned around and winked at Manny.

"I wasn't whining." Manny pushed his hands in his trouser pockets. "I was pissed off having to make sleeping arrangements in bloody Rousseau & Rousseau."

"What sleeping arrangements?" I sat down next to Colin. He took my hand immediately, holding it a bit firmer than usual. Normally, he held my hand to comfort me or for simple physical closeness. I suspected this time he was the one in need of comfort.

Manny didn't notice. "Bloody Gallo refused to be transferred to a holding facility. He threatened to stop co-operating at all if we moved him from Rousseau & Rousseau. I had to make all kinds of promises to Phillip just to get him to agree to keep this international criminal in his conference room."

"You are misrepresenting the situation." I knew this not only because of Manny's nonverbal cues, but also because I knew my previous boss. "Phillip didn't ask you for any promises, did he?"

"Of course not." Manny rubbed his hands hard over his face and pushed them back in his pockets. "I just don't like that we're hosting bloody criminals in his workplace. Phillip was as always gracious about it and even brought in a small folding bed for Gallo."

I looked at Manny, then at Francine and Pink and back at Manny. "You wouldn't have been so accommodating if you hadn't found something that has you worried."

"*I* found it." Francine lifted the smartphone in her hand and waved it around. "So far we've only been able to crack this baby open. The computer and other smartphone are locked up tighter than my great-aunt's diamonds."

"Your great-aunt has diamonds?" Pink asked.

"Another story for another day." Francine swivelled her chair around to face me. "I found a link on this phone that sent me on a bit of a chase, but it led me to a dark website with the details of this meeting the presidents thought was super-duper secret."

I knew that Tor sites were extremely hard to access, but I had to ask. "Have you been able to hack the site? Do you know how many people have seen the information?"

"Haven't gotten there yet, girlfriend. I was just about to get my ninja hacking skills going when you came out of your cave."

"I was in my viewing room." My lips thinned when she smiled widely at me. "Don't use expressions. My focus is on work today, not trying to understand euphemisms."

Her exaggerated wink communicated her good mood. It also assuaged the immediate concern I had that I'd been too harsh. She winked at me with her other eye and laughed. "That website gave pretty much the same information Gallo gave us. Important world leaders will meet to discuss Russia's problems with the West and it will take place Saturday at three o'clock."

"Nothing about where it will be?" I wished Privott had told us. It would go a long way to help us prevent an attack on these important people.

"Nope." She winced. "Sorry."

"Supermodel also found a lot of phone numbers. And she

traced them." Manny lifted an eyebrow at Francine.

"Ooh, I get to explain. Goody. So I traced the numbers and found nothing. There were eleven numbers in total. One was for the hotel where Gallo stayed, two for restaurants and one for a tailor. The other seven are all phones that are not registered to anyone."

"And they're all turned off." Pink pushed the laptop away from him and also turned to face us. "We tried, but can't turn them on remotely, which means that either the SIM cards or the batteries have been removed."

"Burner phones." Manny sat down at the table. "Some countries make everyone register when they buy a SIM card or they can't get on air. At least that makes the job a little bit easier for law enforcement. Here anyone can buy a cheap phone, get a prepaid SIM card and Bob's their uncle."

I grunted. Manny had used this expression twice before. I managed to refrain from commenting.

Pink pointed with his thumb to the computer behind him. "We have an alert on all those numbers. The moment one of them goes live, we'll be on it and hopefully track it. I've been working on Gallo's laptop, but I think I will hand it over to Francine now."

"You have to go." It was clear in his body language.

"I would like to get in at least one hour's training with my team. As soon as Vinnie gets back, I'll go." He smiled when I inhaled. "If you're going to ask when Vinnie will be back, I reckon it will be another fifteen minutes or so."

"Then we might as well get this going." Manny tapped his finger on the table. "Tell us what you found, Doc."

The tension in Colin's hand was distracting. I needed to let go of his hand in order to focus fully on presenting my findings, but felt conflicted. It wasn't often that Colin needed me. Not like this. I swallowed and squeezed his hand the way he always did when I needed more courage. He squeezed back and relaxed the hold on my hand. I glanced at him and felt even more conflicted.

There was nothing out of the ordinary in the way Colin sat in his chair, his ankle resting on the opposite knee. His free hand was resting on his ankle, his shoulders relaxed, his face showing just the right amount of interest, focus and intelligence. But I saw the well-hidden distress and it awakened an uncommon need to keep holding his hand.

"Doc!" Manny slapped his hand on the table. "Stop making eyes at Frey and talk to me."

Colin blinked slowly, then smiled at me as he pulled his hand away from mine. "Millard is feeling lonely, love. Tell him what you discovered."

It was extremely hard for me to turn away from Colin. I reminded myself of the promise I'd made to try my best not to comment on his nonverbal cues, so I forced myself to shift in my chair until I had my back half turned to Colin. That would make it easier to ignore his distress and my irrational need to do something about it.

"Francine, can you bring my computer up on the large screen?"

"Give me a sec." Francine picked up her tablet and swiped the screen. "I'll show you how to do this with your tablet. Easy-peasy."

Before the large screen had finished rolling down the

wall next to the round table, four of my computer monitors displayed in a split screen. "Put monitors one to four up. Please."

Francine smiled at my belated politeness and did as I asked.

"Colin's knowledge of artists and their history has proven essential in finding the common factors that linked these people." I pointed at the top left corner. "The man on the right is Braulio José Benito de Goya y Franqué, Francisco Goya's father. The man on the left is Jan Bartholomeus Rubens, Peter Paul Ruben's father. Both fathers were born on the eighteenth of March. Different years, but same day and month."

"That seems too easy, Doc." Manny's *corrugator supercilii* muscles pulled his eyebrows into what is frequently referred to as 'the thinker's brow'. "Are you sure there aren't any other commonalities?"

"Easy?" Colin straightened in his chair. "It took us two and a half hours before we got to that common factor. First, we checked obvious things in their biographies like education, friends, places they lived and the like. Then we compared paintings. It wasn't as easy as you think, Millard."

"It would take me days to find anything else these men had in common," I said before Manny could respond. "Colin is right. A date of a relative's birthday isn't an obvious common factor one would look at. And it fits perfectly with Gallo's character. He would choose obscure facts like that."

"And don't go thinking to blame Jenny for not looking at obscure facts first. I was the one who insisted on looking at the obvious first. For all we know, Gallo would've used the very obvious because we wouldn't expect it."

I hadn't argued with his sound reasoning then and saw that Manny wasn't going to either now. I pointed at the second split screen. "That's Manet and Cassatt."

"Who are they?" Pink asked.

"Both were elite impressionist artists." Colin's entire body relaxed as he talked about the artists. "Mary Cassatt was one of the few female artists who broke through in a male-dominated industry. She was also one of the few American artists who impressed the French."

"Yes, yes." Manny grunted impatiently. "What do they have in common except for both being impressionist artists?"

I pointed to the bottom half of the large screen. "They painted those paintings."

"Whoop-dee-doo, Doc." Manny's sigh was long and dramatic. "What does that mean?"

"Both paintings are of the city of Toulouse." I didn't give Manny the opportunity to interrupt me again. "Yes, we did look for other commonalities, but this was all we found. Finally, if you look at the bottom left split screen you'll see Horace and Claude Joseph."

Manny tilted his head. "What do they have in common, Doc?"

"They have the same surname." By the time we'd reached these artists, Colin had been too busy on his smartphone to help me. I had been very surprised that the common factor had been so simple.

"Okay, so now we have a date, a city and a surname." Manny's frown increased. "Have you found anything with this info, Doc?"

"I haven't. As soon as I confirmed the brothers' names, I came here to tell you." I looked at Francine. "I also thought you might be much faster at finding out if these three data points will lead us to something."

Francine rubbed her palms together. "Give me a nanosec."

"You've wasted a nanosecond by talking." Even though she did this often, I still despised her outrageous time expressions. "You should ask for a minute. Although five minutes would be more sensible if you want to run a proper search."

"Got it!" She threw both hands in the air and bounced in her chair as if she was dancing. "Who's the queen of all searches? Huh? Who?"

"You are, your highness." Pink stretched his arms out and emulated a bow.

"Supermodel!" Manny waited until Francine lowered her hands and looked at him. "Talk."

She patted her laptop lovingly. "My fabutastic search engine spat out a result two seconds after I put the data in."

"Well? Are you going to tell us?" Manny asked.

"Of course, handsome." She tapped on her laptop and the image of a man replaced my discoveries on the large screen. I estimated the man to be in his late thirties, even early forties. It looked like a surveillance photo taken when he exited a restaurant. He was dressed in jeans and a leather jacket. He appeared athletic in build, but his face was obscured by a baseball cap. Francine continued tapping on her laptop. "Let me see if I can get a better image of him."

"Of who, supermodel?" Impatience made Manny's words sound clipped.

"Ooh! Here we go. I thought we were going to find a birthday for someone. This is a court date when the adoption went through on the eighteenth of March in Toulouse. The judge who presided over that case was Joseph Marc."

"Supermodel, stop with your dramatic presentation. Whose adoption? Who is this person?"

She tapped once more and another image came onto the screen. This photo also seemed to be from surveillance, but this time the man's face was in full view. He had dark olive skin, but his blue eyes led me to believe he was mixed-race. Apart from the small scar above his left eyebrow, his face was flawless. He had the skin and bone structure seen on most male models. His hair was cropped close to his skull, the hints of gray adding to his look of sophistication. Francine cleared her throat dramatically. "Ladies and gentlemen, I present to you Emad Vernet."

Colin's body tensed next to me a moment before I heard his suppressed gasp. It took all my control not to turn to him. Instead I glanced around the room. As much as Colin had tried to suppress his reaction, everyone had noticed it. Francine quickly hid her frown, no doubt to protect Colin from Manny's interest. It was too late.

Manny sat up and leaned towards Colin. "Frey."

I gave in and looked at Colin. He closed his eyes and shook his head. In the three and a half years I'd known him, I'd seldom seen him distressed. But never as distressed as now. His face had lost its usual healthy colour and he was swallowing continuously. He clenched his teeth, his *masseter* muscles bulging on the sides of his jaw. I felt helpless watching his obvious internal torment and did the one thing

I knew helped me. I put my hand on his forearm.

"Frey." Manny leaned even closer. "What the bloody hell is going on?"

Colin took my hand and held it tightly. "Emad Vernet is not someone we want to mess with. If we're going after him, we'd better get it right the first time."

"Okay." Manny relaxed in his chair. "So you know this pretty boy. Tell us everything."

"I can't tell you everything, Millard." Colin shook his head when Manny's nostrils flared. "Not because I'm being difficult. A lot of this shit is classified. Highly classified."

Manny could be rude, unnecessarily provocative and impatient. But he was also one of the most astute observers I knew. He proved that once again by not pushing Colin with his usual sarcasm. Instead he let go of all the nonverbal cues he employed to get information from people. He rested his hands on his thighs, his elbows out, his body language open. "I respect that you deal with stuff that is way beyond our— beyond my—purview. But don't you think that after all this time we've proven to you that you can trust us with this intel?"

Colin pushed his free hand through his hair, his other clutching mine. "Fuck, Millard. This is not good."

"Then tell us."

The elevator doors pinged, drawing our attention. Vinnie stepped out of the elevator and his eyebrows rose when everyone looked at him. "What? Y'all happy to see me?"

"Fuck." Colin's softly spoken exclamation shocked me. I glanced at him and saw that even more colour had left his face, his eyes trained on Vinnie. Waiting.

He didn't have to wait long. Vinnie's attention went to the large screen and immediately his eyes flew wide open. His hands tightened into fists, his knuckles turning white. He stalked closer to the screen and shook a fist at it. "What is he doing on our screen? Did you find him? Where is the motherfucker who put this scar on my face? And who the fuck is he?"

Chapter SIX

"Vin." Colin got up and walked towards Vinnie, reaching out to his friend. "I can explain this."

Vinnie spun towards Colin. "Then you better start fucking talking very quickly, dude. People only say that shit when they're guilty of something."

Manny also got up and stood next to Colin. "Why don't you start, big guy? Tell us what Vernet did to your face."

"Vernet?" Vinnie's voice was mere decibels below shouting. "That's this fucker's name? How long have you known, dude? Why would you keep something like this from me?"

"Why did you keep it from *me*?" Francine joined Vinnie and glared at Colin. "If I'd known you were looking for this person, I would've helped you. You know I would've. Why did you keep this from us?"

"Um. Maybe everyone should take a step back." Pink was standing next to Francine's desk, his hand resting on his holstered weapon. Even though I suspected it was force of habit whenever he found himself in a conflict situation, it did nothing to appease my extreme discomfort that he might aim that gun at my friends.

"Shut up, Pink." Vinnie didn't take his eyes off Colin. "This is between me and my so-called best friend."

"Come on, Vin." The hurt on Colin's face brought an uncomfortable tightness to my chest. "You know I would never do anything to harm you."

"You were keeping this fucker away from me to protect me?" Vinnie was now shouting. "Who the fuck are you to decide what's best for me? To protect me?"

"You're putting words in my mou—" Colin's sentence was cut off when Vinnie punched him hard in the stomach. Colin immediately grabbed his torso as he folded double and dry-heaved.

"Vinnie!" Francine grabbed his arm and tried to pull him back when he stepped closer to Colin. "Don't do this. Hear Colin out first."

"Let me go, Francine. You're gonna get hurt." Vinnie shook her hold off his arm with alarming ease.

The hurt that flashed on her face was immediately replaced with fury. Darkness entered my peripheral vision when Vinnie turned his attention back to Colin. It was a matter of seconds before I would go into a complete shutdown. My non-neurotypical mind could not process this kind of betrayal and aggression between friends. Between *my* friends.

I tried to call out to them to stop, but my mouth wouldn't obey the signals my brain was sending. I couldn't even utter a soft groan when Colin straightened and Vinnie punched him again. This time he used his non-dominant hand, but since it landed on exactly the same spot, Colin not only folded double, but lost his balance and landed hard on his knees.

More darkness overtook my vision, the powerlessness I felt too overwhelming to neutralise with a Mozart composition or deep breathing. I looked at Francine, hoping she would do something to stop this, but she was tapping on her smartphone screen.

I glanced away from her in time to see Pink aim his weapon at Vinnie and shoot.

Chapter SEVEN

"Jenny." Colin's hand on my forearm was warm. Safe. "It's calm now. You can come back to me."

I opened my eyes to an empty team room. I was still on my chair at the round table, hugging my knees tightly against my chest, rocking back and forth. It took the first two lines of Mozart's very short motet Ave Verum Corpus before I could stop the rocking and let go of my legs. It would be a few minutes before the blood circulation in my legs was restored and I would be able to walk.

I focused on Colin's strong hand on my arm to ignore the pins and needles in my legs. It was hard to vocalise the question that was threatening to send me back into a shutdown. "Is Vinnie dead?"

"What? No. No, love. Vin's fine." Colin leaned down and waited until I looked at him. I was surprised to find that my focus was blurred by tears. Colin uttered a surprised sound and wiped the tears with his thumb. "Oh, Jenny. We are such idiots. I'm so sorry we scared you like that. Pink shot Vinnie with the stun gun. It took Vin less than a minute to be back on his feet."

"He's fine? He's uninjured?" I blinked away more tears and stared hard at Colin. I needed to see the truth in his answer.

"Vinnie is at home, cooking dinner. He's fine. Pink feels terrible that he did that, but he didn't know how else to stop Vin."

"You didn't answer my second question. Is he uninjured?"

"Yes. He didn't even fall down completely when Pink stunned him. The strong bastard only went down on one knee and grunted like he was lifting a heavy weight." Colin's smile was self-deprecating. "Two soft punches from Vin and I'm flat on my back."

"You weren't on your back. I saw you landing on your knees."

"And that after Vinnie pulled his punches."

"What does that mean?"

"It means he didn't hit me as hard as he's able to. He was just looking for an outlet. And I was the closest punching bag available."

I stared at him in absolute confusion. "I can't see any anger or resentment in your nonverbal cues. Why aren't you upset that your best friend hit you? Oh, my. Are *you* uninjured?"

"I'm going to have a brag-worthy bruise on my stomach, but I'm not hurt, love. Not even my feelings."

"That's not true. I saw your reaction when Vinnie challenged your friendship."

"Already forgotten. He was just lashing out." He gently rested his index finger between my eyebrows for a second. "Such a big frown. Vin and I have been through a lot more challenging times, love. I know him well. And he knows me. I'm sure by the time we sit down for dinner, he will no longer be pissed off that I didn't tell him about my investigation."

I pointed at his face. "You're not sure about that."

"Not completely. But I'm hoping it will be true." Colin leaned back. "This is a very sensitive topic for Vinnie. I know how he got that scar, because I was there. But I'm not sure Vinnie has ever told anyone else what happened."

"Why not?"

Colin started to say something, then pressed his lips together. After three seconds, he shook his head. "It's his story to tell. You know it doesn't have anything to do with my trust in you, right?"

"Of course." My legs felt fully functional again which reminded me of why I was sitting here. "What happened?"

"Francine happened. She sent an SMS to Phillip, asking for emergency intervention." Colin laughed. "Vinnie was just getting back up after Pink had stunned him when Phillip got here. No one has ever made me feel so ashamed of anything before in my life. He had us all looking at the floor and mumbling apologies."

"That doesn't sound good."

"Then I'm expressing myself poorly." He inhaled deeply like he sometimes did to gather his thoughts. "In his dignified and quiet way, Phillip walked to us and asked us what was happening. Francine was getting herself all worked up again when Phillip told us we should be ashamed of ourselves. In the whole time we'd been explaining ourselves, no one had noticed you'd gone into a shutdown.

"Well, that really put a damper on all our anger. Phillip suggested Vinnie go home to prepare dinner, Manny and Francine go for a drive to calm themselves before going to our apartment and I stay with you."

And this was the reason Phillip was such a successful negotiator. "Where is Phillip?"

"He had to finish the meeting he was in when Francine SMSed him." Colin glanced at his watch. "But he's most likely at the apartment with the rest of them, waiting for us."

I insisted that we left immediately. I wanted to see Vinnie's micro-expressions when I asked him if he was well.

No sooner had I entered the apartment than Nikki stormed in from her side of the apartment. "Doc G! You're home."

"I am." I looked at her and frowned. Nikki's presence in the last two years of my life had taught me more about friendship and love than any of the books I'd read. Growing up as the child of a notorious criminal had given her a different insight into life. At the age of twenty, she was a very mature young woman. She was also one of the most optimistic and resilient people I knew, which was why the slight downturn of the corners of her mouth concerned me. "What's wrong?"

She took half a step back. "What's wrong? Duh! The super-awkward atmosphere. That's what's wrong. I'm so glad you're home. You've gotta fix this. Vinnie's cooking for like a million people and Francine isn't helping him. She hasn't even once suggested using cumin or adding vanilla to his stew. This is not right."

I was torn between my desire to see Vinnie and my concern about the deception cues Nikki was trying to hide with her chatter. The former won out. I lifted one eyebrow and made sure Nikki noticed my expression. "We'll talk."

"Bugger." Nikki had started using Manny's expression to

tease him, but it had soon become a habit. Now it expressed her knowledge that I'd seen through her lies.

I left Colin talking to Nikki and walked towards the kitchen. My apartment had started out with three bedrooms and the kitchen, dining room and living area in an open-space arrangement. Now Colin owned the apartment next door and one of the connecting walls between the apartments had been removed to form one large residence.

Nikki and Vinnie stayed in two of the three bedrooms next door and Colin and I in my apartment. Even though the kitchen on the other side was fully functioning, Vinnie used mine to cook for all of us. He and Colin had changed that living area to an entertainment area with an obscenely large-screen television where they watched sport and mindless action movies.

My living area remained the space where we visited on the two large white sofas. I ignored Phillip, Manny and Francine quietly sitting on one sofa, and entered the kitchen. Vinnie was stirring the largest of the three pots on the stove, every muscle in his body tense. It was always a pleasure to watch the large man cook. He was one of those gifted people who had a natural ability to mix ingredients to bring out the best flavours and produce a meal that could challenge many renowned restaurants.

I leaned my hip against the counter and quietly watched him. He knew I was there. I'd seen the momentary pause in stirring before he'd continued. Yet he didn't speak. Neither did I. The relief I experienced from seeing him unharmed far outweighed the concern I had for the barely contained emotions filtering through his tight facial muscles.

We stood like that for seven minutes. I listened to Phillip, Francine and Manny quietly discussing the meeting between the leaders and Colin and Nikki joking about the three young men who were vying for her attention in one of her university classes. I listened, but didn't look. My interest was captured by the constant increase in Vinnie's muscle tension. Had it been me, I would already have been in a shutdown. Or a meltdown.

"Argh!" Vinnie stopped stirring. Everyone in my apartment stopped talking. After a few seconds, Vinnie shook off the wooden spoon, placed it on the spoon holder and turned off the stove. He stared at the three pots, the muscles in his jaw working. "Fuck this! Just fuck this."

Without another word, he stormed to his side of our joined apartments. Nikki started going after him, but stopped when Colin grabbed her arm. "I don't think it's a good idea, Nix. Not now."

"Vinnie shouldn't be alone." She pulled her arm out of Colin's grip. "Look, I don't know what happened at the office, but Vinnie is taking it really hard. If you don't want me talking to him, then you go."

The strangest emotion welled up in me while listening to the once-timid young woman assert herself. It took a moment for me to recognise the emotion as pride. I was too young to be Nikki's mother and would never presume to know what maternal pride felt like. But I could imagine it was something like this.

"Jenny?" Colin was standing next to me. I hadn't seen him come into the kitchen, so focused had I been on these unfamiliar emotions. "Will you go?"

"Go where?" I looked from Colin towards the living area and realised everyone was watching me.

Phillip got up and walked to us. "Nikki is right. Vinnie needs someone right now. Colin might not be the right person at the moment. I'm sure you can see why none of us would be who Vinnie needs right now."

"He doesn't need me," I said before Phillip could say it.

"Think carefully." Phillip looked steadily at me. "Then tell me again Vinnie doesn't need you."

I didn't need to think carefully. The moment the words had left my mouth, I'd known the untruth they represented. I closed my eyes against this knowledge and my shoulders dropped. When I looked up, Phillip's expression was pleased. I sighed. "I don't know what to say."

"You'll know when you're there."

I didn't share Phillip's confidence. Colin did. "Bring him back to us, love."

I sought out the one technique that always helped me. I only needed to mentally write one line of the beautiful and short choir work Mozart had composed for a church near Vienna. The next two lines were sheer procrastination.

Knowledge was my weapon of choice. Going into any situation armed with as much information as possible, I felt confident about finding solutions. Speaking to Vinnie about whatever was troubling him was most intimidating. I felt ill-equipped to deal with this new situation.

When I opened my eyes and saw everyone still patiently waiting for me, expectation clear on all their faces, I gathered all my courage and left the kitchen. I didn't often go into the other side of the joined apartments. I had no need to. The wrestling matches Vinnie and Colin enjoyed watching on the large television held no attraction for me. Nor did the ridiculous action and romance movies Nikki enjoyed. Our socialising was done in my living area, so I never had the need to visit them in their rooms.

I walked past the comfortable sofas in the entertainment area and focused on Vinnie's closed bedroom door. He had the largest room in this apartment, but didn't spend a lot of time there. He and Nikki were well suited to share this part of our home since they were both very social in nature and spent numerous hours making use of the entertainment area. I stopped in front of the dark wooden door and stared at it. I still didn't know what I was going to say. My extensive studies had never prepared me for being a friend. Only for a better understanding of the neurotypical mind.

I considered how Manny, Francine, Colin and especially Phillip would've handled this. Before I fell into the trap of overanalysing my next step, I knocked on the door and opened it.

Chapter EIGHT

Vinnie was in the far corner of his room where he'd set up his body-building equipment. I walked into the room and closed the door behind me. "Vinnie?"

He glanced up, but didn't answer me. Moving the dumbbell from his left to his right hand, he started doing bicep curls that bulged his arm muscles, revealing their true size. I walked closer and sat down on a small stool by the window. Vinnie was sitting on the bench of his home gym and grunted as he continued his workout.

I had never watched him exercise. It was fascinating to watch the total concentration he gave each movement. I understood this kind of escapism. As a child, my shutdowns had provided a safe place whenever I was overwhelmed with physical or mental stimuli. In my teens and early adulthood, I'd taught myself a few ways to deal with too much stimulation. One of those ways had been to isolate myself. Without any friends or colleagues to provide emotional upheaval, it had been much easier to avoid shutdowns.

Then Colin and Vinnie had entered my life. Suddenly my simple life had been filled with friends, bringing endless turmoil and challenges. Even though it was a daily temptation to escape into the safe place of emotional neutrality, I'd come to value the love of my friends far above the easy, and lonely, life without friends.

With their love, my friends had also brought new emotions into my life. Sometimes those emotions felt like they were belts around my chest, tightening until I felt I couldn't breathe. Like now. The distress on Vinnie's face as he slowly lifted his forearm again increased the pressure around my chest. I felt so helpless. "I don't know what to say."

"Nothing is good." His harsh tone was immediately followed by an expression of remorse. He lowered the dumbbell onto the floor and dropped his head into his hands. His breathing was harsh, every muscle in his body tense. It was almost two minutes before he looked at me. The despair around his eyes left me breathless. "It was my fault, Jen-girl. It was all my fault."

I sat frozen. I didn't know what to do, what to say. For a few seconds, I searched for actions the others would take and decided to approach this differently. I thought of the times Vinnie had comforted me, the times he'd known what to say. I needed the last two lines of the Ave Verum Corpus before I got up and sat next to him on the bench. I glanced at the twenty-centimetre distance between us, inhaled deeply and shifted closer until our legs touched.

Vinnie looked sideways at me, his head hanging low. "I don't want to tell you this, Jen-girl."

"Your nonverbal cues are in conflict. It appears you do *and* you don't want to speak about this."

He snorted. "That about covers it."

We sat in silence for more than a minute. Vinnie's elbows rested on his knees, his hands in rigid fists as if he was attempting to physically keep his emotions under control.

His breath hitched and a short groan came from deep in his chest. His second groan was longer and filled with immense emotional pain.

The tightness in my chest felt like it was strangling me. I swallowed at the tears forming in my eyes. Vinnie had taught me so much about friendship. He'd given of himself without expecting anything in return. Countless times he accommodated my many non-neurotypical quirks and found ways around it to show me his support and caring. This was a moment I wanted to show him my love and support. But it was so hard for me.

With great effort, I reached out and put my hand over his fist pressing into his thigh. He jerked and looked at me, his eyes wet with tears. My own tears spilled over and I squeezed his fist. "I… I don't know what to do. I know it's not possible, yet I have this overwhelming and irrational need to take away your pain."

"Aw, fuck." Vinnie's head dropped low again and his shoulders started shaking. I was terrified. Had I said the wrong thing? Had I just caused him more pain? I started lifting my hand away, but he grabbed it and wrapped my hand in both of his. His grip was almost crushing while silent sobs shook his large frame.

After a few minutes, he wiped his cheeks on his forearms without letting go of my hand and turned to me. "Promise me you won't lose respect for me. I won't be able to deal with that. Anything but that, Jen-girl."

"Respect is earned, Vinnie." I didn't have to think about my answer. "You've earned my respect from the first day I met you. I can list all the ways you've proven yourself to be a man of integrity and honour, but I know you well enough to know you'll be bored by the time I get to the twelfth or thirteenth point."

He gave a half-laugh. "Only you would want to make a list like that, Jen-girl."

"You asked me to promise that I won't lose respect for you. That request doesn't make sense. I judge you by the person you are now, the actions you're taking now, the code you live by now. It is irrational, and frankly unintelligent, to reason that we don't evolve, that we don't grow. A decision you made ten years ago might have been the best decision available to you at that time. It might also have been a really bad decision that negatively affected a lot of people."

As I said this, I realised how much I had changed in the last four years. How much my view on life and people had changed. "If I knew fifteen years ago what I know now, I would've made different decisions. But I didn't have the life experience and knowledge I have now. I can't judge my twenty-year-old self by who I am now. The same way I won't judge your younger self by who you are now. That was then. This is now."

Vinnie stared at me, his eyes clear of tears, but bright. "You are the best person I've ever known, Jen-girl. There's not a bad bone in your body."

"As far as I know, my bones are all healthy." I frowned. "But I don't see the relevance to our conversation."

Vinnie chuckled. "Of course you don't."

This time the silence that surrounded us as we sat quietly was not filled with pain and tension. I was desperate to take my hand from Vinnie's grip and wipe it repeatedly against my jeans. I didn't act on my growing urge. Vinnie was still gripping my hand and I wanted to give him that.

"It's my fault she died. Fuck. She was only seven. Just a little girl." Vinnie's words were so softly spoken, I barely heard them. I had no response to such a declaration, so I waited to hear the context. It took him another two minutes before he spoke again. "It was after Colin got arrested because of me and was forced to work with Interpol. All because of me."

"How many times have both of you said that it was the best thing that happened to both of you?" Early in their friendship, Colin had asked Vinnie to help him steal a Rembrandt painting. They had broken into the museum's conservation centre, sure that the guards were not going to pose any threat. An elderly guard had surprised Vinnie, but had received such a huge fright when he'd seen Vinnie's large body that he'd had a heart attack.

Colin had known that Manny had been investigating him and had phoned Manny for help. He'd sent Vinnie away, protecting him from any consequences. It had given Manny great pleasure to place Colin in cuffs after they'd sent the guard to the hospital. That pleasure hadn't lasted long. The moment Interpol had found out about Colin's arrest, they'd recruited him to help them recover items ranging from stolen classified documents to Nazi-looted artworks. A few times he'd even had to recover kidnap victims.

Vinnie's hands tightened around mine. "If it wasn't for Interpol and our history, we wouldn't be here today, so I suppose something good came from it."

"Tell me about the little girl."

"Becks. Her name was Rebecca Susan, but everyone called her Becks." He swallowed a few times. "She was my neighbour's kid, but spent more time in my flat than with her mom. A right little tomboy. She refused to wear dresses and loved watching Dakar rallies with me."

"Were you living in New York then?" I didn't know every place Vinnie had stayed, but three times he'd referred to New York with great fondness.

"Yeah. She was a little city tomboy." His voice broke and he took a shuddering breath. And another. "I can't tell the story. I just can't, Jen-girl."

"Is this related to Emad Vernet?"

"Yes."

"Do you think knowing this information would help us find Vernet? Stop whatever these people are planning?"

He nodded.

"Would you mind if Colin shared the facts with us? I'll ask him to stay only to the facts."

"No." Vinnie straightened. "No. I will not reduce Becks to facts. No. She was too special for that."

"Then tell me."

Vinnie closed his eyes. "It was a year after Colin had been arrested and started working with Interpol." He turned his head and looked at me. "He was made for this shit, you know. I'd only known him for a short time, but the moment he started working for the good guys, he changed. It was like he'd found his true purpose in life. It wasn't the same for me. I wasn't recruited by Interpol. Not then. I saw how happy Colin was and started trying to get myself out of all the illegal shit I was in.

"I was travelling quite a bit then, following Colin all over the globe as his backup whenever he needed me. I don't know how I'd missed it, but I only caught onto it months after Becks started staying over in my place. Her mom was working three jobs just to make ends meet. They were still struggling financially and her mom took in a boarder. Often Becks' mom would be working night shifts, leaving her little girl alone at home with this man.

"He never tried anything strange with Becks. Believe me, I asked her and then I beat the shit out of him just to make sure he would never even think about it. But he was a drunk. Becks didn't feel safe when he was drinking and she would break into my place when I wasn't there and sleep there. I caught her one night when I came home."

His expression softened. "This tiny little thing sleeping in my big bed. I left her there, but watched over her the whole night. When she woke up in the morning, she was unapologetic and told me that I should thank her for looking after my place while I was gone.

"It took some doing, but I cleared it with her mom that she could stay over in my place. Becks didn't want her own room in my flat, so I put an extra bed in my room. She became the reason I loved going home. In that one year, I smiled more than I remembered doing in my whole adult life."

I didn't prompt him when he stopped. I allowed this information to settle in my mind. I wasn't surprised that Vinnie had concerned himself with the wellbeing of a young child. Even though Nikki wasn't a child, Vinnie was more protective of her than any of us. If Becks had still been alive, she would've been Nikki's age. I wondered how much Nikki reminded him of Becks.

Vinnie groaned softly. "Colin was asked to steal back art that had been smuggled across the US border. We didn't often do jobs in the US, so it was a novelty. As usual Colin did his due diligence, being more careful than the most paranoid spies. If only I'd been as careful."

His head dropped back and he looked at the ceiling. "Fuck it, this is hard."

"You loved her."

"I did." He looked at me, his eyes wet with tears. "I loved her like she was my own, Jen-girl. It still tears me apart. She shouldn't have died. It should've been me."

I didn't say anything. There was nothing I could think of that would be appropriate.

"Colin had found out what the man who'd smuggled the artworks looked like." He was whispering, his face tense. "We didn't know his name. Not then. All Colin knew was that he worked with somebody else. And what he looked like. Colin asked me to reach out to my contacts to see if anyone had any information about a smuggling team, with one man who was mixed race with blue eyes and a scar above his left eye.

"I wasn't careful enough. Paranoid enough. Later I found out that one motherfucker told this Vernet I was looking into him. He even gave Vernet my address." Tears streamed from his eyes. "Fuck. Becks was in my bedroom when the bomb went off. It was meant for me, Jen-girl. For me! She should not have died. Not my little Becks."

Raw sobs tore through his body. I sat frozen. His pain paralysed me. How could anyone ever find any words to address such anguish? Such deep guilt? My discomfort with my hand clutched between his suddenly seemed insignificant. I couldn't bring myself to embrace him, but hoping that in some miniscule way I could convey my understanding and love, I leaned against his side. Then I leaned in harder.

It took Vinnie a while to compose himself. Not once did he let go of my hand. Still holding it between his, he pressed his one hand hard against his mouth. People often did this to prevent themselves from speaking, to control whatever it was that wanted to spill from their lips. After a few moments he lowered our hands. "Colin and I were in the living room. The bomb had been set to go off when someone got onto my bed. For some reason Becks must've decided to sleep in my bed. I was standing close to the room, Colin was sitting on the sofa and only got a few scratches. There was nothing left of my bedroom. Nothing left of Becks. He took her from me."

"And you?"

Vinnie turned his face so I could see the scar running from the top of his left temple, down his cheek, jaw and neck under the collar of his t-shirt. "This came from the door of this stupid model race car Becks always carried around with her. I bought it for her that first Christmas. The blast blew the car apart and turned the door into a rotating blade. It ripped me up. It took the doctors three hours and a hundred and nineteen stitches to make me look like this. I would take twenty scars like this if it meant Becks wasn't on my bed that night."

"That's why you're so protective and aware of security."

"Yes." He turned fully to me. "Colin is a real bastard, Jen-girl. He didn't leave me alone for a moment after that blast. He didn't allow me to go and find Vernet, even though we had multiple photos of him and a good guess at his location. He didn't allow me to push him away and not care. But it wasn't until you, Francine and Nikki that I cared so deeply again for anyone. You made me care again. I can't lose that. I can't lose any of you. It will kill me."

"You won't lose me. Or them. They love you. They asked me to speak to you because they want you in there with them."

Vinnie's eyes filled with tears again, but he shook his head and straightened. "How many Mozart thingies did you have to write before you agreed?"

"Three lines of a Mozart motet."

The smile that lifted Vinnie's cheeks and crinkled the corners of his eyes was genuine. I returned it and his smile widened. "I'm glad it was you."

His nonverbal cues alerted me that there was more to his statement. "Glad it was me who did what?"

"I've never told anyone else about Becks. I never even spoke to Colin about her after that day." He squeezed my hand and let it go. A small smile lifted the corner of his mouth and I realised he was looking at me wiping my hand hard against my thigh. I stopped and his smile disappeared. "Thank you for… fuck, thank you for everything, Jen-girl."

I'd never said this before and it felt very uncomfortable, but I knew it was important. "I have a very deep affection for you which Colin has told me is love. Not like I love Colin. Or Francine. Or Nikki. It's different. But it's there."

Vinnie's *mentalis* muscle caused his chin to quiver. He

pressed his lips hard together and stared at me with wide eyes.

He didn't need to speak. I saw it all on his face. And was certain that he would be too emotional to continue this line of discussion. I shifted away from him. "Your dinner is getting cold."

His smile was small, but grateful. "And it's most likely ruined by Francine and her stupid spices."

Chapter NINE

"I listened to Colin. I didn't look for the Vernet dude. I didn't even know his name." Vinnie's shrug was unconvincing. He was not uncaring about this failure. He looked at Colin. "You never told me you were looking for him."

We were sitting at the dining room table. Only Phillip and Manny had finished their meals. Francine had been listening to Vinnie retell his history with Becks, tears streaming down her face. Nikki had pushed the food around her plate for a few minutes before putting her knife and fork down and giving Vinnie her full attention. Her eyes were wide, her expression mirroring what I'd felt witnessing Vinnie's emotional anguish.

Vinnie's retelling was not as emotional as it had been when he'd told me. Yet it deeply affected everyone around the table. Nikki was using my linen napkin to wipe the tears from her cheeks. Francine had accepted the handkerchief Manny had offered her and was carefully dabbing under her eyes. Phillip sat motionless and Manny was slouched in his chair, his lips pressed in a hard line.

Distress was clear on Colin's face and most likely the reason his food was untouched. I hadn't even dished up when Vinnie and Nikki had finished setting the table and everyone had quietly taken their seats. The powerlessness I felt in the face of my friend's suffering had robbed me of my appetite.

Colin shifted in his seat. "I never stopped looking for him, Vin."

"Then why did you tell me to back off? Why did you tell me that revenge was not going to bring Becks back?"

"Because it was and still is true." Colin rubbed his hands against his thighs. "You were in no condition to go looking for revenge. Not after the blast."

"There's more." I sucked my lips in between my teeth when I realised I had just commented on Colin's nonverbal cues when he'd asked me not to.

"Might as well spill now, dude. My guts are all over the table in any case."

Colin nodded. "You would've killed him, Vin. Hell, *I* wanted to kill him."

"Then why stop me?"

"Because you would've lost more than just Becks. You're not a stone-cold killer, Vin. If you'd gone after Emad Vernet and acted on your grief, you would've dishonoured Becks' memory. It might've given you some form of comfort, but later it would've eaten away at your soul."

"And you decided what would be best for me? What the fuck, dude? I don't get it when people think they know what's best for another person."

"Is Colin wrong?" Francine crumpled the handkerchief in her hand. "Would you have been the person you are today, the person we love, if you'd gone after Emad and killed him?"

"Fuck, I don't know." Vinnie crossed his arms. "You're ganging up on me now? Were you in on this with Colin, looking for Emad behind my back?"

"Don't go getting all defensive now, big guy. I didn't know anything about Colin's secret search." She glanced at Colin. "You and I are going to have a very long chat about that."

"Do you three want to hug or can we discuss how this fits in with the case?" Manny looked from the one to the other. "No hugging then? Good. Then tell me why you didn't find this guy, Frey. It's been a bloody decade. Aren't you supposed to be one of the best criminals in the world, finding lost things?"

Colin glared at Manny. "You are such an arsehole, Millard."

"Thank you. Now answer my question. Why did you fail so miserably?"

"He's untraceable. I have stacks of photos of this guy, but can't find him on any law enforcement database." He looked at Francine. "I was really shocked that you found that photo of him so quickly. I'd tried every way I know and hadn't gotten anywhere."

"And that's why you should've asked for my help. I don't understand why you didn't."

I did. "If Colin had asked you to find someone in a photo, your curiosity would've led you to more searches and you might have found out about Becks. Colin knew Vinnie didn't want anyone to know. He wasn't going to betray that trust."

Manny looked at Colin. "You didn't find him with facial recognition software? Airports? Anywhere?"

"When I say I tried everything, I mean it." Colin turned to

Francine. "I used the FBI's facial recognition programme to scour Facebook and other social media in case he appeared in someone else's photos. Nothing."

"How the holy hell is that possible?"

"That's a good question." Colin shook his head. "I've worked through all possible scenarios. This is only possible if he is under someone's protection. No single person has the resources to protect himself from the best searches law enforcement has to offer. I'm wondering if he's working for some agency, maybe has some security clearance that allows him to be this invisible."

"Tell me everything you know about him, Frey."

"For starters, he's not on any law enforcement agency's radar. For about two years after the blast, I looked often to see if any agency was looking for him. Not one. The last few years, I've not been checking as frequently, but when I checked a couple of months ago and again yesterday, there was still nothing."

"And of course you have much better access now." Francine picked up her tablet. "But you don't have my ninja hacking skills. Maybe the agencies are hiding him somewhere."

"Stop for a moment, Francine. Don't run a search right now." Colin leaned forward and rested his forearms on the table. "In my search for Emad, I found a few important connections. One in particular that I think might be the reason he's unfindable."

"Ooh, the plot thickens." Francine put her tablet on the table. "Go on."

"I'll give you the whole file I've compiled on Emad, but a

very important part is his half-brother. See, Emad was born in Egypt to his French mother and Egyptian father. It was his mother's second marriage. Her first husband was the French ambassador stationed in Egypt and was ten years his wife's senior. When they arrived in Egypt, they already had one son, Claude.

"In the second year of the ambassador's mission, the wife started an affair with their Egyptian driver. Apparently it was true love and within a year she was divorced and married to the Egyptian. Emad was their child. For the next five years, Claude never saw his mother again. Part of her divorce agreement had been to give the diplomat husband full custody of her first son.

"She became very sick and her true love lost interest in her. She died that same year and Emad had nowhere to go. His Egyptian family didn't want him and the mother had cut all ties to her family and friends when she divorced the diplomat. I'm not sure how, but Claude's father heard about his son's half-brother being homeless, flew to Egypt and used all his contacts to adopt the boy. Two weeks after he and Claude arrived in Egypt, they left with a new addition to the family."

"Something tells me the diplomat is important." Francine's hand rested on her tablet as if ready to start an immediate search.

Colin inhaled deeply and nodded. "The diplomat is Alain Vernet."

"Mother Mary and all the saints!" Manny rubbed both hands over his face. "Tell me you're joking, Frey."

"Couldn't make this stuff up even if I tried, Millard."

"Um, who's Alain Vernet?" Nikki shrugged when everyone looked at her. "You guys know I don't follow politics. I only care about shopping and celebrities and reality shows."

"That's not true." My frown deepened when Nikki smiled. "That was not funny."

"I thought it was a little funny." Francine held her thumb and index finger half a centimetre from the other and winked at Nikki. "Alain Vernet is an old guy very few young people know about, even young people with an interest in politics. Colin can correct me if I'm wrong, but he's been on the advisory board for the United Nations for the last two decades. Currently he's on the Advisory Board for Human Security."

Colin nodded. "I only found out about Claude and Alain Vernet about three months ago. When I was in Italy to authenticate that Rembrandt for the national museum, I was chatting to the auctioneer's wife. Her passion is not the art her husband so carefully sources from all over the world. It is anything and everything to do with Egypt, preferably ancient Egypt. She told me her interest was piqued by a boy in her class when she was in grade two. His dad was a French diplomat, but this boy had Egyptian origins. He talked a lot about spending his early childhood there and that he was now living with his new dad and new brother."

"What made you think she was talking about Emad?" Phillip asked.

"She mentioned his dark skin, blue eyes and the scar above his left eye. It sent all kinds of alarm bells ringing. It wasn't very hard to get the name of that little boy and find out the rest of their family history. At first I was fired up"—Colin

looked at me—"excited to have finally found this smuggler's true identity. But the more I found out, the more I realised that we were walking into a minefield of problems."

"Especially if we're going to take on Alain Vernet's son," Francine said.

"Sons," Colin corrected. "Claude is the black sheep of the family. And he's Emad's partner in crime. Claude was very easy to find. He's all over the criminal database in France."

"Only arrested or convicted as well?" Manny asked.

"Oh, Claude spent time in prison. Alain Vernet bailed his firstborn out and made arrests and other problematic situations go away until Claude was twenty-one. Three weeks after his twenty-first birthday, Claude was arrested for starting a fight in a club and beating the bouncer into a coma. The bouncer needed surgery and three months of physical therapy. The records show that Claude phoned his father shortly after his arrest, but there is no record of Alain visiting the police station or having any other contact with his firstborn."

"Tough love." Nikki nodded.

"Claude served three months because he didn't have the money to pay the fine he got. The rest is my speculation. I think Claude and Emad are very close as brothers. After Claude left prison, he started his smuggling business with the help of his younger brother. From what I found, it looks like Alain Vernet had completely cut Claude out of his life and spent all his energy on Emad.

"While Claude was out making a name for himself in the criminal world, Emad was studying law. With his dad's connections, he got a prime position in a prestigious legal firm. He earned his promotions with a very sharp mind and a high success rate in negotiating profitable contracts for his clients. He is also fluent in his biological father's mother tongue, Arabic, and proficient in Chinese, Spanish and English. Needless to say, that caught the attention of the DGSE."

"The Directorate-General for External Security? He's a spy? With spy training and spy skills?" Nikki's eyes were wide. "I know it shouldn't be, but it's like really cool."

"Not if being a spy gives Emad the opportunity to break the law." Manny breathed heavily through his nose, his lips tightly pressed together.

"It would be the perfect cover." Vinnie spoke for the first time since Colin started his explanation. "Emad gets to travel the world. His job gives him all kinds of criminal contacts. And he has the resources to take his brother with him without anyone noticing."

"That's what I was thinking too." Colin's eyes narrowed when Francine picked up her tablet, but he turned his attention back to Vinnie. "I only got my hands on this info the last few weeks, Vin. I didn't want to open old wounds without enough evidence. When I found out who their father is and that Emad works for the DGSE, I didn't want to do anything that would raise red flags and put any of us in danger."

Something that had been mentioned earlier bothered me. "How is this related to the spider tattoo?"

"When I looked through Claude's arrest records, I made sure to memorise all the photos they had of him." Colin tapped on the inside of his wrist. "That's where I saw the tattoo. I have all that info and the photos in the file as well."

I stared at Colin's face. "Your tense lower eyelids and raised upper eyelids exhibit fear. Why?"

"Fear, Frey?" Manny closed his eyes for a second. "What the bloody hell is going on?"

"Last week, I uncovered connections between Claude and Fradkov."

"What the fuck, dude?" Vinnie's eyes were wide. "Fradkov is BFFs with Russia and North Korea."

Fortunately, Francine and Nikki had used that ridiculous acronym enough times for me to understand. "Your statement doesn't make sense. A person can't be friends with a country. Is Fradkov best friends with President Andreyev and Kim Jong-un? Or are you being hyperbolic?"

"And that's why you should've come to me, Frey." There was no bluster in Manny's tone. He rubbed his hands over his face. "Holy frigging hell. Fradkov is a name few people have the courage to say out loud."

Colin straightened. "You know about Fradkov?"

"Unfortunately. He's one of the most powerful men on this planet. He has single-handedly destroyed entire regimes. On request—and by request, I mean gigantic payment—he'll build a new regime. One willing to play nice with those who paid to kill off the old and establish the new government."

"I've never heard of such actions." I made a point of staying up to date with current political affairs.

"Of course you wouldn't have heard about this." Francine looked up from her tablet for a moment. "These are all conspiracy theories. No evidence has ever been found to connect Fradkov to any of these revolutions."

"When supermodel says revolutions, you can bet your last penny that most of those were bloody." Manny glanced at Francine's tablet when she picked it up again, then looked at me. "I'm no psychologist, but that bastard is psycho. His only loyalty is to his bank account. If a corrupt government wants to get rid of a whistle-blower or a nosy journalist, he'll happily assassinate that person. For the right price, of course."

"You know much more about him than I do, old man." Vinnie sat back in his chair. "All I knew was that he is a master at destroying careers by planting carefully crafted evidence to discredit some dude. I also know Fradkov was born in Cuba, spent some years in South America and studied politics in the US. That's it."

"When he graduated, he was offered professorship at Harvard, but he declined," Manny continued. "Up to this point all agencies have info on him. But he disappeared after he got his doctoral degree. Gone. There have been rumours floating around that he's on the payroll of the CIA, MI6, the FSB and several other national security agencies."

"And he collects art." Colin's quiet statement caught everyone's attention. "More specifically, he collects Vecellios."

"Bloody hell, Frey." Manny slumped in his chair. "Can this get any worse? How the hell do you know he collects art?"

"A few months before you arrested me, Fradkov hired me to authenticate three paintings. Two of those were Vecellios. The other was a Bellini, another famous Renaissance artist. We had an hour-and-a-half conversation about Renaissance art. He's a well-spoken, highly educated man."

"You liked him." I saw it in Colin's expression.

"I did. There was no indication that he was anything other

than the businessman he introduced himself to be. Most definitely not a political assassin."

It was quiet around the table for two minutes. Then Manny pressed the heels of his hands hard against his eyes for a moment. "We need to find out what kind of connection Gallo has to Emad and Claude. Then we need to find out if and how this is connected to the meeting between the leaders. And if or how Fradkov fits into all of this."

"I'm going to make you pay for not trusting me for a very long time, Colin." Francine looked up from her tablet. "I would've been able to find a lot more info if you had asked me. Your computer skills are no match for mine."

"You found something." I saw it in her nonverbal cues.

"Not something, girlfriend. Someone." She flipped her hair over one shoulder. "I found Emad. I know where he is."

"For the love of all the holy saints, please tell me you didn't sit here next to me and hack the DGSE's site." Manny glared at Francine.

"Okay. I won't tell you." She looked at me. "I'll tell you. It wasn't even fun hacking them. Their security is no challenge. Anyhoo, I found a file on Emad. It has all the identities officially created for him."

"At last count I had seventeen," Colin said. "How many are on his file?"

"Twenty-one. We'll compare notes later. I'm thinking you would be more interested to know that our boy is on his way back to France. He's just spent a week in South Korea as Pierre Baert." She glanced at her tablet. "His flight lands in five hours at Charles de Gaulle."

Manny took his phone from his trouser pocket. "I'll get

Daniel to organise a GIPN team in Paris to go to the international airport and meet Emad there."

"Bring him here." Vinnie's voice was low.

"Not for you to torture him and make him cry for his mommy." Manny lowered his chin and stared at Vinnie. "You going to keep your shit together, big guy? If these idiots have something planned for the leaders' meeting, we need to focus on that. I need your mind in the game and not on taking revenge. There will be time for that later."

Vinnie clenched his jaw so tight, I wondered if he was causing damage to his teeth. After a few seconds, he nodded stiffly. "My mind is in the game."

"Good. Something tells me the next few days are going to be like nothing we've experienced before." Manny glanced around the table, then at his smartphone's screen, and nodded. "I think we're done here for the night. Emad will be here in the morning. Let's get some sleep and gain some control over our emotions."

"Listen to you use the royal 'we'. It's so sexy." Francine reached over and played with Manny's earlobe. "Shall *we* go home and lose some control before *we* get some sleep?"

"Get off me, woman." Manny pushed her hand away without looking at her. "I'll get Daniel updated and also brief Privott on what's happening. Tomorrow is going to be a tough one."

Chapter TEN

"Criminal!" Manny snapped his fingers in front of Vinnie's face. "Do you have control of yourself?"

Vinnie's nostrils flared and he swallowed repeatedly as he looked at the only wooden door on this floor of GIPN's headquarters. The GIPN building was just outside the centre of the city, strategically positioned to reach most areas as soon as possible. It was a modern building with an industrial finish.

This floor was where Daniel and his team spent their time when they weren't in the field. There were three rooms, separated by glass walls. One of those rooms was occupied by four men and a woman, all dressed in the GIPN uniform. It looked like they were planning an extraction strategy if I went by the maps and schematics displayed. Another room had gym equipment, currently being used by two men.

Industrial carpeting covered the floor throughout this whole space, ventilation and other pipes ran along the ceiling. I liked the minimalistic finishings. I especially approved of the smart usage of the glass walls to keep conversations confidential and cut down on the overall noise of a group of people occupying the same area. We were in a large conference room, also cordoned off with glass walls and a glass sliding door.

Only one room on this floor had brick walls and a solid wooden door. Emad Vernet was in that room.

Vinnie took a deep breath and turned to Manny. "I'm good. I've got control. I know we'll find a way to make that motherfucker pay for what he did."

Manny looked at me. I nodded. "He's being truthful."

"Good." Manny pointed at the large glass table in the centre of the room. "Now sit your arse down. We've got work to do."

Vinnie glanced once more at the closed door, then at the GIPN officer standing guard, before he sat down next to Daniel. As soon as Emad's flight had landed, a GIPN team stationed in Paris had boarded the plane and taken custody of Emad. Daniel had shown no deception cues when he'd said he trusted that team with his life.

They had transported Emad to GIPN's headquarters here in Strasbourg and Daniel had informed us early this morning that the diplomat's adopted son was ready to be interviewed as soon as we could get here.

Francine hadn't joined us, still working on decrypting Gallo's computer. Manny had said that she'd only slept four hours before she'd returned to the messy workstation in her living room. He put his smartphone on the centre of the table and tapped on the screen. A second later, a ringtone sounded in the room and was immediately answered.

"Hello, my lovelies."

"What did you find, supermodel? And keep it clean. You're on speakerphone."

"You know our deal, handsome." Francine's was one of the few female voices I enjoyed listening to. It had a breathy quality and her alto pitch never vexed me. Although her irreverence and melodrama frequently did. "You show me yours and I'll show you mine."

"We don't have time for this now, supermodel."

"Time for what?" I asked.

"Oh, hey, girlfriend." The sound of Francine's bangles came through the speakers of the phone and I wondered if she was waving at her phone. "I want to know what Daniel's palace looks like."

"Why would Manny know that? We are not in a palace. And I'm not sure Daniel owns…" I sighed. "What did you mean?"

"Oh, for the love of all that is holy." Manny grabbed his phone and tapped a few times on the screen. "Here. Look."

He got up from the table and did a slow turn while holding the phone in front of him. When he was at an angle where I could see the screen, I realised he was now on a video call with Francine.

"That's all you're getting." Manny tapped his phone again, put it on the centre of the table and sat down. "What did you find?"

"Enough evidence to put Gallo away for the rest of his life."

"What evidence?" Colin asked.

"Ooh, juicy stuff." Francine's voice rose in the way it did when she got excited about celebrity scandals. "It took some doing to decrypt his computer. It had some military-grade encryption going, but nothing this queen of all computers couldn't crack. Anyhoo, I found all his financials, all his accounts, all kinds of stuff on his businesses. It confirmed a lot of what we found in the last ten months."

"None of that is useful in this case." I found it most exasperating when people felt the need to build a dramatic introduction to their findings. "Stop wasting time and tell us what you found."

"You and handsome are such spoilsports." She sighed loudly. "Fine. I'll tell you. I found a bunch of hidden files with more encryption. I only managed to crack one of those babies wide open. But I got us three recordings."

"Video recordings?" I wondered if everyone had heard the hope in my voice.

"Nope. Only voice recordings of three short phone calls."

I barely stopped the groan from leaving my lips. Without the context of body language, it was difficult for me to understand people's communication. Only listening to someone's words and tone made it so much harder for me to know whether they were being truthful or whether I should investigate deeper to find their true intentions.

"Let's hear them." Manny leaned towards the phone, tilting his head.

"Coming right up." The clicking of a mouse sounded for three seconds. "Okay, here's the first one."

At first, I thought it was Manny's phone ringing, but then I realised it was the recording. The call wasn't immediately answered.

"Yes?" The curt answer came from a male voice after the seventh ring. I couldn't tell anything from that one syllable. Especially when there was so much static on his side of the conversation.

"It's done." This male had a deeper voice, his accent undefined.

"Everything. You did it all?" The first man's accent came through strongly. I knew an expert at the Strasbourg University who would be able to pinpoint this man's origins, sometimes even the suburb of his hometown, by listening to his enunciation. I didn't have this ability. But his Russian accent was unmistakeable.

"Of course." The deep voice sounded insulted, but I didn't know if it was sincere or a pretence to maintain an image of arrogance and control. "It went down without a hitch. As predicted, we have plenty of leftovers."

"Good. You must stand by now. I'll contact you with instructions." The static couldn't hide the slight lift in the Russian voice. Despite his attempt to sound bored, he was excited. Colin frowned and leaned forward. Then he shook his head and sat back in his chair.

"You have two weeks. Then I'm selling the leftovers. I'm not sitting on my hands for months on end."

There was silence for seven seconds. "I will contact you this week."

A few clicks sounded through Manny's phone and Francine's bracelets jingled. "Okay, my lovelies. That is the first recording. Do you want to hear the next one or do you first want to discuss this one?"

"Doc?" Manny looked at me with raised eyebrows.

I took a moment to consider the best course of action. "Play the next one."

"Done, girlfriend." Another few clicks sounded and I readied myself to listen to every nuance.

This time the call was answered after the first ring.

"Is it there?" It was the same deep voice from the first

recording. His voice sounded more animated, as if he was speaking to someone he trusted.

"Yes. He transferred it thirty minutes ago." The new male voice had a similar accent to the deep voice, but the differences were there. I wondered what the sociolinguist would say about this.

"He said it will go down this week."

"Fantastic." The relief and excitement sounded genuine, but I couldn't be sure. "Then we'll get the rest and we can blow this joint."

I gasped at the last few words. The recording ended and I held up my hand. "Wait before you go on, Francine. Tell me what he meant when he talked about blowing this joint."

"Usually that means someone is happy to leave a place, Jen-girl." Vinnie narrowed his eyes at the smartphone. "And I really hope that is what this dude is trying to say."

"Because the alternative could be that they intend to blow *up* a place." Daniel pulled his smartphone from one of the many pockets in his combat pants. "We might need to mobilise the bomb squad just in case."

I had many more questions, but they would have to wait. "Play the next one, Francine."

"Here it is." More clicks and once again the ringing of a phone sounded.

"Yo." The third male voice sounded relaxed.

"Do you have the blueprints?" It was the deep voice again.

"Yup." The short answers frustrated me. I could tell almost nothing from these short sounds.

"Meet me at Oh-Suh at eleven tonight."

"Hmm. You see, I'm thinking you need to make it more

worth my while." At last I could tell that this man had a German accent. He was very confident. The pitch of his tone didn't increase. This sentence was spoken with the same slowness as the first two words. "I'm doing this because I believe in what you're trying to accomplish, but if anyone ever connects me to this, my career and possibly my life will be over."

"We have an agreement." The deep voice's tone left no opening for negotiation. "Back out now and your career and life will be over much sooner than you're expecting. Be at Oh-Suh at eleven."

The call ended and Francine's bracelets jingled again. "That's it. So? What do you think?"

"Well, I think that I wouldn't want to push the guy on all three calls," Daniel said. "Not with that 'or else' he ended the call with."

"He didn't say 'or else'." Not in any of the three recordings.

"It was implied," Colin said with a smile. "I agree with Daniel. That man doesn't sound like he should be trifled with."

I organised my thoughts, my questions. "Francine, do these recordings have time stamps?"

"They do." More bracelets jingling. "All of them were recorded four days ago. The first one at eleven o'clock in the morning, the second an hour later and the third fifteen minutes after that."

Vinnie leaned forward. "If the dude from the first recording was going to contact the other dude this week, it means whatever they're planning is going to take place in the next three days."

"Or sooner." Manny scratched the stubble on his jaw. "If all this is connected, then it's going to happen tomorrow when the leaders are meeting."

"We don't have enough evidence to connect all the people and other elements." I wished we had more information, more data. "Francine, did you find anything else on the computer?"

"Not on Gallo's computer, no. There are a few more encrypted files, but there's an almost one-gigabyte file that I'm really interested in. What would take so much memory? Something delicious, that's what."

"Try to decrypt it as soon as you can. It might give us more useful data."

"I'm all over it, my bestest bestie. But I'm also going to look until I find some footage of the last two men meeting at Oh-Suh."

"Do you know this place?" Colin asked.

"Oh, do I ever. Only true hackers know of Oh-Suh. It's a play on OSU, which stands for Officially Sanctioned User. It's an underground club that you can only get into if you're able to hack the security system. They change the system every night and it's never an easy hack. Fortunately, it's totally worth it. It's one of the best clubs I've ever been to."

"Does this mean those two men are hackers?" Daniel asked.

"I know you're going to hate me saying this, girlfriend, but that is my guess. The hackers really want to keep this place secret. But I know where it is and I'll find those two on a camera coming or going."

"Do that, supermodel. We need to put faces to these

voices." Manny looked at me. "Is it possible that the man on all three calls could be Emad and the second recording's voice could be Claude? Or vice versa?"

I leaned away from him. "You know I don't speculate. We need recordings of Emad and Claude so we can compare their voices."

"We've recorded the trip from the airport as well as the whole time Emad has been in the interview room." Daniel nodded towards the closed room. "Francine, you can use that to compare."

"Do we have anything on Claude?" she asked.

"I'll get the prison where he served his term to send you any recorded material they have." Daniel got up. "I'll call them now. Give me a few minutes."

"Okay, what do we know?" Manny looked at me as Daniel walked towards the gym area, already talking on his phone.

I didn't respond. We had three recordings that would require speculation to put the conversation snippets into context.

"We know that the dude on all three calls did something that is going to be used in some event going down this week. And that there are leftovers of something." Vinnie thought some more. "We also know he has a partner and they're getting paid big bucks for the thing they did as well as the job they're going to pull off."

I didn't argue. Those were easy and rational conclusions to draw from the conversations.

"And that confirms my theory that one of the brothers is on all three calls and the other on the second call. Doc, what can you add?"

I looked at the phone. "Francine, are you still there?"

"Like I would leave this conversation. It's far too interesting."

"Are there any other recordings on Gallo's computer?"

"Nope. I've checked. I also looked for any access he had to cloud accounts and I did get lucky there. I found his CatchDunk account."

"What on God's green earth is that?" Manny asked.

"It's a clever way to back up every single activity that takes place on your smartphone," Francine said. "Photos, text messages, application information, GPS, just about anything you can imagine is saved on the third-party firmware. It can be a lifesaver if your phone is stolen, broken or lost. If your entire history is saved in the cloud account, you can retrieve it and will have lost nothing."

"Have you accessed it yet?" I didn't ask her if she was able to.

"No. I thought you guys would want to know about the recordings first."

"You're right." Manny leaned closer to the phone. "But now you can start getting into that Catdoo."

"CatchDunk, handsome. And this is priority as soon as I end the call."

"Then end the call. Don't worry, I'll do it." Manny picked up his phone. "Call me when you've got something."

Francine started to respond, but Manny had already ended the call. He rubbed his hand over his short hair and got up. "Doc, we need to find out what secrets Emad will share with us."

Daniel returned and sat down. "I've sent three recordings

of Claude to Francine. It will be more than enough for her to compare the voices."

"What about recordings of Emad?" I asked.

"Also sent. Francine now has enough sound files of both to compare and get an accurate match."

I frowned. "You are convinced that the voices belong to Emad and Claude."

"I haven't had much contact with Emad, but did listen when one of our guys offered him something to drink." He lifted one shoulder—not completely convinced of what he was saying. "I wasn't paying attention to his voice, but I'm pretty sure he's the second voice on the second recording."

"Then I reckon the dude on all the calls is Claude." Vinnie glared at the wooden door. "I wonder where he's hiding."

"Doc? Are you ready?" Manny stood in the doorway, his feet pointing towards the closed room.

I got up. "I don't want to talk to him."

"Good." Manny waited until I passed him, then fell into step next to me. "I don't want you to talk either. I just want you to do what you do best."

I slowed down to a stop and waited until I had Manny's attention. "Have you ever interviewed a spy before?"

"Don't worry about my skills, Doc. I've done this before."

I closed my eyes for a second. "You are one of the best interrogators I've seen. I'm not doubting your skill. I'm taking into consideration that Emad has been trained to deceive."

"Then you'd better be watching closely, Doc." Manny continued walking to the closed room. "We don't want him to fool us."

I mentally wrote two bars of Mozart's Piano Sonata No.11 in A and followed Manny. The GIPN officer stood aside for Manny to open the door. He walked in without waiting for me.

I followed and took a second to take note of the differences between this room and the conference room we'd come from. This windowless room had a steel table, four chairs and nothing else. A solid-looking ceiling finished the room off to look like a generic space found in any office building, not the modern industrial appearance of the rest of the floor.

Manny pulled out a chair and sat down, glaring at the man on the other side of the table. Photos were deceptive in many ways. They caught mere moments in a person's life and without context it was hard to truly determine what the person on the photo could be like. Sometimes photos taken by amateurs were unable to truly capture the beauty of a person. Such was the case with Emad Vernet.

His strong facial bones, olive skin, blue eyes and confident bearing combined to make a very handsome man. His condescending smirk detracted from his appeal and the slight wrinkles in the skin meant it was an expression he often wore.

He shook his hands and the cuffs rattled where they were attached to the loops on the tabletop. "Why am I cuffed?"

"It's a silly little thing we do when we arrest arseholes." Manny spoke slowly as if talking to someone far below Emad's intelligence. "It's to make sure you stay put."

I sat down next to Manny, not taking my eyes off Emad. He wasn't fast enough to hide the flash of surprise followed by amusement. His contemptuous expression returned as he first studied Manny before turning his attention to me. "Who are you?"

"Ah, ah, ah." Manny waved his index finger side to side. "Handcuffs also mean that we get to ask the questions. Not you."

"I won't be answering any questions without my lawyer." He rested his hands on the table and leaned back. I didn't need to wait for Francine to confirm the identity of the voice on the second recording. It was without a doubt Emad Vernet.

"Poor boy." Manny's sympathy would fool anyone who wasn't an expert in recognising deception. Or someone who wasn't a spy. "It's sweet that you think this is like one of those silly American telly shows. You're not in the country of the free and brave, son. You're in a place where you're going to be crying for your mommy soon."

Emad's laughter was genuine. As was the unease that followed when he saw Manny's expression. He swallowed and took a slow breath. His facial muscles relaxed into a neutral expression and I knew our interview was over. He had seen something in Manny's expression that had caused him to call on his training. From this point on his nonverbal cues could be hard to read. I accepted the challenge.

"Why were you in South Korea?" Manny didn't sound very interested in the answer. He was equally skilled at deception.

"Lawyer." The intonation in Emad's voice was neutral, his expression revealing nothing.

"Were you there to meet with your buddy Fradkov?"

"Lawyer."

"Did your brother join you?"

"Lawyer."

"What are you smuggling this time?"

"Lawyer."

"Is it diamonds? Art? Girls? Cigarettes?"

"Lawyer."

"Is your half-brother's father helping you two?"

"Lawyer." No matter how well someone managed to control their facial muscles, it was almost impossible to control one's pupils. That was how I saw Emad's anger. His pupils constricted when Manny purposely distanced him from his adopted father. He hadn't been pleased.

Manny slumped deeper into his chair. "You should know that you're done. Whatever you and your criminal brother thought to smuggle into this country—it's not going to happen."

"Lawyer."

"We know you have plans for next week. Since you're not leaving here, you better hope your brother can pull it off alone."

"Lawyer."

"And you also better make peace with the fact that he'll be the only one enjoying the fruits of your labour."

"Lawyer."

"Well, thank you for your co-operation, Emad." Manny got up, looked at Emad's handcuffed wrists and chuckled. "Don't go anywhere."

"Lawyer."

I followed Manny out the room already thinking that I needed to see more footage of Emad. I needed a baseline before I studied this interview again. The door shut behind us and the GIPN officer took his position in front of the door again. I glanced at the conference room and wasn't surprised to see everyone watching us approach. Against the wall was a monitor showing Emad glaring at his handcuffs. They had been watching the interview.

Manny waited until we were in the room before he turned to me. "What did you see, Doc?"

I sat down next to Colin. "He was angry when you didn't acknowledge Alain as his father, but only as Claude's. His reaction when you mentioned smuggling something into France was smug, victorious."

"Hmm." Manny nodded. "So they're not here to smuggle anything in or out. What about his brother pulling this thing off alone?"

"He wasn't comfortable with that. He also showed contempt when you mentioned the event taking place next week. He thinks you're incompetent."

"Good." Manny rubbed his jaw. "I want him to think he's better than us. Hopefully, he'll slip up and give us something really useful. But at least we know that this has to be a two-man job. At least. What about the payment?"

"Are you referring to 'the fruit of their labour'?"

"Yes."

"Again his reaction was smug." It was incredibly hard to get past my loathing of hypothesising, but I reminded myself that our team worked best when there was a flow of ideas. I inhaled deeply and pushed the words out. "Upon reflection, I believe it is a rational conclusion that Emad believes he will not be detained for long. He displayed pleasure at the thought of the payment."

"Do you think we'll get anything else out of him, Doc?"

"Possibly, but it will have to be a continuance of this interview style."

"Your face is telling me you don't think we should do it."

I almost smiled at the reversal of roles. "You're correct. This interview was successful because you didn't share a lot of information. In order to elicit more reactions from him, you would have to reveal more."

"And that would give the smug bastard enough to know we're lying or that we know too little or too much."

I thought about our next steps. "I need to see more footage of Emad. We need to speak to Alain Vernet, but first I need to see footage of Alain before we interview him."

"I'll get supermodel to have it ready when you get to your room." Manny took his smartphone from his pocket, tapped on the screen and put the device to his ear.

I got up. "I need to leave now."

"I'll bring the old man." Vinnie swallowed a few times, hatred in his expression as he glared at the closed door. "It's better that I don't stay here much longer."

The torment in Vinnie's expression brought that uncomfortable tightening around my chest. I had not considered the effect it would have on Vinnie being so close to the man who had killed Becks and scarred Vinnie for life. I walked to his chair and stood awkwardly next to him. I knew how much he would appreciate a hug, but I couldn't. I put the tip of my index finger on his shoulder.

He turned his head to look at my finger and his breath hitched. When he looked up at me five seconds later, the pain was replaced by affection. "Thank you, Jen-girl."

I nodded and turned to the door. Colin was waiting for me,

his expression soft. I hoped he wouldn't want a conversation about friendship and feelings while driving to the team room. The last twelve hours had been draining enough having to deal with the emotions of the people I cared for. I wanted to focus on finding out what the Vernet brothers were planning. And what Gallo really wanted.

Chapter ELEVEN

"You're too close." I gripped the car seat with one hand and my seatbelt with the other. I cleared my throat and tried for calm. "And you're speeding."

Colin glanced at the digital display on the dashboard and smiled. "Two kilometres faster than the speed limit is not speeding, Jenny."

"Technically it is." I pushed deeper into my chair. "And you're still too close."

Colin chuckled and slowed down enough to put another two metres between us and the Volvo in front of us. He nodded towards the dashboard. "See? I'm driving exactly fifty kilometres an hour."

I sometimes wondered if he tailgated on purpose. It always moved my attention from whatever I was obsessing about to fretting about the distance between the two vehicles. I studied him. "You don't have to distract me."

His smile faltered. "Maybe I want to distract myself."

"From what?"

"What do you think, love?"

I considered the possibilities and eliminated most. "You're concerned about Vinnie."

"He never talked about that night, about Becks' death." His voice was low. "He never asked me to stop talking about it. He would just leave whenever I brought it up in conversation. Every single time. After the third or fourth time I realised we were never going to discuss it again and I left it."

"But you didn't leave it."

He was quiet for a few seconds. "Now I don't know if I should've left it. Vin is very upset that I did this behind his back."

"It could be that the negative emotions he's experiencing are not necessarily aimed at you. It could also be that he doesn't want to face a very painful part of his past." I shrugged when Colin glanced at me. "I'm not speculating. In situations like this, people seek an easier target to aim their anger at. You were the one to use the analogy of being the closest punching bag. This could be the case again. You're convenient."

He laughed softly. "Just what every man wants to hear. I'm convenient."

"I didn't say it with the same negative intonation and facial expressions you used." I crossed my arms over my chest when I noticed his smile. "You purposely misinterpreted my meaning."

"You left the door wide open for that, love."

Apparently I did this often. Colin had used the open-door expression enough times for me to comprehend its meaning. I had no response to that and sat quietly, watching him drive to the team room. I seldom entered a vehicle as a passenger. Most drivers sent me into a state of panic or close to a shutdown with their disregard for the laws and the safety of everyone else on the road.

It had taken Colin only a few trips with me as a passenger

to adjust his driving style to something that I preferred. Two months ago I'd mentioned it and he'd been pleased that I'd noticed it. I'd felt guilty for not mentioning it earlier. It was hard to always remember to acknowledge the small and often big sacrifices my friends made for me.

The ringtone of Colin's smartphone interrupted my musings. He glanced at the display and pressed the button on the steering wheel to connect the call. "Whatcha got, Francine?"

"Well, aren't you just down to business? I expect it from Manny, but not you. What about a 'Hello, Francine'? Or a 'How are you doing, greatest goddess of all the interwebs'?"

I sighed. Francine was in a playful mood. "Hello, Francine."

"My bestest bestie! I knew you would be the one to treat me right."

My head dropped forward and I sighed again. "Is there a purpose to this call?"

"Of course there is. Firstly, to brag about my super-duper hacking skills. Secondly, to hear your pretty voice."

I didn't respond. It would only encourage her. Instead I looked at the display on the dashboard and thought of the dangers of talking on the phone while driving. My small city car had Bluetooth capabilities, but I never used it. I tended to become too focused when talking on the phone, which impeded my concentration on whatever else I was doing. It confirmed the studies that proved that talking on one's phone, even when using a hands-free system, could impair one's driving as profoundly as driving while inebriated.

"Want me to tell Millard that you hacked his investment account? Again?" Colin's smile negated his threat. "Or should I tell him that you changed his investments? Again?"

"How do you...?" Her bracelets jingled over the phone as if she was waving her hands. "Oh, never mind. Manny might shout and scream at me, but when he realises that he's making more money, he'll stop. I hope. Hmm. Maybe he won't. You play dirty, my good-looking friend. I like it."

"You have five seconds to start spilling or I end this call and phone Millard."

"Fine. Fine. Whatever." She huffed loudly. "I used the recordings of Emad and Claude that Daniel sent me to confirm their identities. Claude is the one with the deep voice, the one who talked on all three recordings and Emad was the other voice on the second recording."

"If Claude agreed to meet the person in the third recording, we can assume he is in Strasbourg," Colin said. "Those brothers are tight. I was asking around about the smuggling just after the explosion in Vinnie's apartment. Everything I got pointed to those two never being apart for too long. I'm sure Claude is here."

"That's my thinking too." Francine cleared her throat. "We've got to put them away, Colin. For Vinnie."

"We will." He was convinced.

"Good. Girlfriend, I'm getting you some interview-type footage of Emad as well as daddy dearest. It will be waiting for you when you get here. Next on my list then is finding footage of Emad and blueprint guy before, during or after their meeting. There are enough security cameras, ATM cameras and city CCTV footage to find them somewhere." Her inhale was deep enough to sound over the system. "I will not rest until I find it."

"Do you have any other useful information?"

"Not yet." Her tone softened. "Colin, how's Vin han—" Her question got cut off and silence filled the SUV.

"Huh. We lost the connection." Colin frowned at the display and pressed a few buttons on the steering wheel. His frown deepened. "I'm not getting through to her. Have a look, please?"

I took his phone from the dashboard holder and swiped the screen. "There's enough battery power and you seem to be connected to the internet as well as having a strong phone signal."

"Phone Francine again." Something in his tone made me look away from the phone, but he appeared puzzled rather than concerned.

Even though Colin had a different phone than mine, the operating system was similar enough to navigate. I went to his call history and tapped on Francine's name. The screen changed as if to put the call through, but almost immediately returned to the call history screen. I tried again with the same results. "It's not working."

"Hmm." Again the strange tension in his tone caught my attention.

I studied him closer. "After being with me for more than three years, you should know that you cannot hide your micro-expressions from me. Your *masseter* muscles in your jaw only tighten like that when you are deeply concerned about something. What is wrong?"

"Is your phone working? See if you can get Francine on the line."

When we were stressed, our muscle tension increased,

especially around our throats. This exact effect was causing Colin's voice to sound strangled. Adrenaline shot into my veins and my heart rate increased. "Tell me what is wrong."

He lifted his hands from the steering wheel. "I don't have control of the car."

My first instinct was to grab the steering wheel to make sure the SUV wouldn't crash into the car in front of us. As I reached for the steering wheel, it turned, accurately manoeuvring around a car that was slowing down to turn into a side street. I jerked my hands back and stared at the steering wheel. "No. No, no, no."

"Jenny." Colin's voice didn't penetrate the panic building in my mind. He grabbed my forearm tightly. "Jenny!" The urgency in his tone managed to draw my eyes away from the steering wheel to his face. He kept glancing back at the road, but waited until he was sure he had my attention. "You're going to have to try really hard to stay with me. We seem to be driving safely and calmly at the moment, so I don't want to fight the steering wheel. But I don't want to take my attention away from this. I need you to call Francine on your phone. Can you do that for me?"

I was grateful he had spoken so much. It had given me enough time to focus on his words and force Mozart's Symphony No.6 in F to play in the back of my mind. I nodded and reached into my handbag. "Put Mozart's symphony number six in F on the system. It doesn't need to be loud. Please."

"Of course." He had loaded many of my Mozart favourites onto his entertainment system. The soothing sounds of this composition filled the SUV before I swiped the screen of my smartphone. The immediate relief in my mind was staggering. Mozart's music always had that effect on me. It was as if countless strings in my mind untangled from a chaotic mess, straightened out and gently flowed in tune with the music.

I filled my lungs deeply and called Francine. She answered on the first ring. "Hey, what happened?"

"Put her on speakerphone, Jenny." Colin waited until I held the phone between us. "Francine, I think my car is being hacked as we speak."

"What? Manny is with me. I'm putting you on speakerphone." Frantic typing sounded over the speaker. "Oh, my God. Yeah, I'm being blocked from your phone. As far as my system knows, your phone isn't even turned on."

"Turned on." Colin turned to me. "Jenny, turn my phone off."

I grabbed his phone from my lap and pressed and held the power button down. A few times. "It's not turning off."

"I'm assuming the hacker got access through your Bluetooth." Francine was still typing and clicking in the background. "Even if you turn your phone off now, he is in your car system."

"Can he access my phone?" I didn't want someone controlling my phone. But more importantly, I didn't want to lose contact with Francine.

"Do you have your Bluetooth or internet enabled?"

"Not Bluetooth, but internet."

"Turn that off now." The urgency in her voice sent a fresh spurt of adrenaline into my system.

I took a deep breath and focused on how similar the

symphony's soft sounds were to one of Mozart's operas, especially the fluttering flutes and fast shimmering strings. Finding the right settings and turning off the internet on my phone didn't take long. I leaned back against the seat. "It's off."

"Well, let's just hope he's too busy driving your car to worry about another phone."

"What about Colin's phone?" I looked out of the side window. "Should I throw it out the window?"

"Can't do any harm." She huffed. "Except to the phone. Do it."

I pressed the button to lower the electrical window. The window didn't move. I pressed again. And again. "The window isn't working."

Colin tried his with the same result. Then he pressed the button to unlock the doors. Nothing happened. "He's got us locked in here, Francine."

An involuntary whimper escaped from my tight lips. Blackness entered my peripheral vision and I could barely hear Mozart's symphony over the pounding of my heart.

"Jenny. I need you with me." Colin's hand covered my fists. "You've got to fight this."

I knew that I would be a liability if I were in a shutdown and Colin had to make a crucial decision about leaving the car or taking some other action. If only I truly had control over my mind. I didn't. Over the years, I'd learned many ways to minimise the possibilities of shutdowns and meltdowns. I'd taught myself ways to manage the panic that was a constant companion, but I couldn't control my mind when it reached saturation point.

"Jenny!" Colin shook my fists. "Fight it. I need you."

I forced myself to feel his hand on mine, to hear each note played by each instrument as the sounds filled the SUV. Slowly, the blackness receded a bit. "I'm trying."

"I know, love." He put my smartphone on the anti-slip pad on his dashboard and pulled my left fist towards him. "I need my hands here in case I need to steer. But I also need you here. Can you hold onto me?"

I knew he was doing this as much for me as for himself. I never reached out to touch someone, but pressing my fist hard against his thigh gave me surprising comfort.

"I can't locate your car, Colin." Francine's tapping and clicking had not slowed down.

"He must have disabled all tracking devices in the system."

"Frey, I've got Daniel on the phone." Manny's tone was calm. "Where are you?"

Colin looked at the side street we just passed. "We're going south on Rue du Roland. Just went by Rue du Bois."

"I'm sending Daniel's team to you. The big guy already left the building and is most likely halfway on his way to you already."

"I don't know if that's wise, handsome," Francine said. "If someone's got control of Colin's car through Bluetooth, he has to be within a hundred metres of the car if he wants to maintain control. We don't know what he'll do if he sees Vin."

"The hacker is here?" I didn't like the breathlessness in my voice, but my throat felt as if someone had their hands around it and was squeezing hard. I turned in my seat and looked behind us. "There are a lot of cars around us."

"Let me get on the city cameras and see if I can spot him."

"I'm still sending Daniel out." Manny sounded resolute. "They can keep their distance until we know exactly what we're dealing with."

"You just passed Rue Coli. I see you." Francine sounded relieved.

"Good. Now find who's doing this." Colin's eyes narrowed. "I don't know where he is taking us. This direction will take us to the Institute of Technology or the golf club."

"Okay, I know where you are. I'm checking the cars on the street with you." The quality of Francine's tone was the same as when she was thinking aloud. Frequently it frustrated me because she would present many irrational theories until she settled on something much more worthy of saying out loud. Today, I was glad she was thinking aloud. It gave me something else to focus on. "Hmm, it can't be the red Subaru that's been behind you for a few blocks. The old lady is holding that steering wheel as if it is a wild horse..." Her voice tapered off.

"What about the blue Ford?" Manny asked.

"Nah. That car is older than you, handsome. And that man driving has a phone from the last decade on the dashboard. Do people still use those little tap-three-times-to-get-a-letter pho... Hmm... Ooh! Look! Look!"

"Look at what? I can't see what you're seeing." I didn't succeed in keeping the panic from my voice.

"A drone, girlfriend. It's a small little thing, but it's flying just above your roof."

I stared up at the roof of the car in abject horror. I didn't know how to protect myself from objects that could fly away from me. Or that could control the vehicle I was in.

"Any way you can hack it or disable it?" Colin jerked and glanced at the display behind the steering wheel. "We're picking up speed."

I pressed my fist harder against his thigh and looked at the display. "We're now doing seventy kilometres an hour. This is illegal. This is a fifty-kilometre-an-hour zone."

"The bloody bastard doesn't care about laws, Doc. Supermodel, is the bastard listening in on us?"

"Most likely." Regret was clear in her tone. "Nothing we can do about that right now."

"Get us out of here, Francine." Colin sounded panicked, but his nonverbal cues didn't confirm his tone. With one more glance at the dashboard and the street, he took my phone from the non-slip pad and tapped on the screen. I inhaled and he glanced at me. The quick shake of his head was enough for me to exhale and hope he had a plan. The speedometer was now reading eighty-one kilometres an hour. I grabbed my seatbelt with my right hand and held tight.

"Where do you think he's taking you, Frey?" Manny's tone was off.

"The golf club." Colin tilted my phone so I could see the screen. He had typed 'IOT' and sent it as a text to Francine. Understanding came to me. He was lying in case the person hacking the SUV was listening to us, but Francine would now know we were going to the Institute of Technology.

This deception added to my distress and my breathing hitched. Colin put the phone back and placed his hand over my fist on his thigh. "I think he's taking us to a quiet alley like in Norbert Sartre's case. But I don't know what he thinks he'll find. We're not transporting any art or diamonds."

The SUV swerved around an Audi into oncoming traffic. A delivery vehicle flashed its lights at us and both it and the Audi hooted at us. The front of the small truck lowered as the driver braked, his eyes wide with fear. I was sure my eyes were just as wide, my fear much stronger than the middle-aged man's. He wasn't in a vehicle that had become a moving prison. And a weapon.

"Shit!" Colin pulled hard at the steering wheel, but the SUV continued racing towards the truck. The Audi had slowed down to give us space, yet the person controlling the SUV didn't steer us back into the right lane. I couldn't breathe, couldn't move. All I could do was stare at the truck's grille coming towards me and listen to the last few bars of the symphony's Andante.

Over the speakers, Manny was shouting at Francine to do something, Colin was swearing and pulling at the steering wheel and all I could think of was that I had never asked Nikki why she looked unwell last night.

A moment before I accepted the inevitable and gave myself over to the safety of a shutdown, the SUV swerved into the right lane and flew by the delivery vehicle.

"Fuck!" Colin pounded the steering wheel with the heels of his hands. "Jesus Christ."

"Supermodel!" Manny's tone was the one he used to issue orders.

"On it." Her voice was hoarse. "Hold on, Genevieve. Just hold on."

I looked at the grip on the passenger door and wondered

why Francine would think holding on to any part of this vehicle would save us from a collision at eighty kilometres an hour. I glanced at the display. Not eighty kilometres an hour. We were racing down the street at a hundred and three kilometres an hour.

The SUV slowed down marginally, but still slid across the street when we went around a bend in the road. The rest of this street was eerily quiet. Even though I wasn't familiar with this area, I knew the cross streets had enough traffic during the day to send a car into our path at any moment. If that didn't kill us, the building at the dead end of the street would.

"Jenny, be ready." Colin stared at a far point in the street and I followed his gaze. At first, I could only focus on the solid wall coming closer with each racing heartbeat. Then I saw a familiar pick-up truck parked in front of it. Vinnie was leaning with his torso on the hood of his truck, aiming a rifle at us. I pressed deeper against my seat and realised Vinnie wasn't aiming at us, he was aiming above the SUV.

The loud clap of a gunshot resounded between the buildings, but the SUV didn't slow down, didn't change direction. Vinnie reloaded. At the speed we were travelling, we were going to crash into that wall in seven seconds. If Vinnie's next shot didn't disable the control someone else had over the SUV, we were going to crash and kill Vinnie in the process.

The muzzle flashed a moment before the SUV lurched. I was thrown forward with an immense force and immediately jerked back by my seatbelt. The tyres screeched across the street. We had too much momentum. The building and

Vinnie's truck were coming closer too fast.

"Shit!" Colin fought the steering wheel as the SUV veered towards the building on my side. Vinnie stood up from behind his truck and ran to the opposite side, putting him out of our collision course. He pointed at his truck and I didn't understand what he was trying to communicate. I couldn't move, couldn't breathe, couldn't speak.

The strings and the wind instruments created perfect harmony. Nikki would be well looked after by Phillip, Manny, Francine and Vinnie. My largest regret as the tyres continued to screech and the SUV slowed down too slowly was that Colin wouldn't be there to see Nikki become the successful artist she was setting out to be.

As the safety of a shutdown swallowed me in, I also regretted not having one last opportunity to tell Colin I loved him.

Chapter TWELVE

"Jenny?" A cold hand touched my face. "Honeybuns?"

The intense irritation I experienced whenever Colin used this term of endearment jerked me fully out of my shutdown. I pulled my face away from his hand and opened my eyes. "Don't call me honeybuns. And don't touch my face. Your hand is cold."

"Cold, but alive, love."

His words triggered an avalanche of memories. I gasped and looked around me. I was still in the passenger seat of Colin's SUV. Or at least, what was left of it. My throat tightened when I saw the twisted metal through the cracked windscreen. The SUV's front was one third of its original size and I didn't know if it would be possible to repair the side of Vinnie's truck. Somehow the deflated airbags made the severity of the crash more real for me.

My arms were wrapped around my knees, my legs tight against my chest. It took two lines of Mozart's Symphony No.41 in C to stop rocking back and forth. Yet I couldn't let go of my knees. I turned awkwardly towards Colin and stared at him. He was standing next to the SUV, slightly bent over to be eye level with me. I frowned. "You have blood on your face."

"Huh. They didn't clean me up properly." His eyes

widened at my expression and he put his hand on my forearm. "Hey, I'm okay. Look." He turned his face to show me his left temple. "It is a small cut. The medics already sorted it out."

"What about your hand?"

"Can't hide anything from you, can I?" His smile was soft. He held up his hand for me to see. The white bandage made his lightly tanned skin look darker. "This is just a cut. Well, actually three cuts. Everything happened so fast, I didn't even know I'd cut my hand until Vinnie pointed it out. Fortunately, the cuts on my hand and the one on my face don't need stitches."

"Vinnie." I looked behind Colin. "Is he okay?"

"Everyone's okay, love." He shifted to the side so I could see past him. "They're just worried about you."

The quiet street had been transformed into a hub of activity. I counted five law enforcement vehicles, their lights flashing, but wouldn't be surprised if there were more. The one closest to us looked like one of Daniel's GIPN trucks. That was where everyone was congregated.

Vinnie and Daniel were talking quietly, Manny was scowling while listening to someone on his smartphone and Francine was staring at us, her tablet hanging loosely in her hand. Their presence, the vehicles and all the activity brought a question to my mind. "How long was I shut down?"

Colin glanced at his watch. "Almost two hours."

No wonder my body felt so stiff. I inhaled deeply and focused on relaxing my arms. It took longer than I liked, but eventually I was able to let go of my legs. Colin tilted his head and, when I nodded, helped me lower my legs to the side of the SUV. Full physical awareness returned to me. "I'm cold."

"I'm sorry, love. We put blankets around you, but you kept throwing them off." He started at my feet and visually inspected me all the way to my face. "Can you feel any injuries?"

"I don't think so. I'm still not feeling my feet, but that's just lack of blood circulation."

"Shit." Colin pushed his fingers through his hair—a gesture he only employed when in high distress. "Dammit, Jenny. It nearly killed me not knowing if you got hurt. You wouldn't even let me touch you."

"I think I'm fine." I wiggled my toes, stared at my hands as I stretched out my fingers and rolled my shoulders. "I feel fine."

"We need to get you checked out."

My reaction was immediate. "No. No. No, no, no."

"Please, love. I need to know you're okay."

"No." I pressed my lips tightly together to prevent that one word from repeating itself. When I regained control, I looked at him. "The thought of going to a hospital or having someone touch me is bringing on a shutdown. My brain is too overwhelmed. I can't. I just can't do this right now."

He took both my hands in his and pressed them against his forehead. He looked up after three seconds, his expression determined. "You will not leave my side. You will not complain that I'm watching you all the time. You will admit when you're not feeling well. And the moment I notice something isn't right, I'm taking you to the hospital and you'll just have to Mozart your way through it."

"Don't use Mozart as a verb."

He smiled and straightened. "Good. I'm glad you agree."

"I didn't agree to anything."

"You didn't argue." He gave a half shrug. "In Jenny-language that means you agreed."

I inhaled to scold him for his assumptions, but noticed his micro-expressions. "You're trying to distract me by teasing me. It almost worked."

"Not almost. It did."

I followed his pointed look and sighed. He was right. The terrified posture of my shutdown had completely disappeared. I had both feet on the floor, my fists on my hips and my back straight. I got up and winced when the pins and needles in my legs gained intensity. But I continued glaring at Colin. "You're smug."

"A little." He stepped closer and gently touched my chin. "But I'm much more relieved that you're okay."

"How are you doing, Doc?" Manny was standing behind Colin, the others next to him. Colin turned around, took my hand and pulled me to stand next to him.

"I feel fine." I lifted my free hand to stop Manny when he looked behind him. "Don't even suggest the paramedics examine me or that I should go to a hospital. I agreed that Colin can take me to the hospital if I don't feel well."

"Doc." Manny's tone carried a warning.

"We'll all keep an eye on her, old man." Vinnie pushed Manny out of the way and took his place in front of me. He stared at me for a moment, then grunted loudly. "You're not up for some Vinnie-love, are you? Huh. Didn't think so. Well, just so you know, the moment that wild look is out of your eyes, I'm hugging you."

I turned to Colin. "Do I have a wild look in my eyes? What does it mean?"

"It means that we can see you just had a close call, girlfriend." Something in Francine's voice caught my attention and I looked at her.

Then I pointed at her face, but looked at Colin. "Is that the wild look Vinnie is talking about?"

Colin glanced at Francine and nodded. "We all got a fright, love."

"I was watching this on my computer." Francine's tone sounded thick with tears. "It was the most horrifying thing I've ever experienced."

"Pah!" Vinnie bumped Francine with his shoulder. "Horrifying? You don't know what that means until someone tries to put Indian spices in your Auntie Helen's *Italian* family recipe."

I was grateful for Vinnie's attempt to lift the mood. It had been a traumatic experience and I didn't want to micro-analyse emotions now. I wanted to focus on things that made me feel safe. Things that engaged my cerebral cortex. Things like the many questions I now had. "It doesn't make sense."

"I agree, Jen-girl. No one should destroy a family—"

"She's not talking about your cooking, big guy." Francine lifted her tablet. She was wearing gloves with special pads on the fingertips that allowed her to use the touchscreen of any device. "What doesn't make sense, girlfriend?"

"The evidence we had pointed to Gallo being responsible for hacking Norbert Sartre's car." I shifted from side to side to get more blood flowing to my legs.

"He admitted as much," Colin said.

"He needs us, needs me to play this game he's been planning." I shook my head. "It just doesn't make sense that he would want to kill us."

Manny nodded towards his car. "Then let's go ask the bloody bastard."

I leaned into Colin's side. "No."

"Why not, Doc? I think it's a good idea to ask that psycho if he did this."

"It's not about Gallo. I agree with you that speaking to him will give us valuable information." I looked at his car with wide eyes. "I can't get into a car with you."

Vinnie burst out laughing. "Take that, old man!"

"Bugger off, criminal." Manny looked around and called Daniel over. "Can you drive these divas to our place?"

"Sure." Daniel faked innocence as he looked at Manny. "Do you want to sit in front or in the back?"

Laughter filled the street, Vinnie's the loudest. I didn't fully understand the humour, but I did understand the value in comic relief after a difficult, or even traumatic, event.

"You can all go to bloody hell." Manny stormed to his car, but his outrage didn't convince me. I'd seen the corners of his mouth twitch. He glared at Francine while unlocking his door. "Are you coming with me or driving with the comedians, supermodel?"

"I'll come with you, handsome." She waited until I acknowledged her expression of relief and affection before she walked to his car. "I find your driving and grumpiness very sexy."

They got into Manny's sedan, their bickering changing

topics faster than I cared to follow. Daniel confirmed that we were no longer needed at the accident scene and I grabbed my handbag from the SUV before following him to one of his team's SUVs. I glanced inside to confirm that the interior wasn't as messy as Manny's car, then turned to Daniel. It was hard, but I took three seconds to carefully form my request. "I need Colin to drive. Um… please."

Daniel lifted one eyebrow. "That's against regulations, Genevieve. Only GIPN personnel are allowed to drive these vehicles."

"Dude." Vinnie grabbed the keys from Daniel and handed it to Colin. "You've seen how my man handles a car. He'll get your GIPN wagon there in one piece."

Daniel nodded and got in the backseat with Vinnie. Colin and I got in the front. I pulled the seatbelt across my torso. It was as if a light was switched off the moment the buckle clicked into place. I grabbed the seat with both my hands and focused on my breathing. No one spoke. Colin fiddled with his smartphone for a few seconds until the overture of Mozart's *Zauberflöte* came through the small speakers.

It took three bars before I was able to take a deep breath and another two bars before I could let go of the seats. I pressed my fists into my thighs and blinked when Colin put his hand over them. "Are we good to go, love?"

I looked at his smartphone on the dashboard, then at him. The concern in his face was deep. "Thank you."

He smiled at me. "And in Jenny-language that means…?"

"Thank you for knowing what I need." I twisted in my seat to look at Daniel. "And for breaking protocol for me."

Daniel nodded. "Anytime, Genevieve."

Colin squeezed my hands and put both hands on the steering wheel. "Okay, let's go ask Gallo some questions."

It took seven minutes before I could open my fists and another two minutes before I could take my eyes off the road in front of us. I took Colin's smartphone and turned off Mozart's brilliant display of contrapuntal skills. The men were talking about the business opportunities of securing vehicles from being hacked. I had different concerns.

I took my smartphone and swiped the screen. Two seconds later, I pressed the phone against my ear and waited. It took only four rings.

"Hey, Doc G. What's up?"

The relief of hearing Nikki's voice was physical. Tension I didn't know I had released and my shoulders dropped. "Hey, Nikki. How are you?"

"Um. Fine?" She drew out the last word and hesitated for a second. "Is everything okay, Doc G?"

"Now it is, yes." I settled back in my seat. "But I want to know if you are sick."

"Um. What?" Her voice rose a pitch. "Why would you think I'm sick?"

"You answered my question with a question." I narrowed my eyes. "And you start singing your sentences when you're lying."

"Ah, shittidy shit." She sighed heavily. "I'm not sick, Doc G."

"Don't lie to me. I can't see you to know if you're telling the truth."

"I'm not lying." Her tone sounded sincere. "Something is up, but I'll tell you later, okay?"

"You're not sick?" I had to make sure. Going only on her words and tone of voice made it hard for me to determine the truth.

"Where are you?"

"In a car with Colin, Vinnie and Daniel. You didn't answer my question."

"Because I was going to suggest that we Skype and you can see that I'm telling the truth." A small hitch in her tone stopped my suspicion. She was hurt.

"I…" I carefully considered my words. "We don't need to Skype. I trust you."

"I love you too, Doc G." She made a kissy sound over the phone. "I'll speak to you tonight, 'kay?"

"Okay." I ended the call and realised the men had stopped talking.

"What's going on, Jen-girl?" Vinnie's tone was hard, worried. Colin turned into the street that would take us to Rousseau & Rousseau and our team room.

"I thought I saw something last night." I shrugged. "Nikki says she isn't sick. I believe her."

"But you think something else is wrong." Colin parked in front of our building.

"Maybe not wrong. I'm not sure. She said she'll tell me tonight."

"And you'll tell us if something's wrong." Vinnie leaned forward until his face was next to mine. "You'll tell us, right, Jen-girl?"

I jumped in my seat when someone knocked against my window. I turned and looked into Manny's annoyed face. "Are you going to chat like teenagers all day or are we going in?"

Grateful for the interruption, I unbuckled and opened the door. Vinnie's hand grazed my shoulder as I got out and I looked back. His depressor *anguli oris* muscles were turning the corners of his mouth down, a frown pulling his brows together.

Ignoring Manny's heavy sighs, I waited for Vinnie to get out. I stepped closer and waited until I knew he was truly listening to me. "If there is something amiss, but more importantly, if Nikki allows me to tell you, I will."

"What's wrong with Nikki?" Manny snapped his fingers in front of my face when I didn't answer him. "Missy, you better tell me right now."

"Wait. What?" Francine pushed between Manny and Vinnie. "Is Nikki okay?"

I wasn't going to repeat this argument. I walked to the heavy wooden door leading to Rousseau & Rousseau's foyer. With my hand on the door handle, I turned around and addressed everyone. "Nikki told me she isn't sick. I believe her. If there is anything wrong that she wants to share with you, she can tell you. I will not discuss this any further. We need to speak to Gallo."

As expected, it wasn't the end of the discussion, but I ignored any more attempts from Manny, Vinnie and Francine to get information from me. Colin stepped between me and the others when the elevator doors opened and glared at them. "Get the next one."

He smoothed his eyebrow with his middle finger as the doors closed and chuckled when both Manny and Vinnie swore at him. I was leaning hard against the wooden panel facing the doors. "I made a mistake phoning her while

Vinnie was there."

"No, you didn't. If something is wrong, Vinnie won't be far behind you seeing it." He frowned. "You think it's serious?"

I lifted one shoulder. "It could be boyfriend problems. Someone from the art faculty."

"Another student?" Colin waited until I nodded. "How long has this been going on?"

"Three months." I thought about it. "And eleven days. In the beginning, she thought he was perfect for her, but the last three weeks she's been saying that they're just good friends. She was truthful when she told me they have a lot of fun together and she's happy to be without a boyfriend at the moment."

"Huh. Why didn't she tell me about this boyfriend-friend?"

I had asked her the same question. "She's embarrassed that she can't keep a boyfriend for a long time."

"Silly girl." Colin waited for me to enter the reception area of Rousseau & Rousseau when the elevator doors opened. "No one is supposed to have long-term relationships when they're students."

"That is a broad generalisation that I don't agree with." I waved my hands sideways as if to cut through the air. "And I'm not going to argue about it now. Hello, Timothée."

"Doctor Lenard." Tim nodded at me from behind the heavy reception desk. The muscles in his face and shoulders relaxed when he looked at Colin. "How are you, Colin?"

"Well, thanks, Tim." Colin's smile was genuine. He liked Tim. "Is Monsieur Gallo behaving himself?"

Tim turned his computer monitor around for us to see. "He's just been sitting there. Every now and then he sips some water, but he hasn't eaten anything today."

I looked at the monitor. Gallo was sitting in the same chair as yesterday, wearing the same suit. I expected to see exhaustion in his expression and his body language. Not pain and sadness. The elevator opened behind us and Vinnie's loud laughter filled the reception area. It must have also reached the conference room, because Gallo's body jerked and his eyes went to the door.

Francine was teasing Manny and Vinnie was still chuckling, but I was more interested in Gallo's body language. He pulled at his cuffs, straightened his shoulders and lifted his chin. The pain was still there, albeit hidden, but the sadness had been replaced with excitement. I despised the games people enjoyed playing.

"You ready for Gallo, Doc?"

I straightened and looked down the hallway. "Yes."

"Let's do it." He turned to Francine. "You have one minute to get to the team room and record this."

"*You* have one minute to get in the conference room and interview him." She lifted her tablet, her expression insulted. "I can do my job from here."

Manny sighed heavily and walked towards the conference room. I followed. Vinnie and Colin were behind us. Manny turned around at the door, his expression professional, his voice low. "You two stay out here. I don't want to distract Gallo with your presence. Let's see if Doc and I can get as much as possible from him."

"We'll be right here." Vinnie leaned closer to me. "You shout and we're there."

"You sure you want to do this, love?" Colin put his

bandaged hand in his trouser pocket. "We had an eventful morning."

"Gallo has answers we need." And I didn't know how much longer he would be able to provide us with any useful information. "I want those answers."

"There you go, Frey." Manny opened the door and walked in. "Gallo! You look well rested."

"And you look as backwoods as always." Gallo's haughty tone was forced. It was easier to hide the expression of pain on one's face than disguise the tone in one's voice.

Manny sat in the same chair he'd occupied yesterday and I took the chair next to his. As usual Manny was slouching in his chair, but he wasn't as successful in looking bored. His anger was too close to the surface to hide. I leaned one elbow on the table and studied Gallo. I didn't want to miss a single micro-expression. "Do you want me dead?"

Gallo blinked twice and the *corrugator supercilii* muscles close to the centre of his eyebrows twitched. He was confused. "No. I used to dream about killing you slowly, but not anymore."

Manny shifted, his fists bulging in his trouser pockets. He had not been pleased that I had asked Gallo a question, but Gallo's answer had brought Manny's anger in full view. I didn't want him to agitate Gallo. His answers were too important. I leaned forward. "Why did you hack Norbert Sartre's car?"

"Hmm." Gallo's eyes narrowed and he looked from me to Manny and back. "You're asking me questions and the idiot is looking like he's dreaming about torturing me. What happened?"

"Answer my question." I wasn't going to allow him to lead this conversation.

Gallo tilted his head and looked at me. "Okay, I'll play for now. I hacked Norbert's car because I wanted your attention."

"My attention or my help?" I saw the truth in the quick widening of his eyes. "You need my help."

"If you say so."

"What is your relationship with Emad and Claude Vernet?"

Manny shifted again in his chair and turned his head to glare at me. I didn't care that he didn't approve of my questions. I was tired of playing games.

Gallo's smile was smug. "Aha. So my first clue helped you find those two. Have you located them?"

"Answer my question first."

"No." He shook his head slowly. "I don't think I will. Not yet anyway. I want my first favour, then I'll tell you everything I know about the Vernet brothers."

"A favour by definition is an act of kindness beyond what is due or usual. You're not asking for a favour."

"Call it what you want to. No, wait. You could call it your atonement for destroying my family."

"Those men weren't your family."

"They were." His lips thinned and sweat beaded on his forehead. He took a shaky breath and unclenched his fists. "And you will do this or you won't get anything else from me."

"Stop making threats and tell us what the hell you want, Gallo." Manny's voice was rough with suppressed fury.

Gallo smiled. "I want student visas for Davi Ribeiro and

Alda Ribeiro. They must have unhindered access to study in France."

Those names were familiar. It took me two seconds to place them. "Those are Vitor Ribeiro's children."

Vitor Ribeiro was one of the four men who had been co-conspirators with Gallo in many crimes. Of all Gallo's so-called brothers, Ribeiro was the only one who'd had children. But he wasn't the only one who had died in the last year. The police in Rio de Janeiro believed that Gallo had poisoned Ribeiro for agreeing to co-operate with them. It had been the poisoning of another close friend, Mateas Almeida, that had brought that case to our attention.

"No." Manny sat up. "That's not going to be possible, not with the current immigration situation in Europe."

Gallo exhaled slowly and leaned back. "Then you're not getting anything else from me. Good luck with trying to save the leaders and all the other thousands of people who will die."

There was only truth in Gallo's nonverbal cues. I didn't yet know the reason he wanted the children of the friend he called his brother to come to France. I turned to Manny. "If their background checks do not raise any concerns, can you guarantee visas for them?"

Manny's eyes widened, then narrowed. "Outside. Now."

Gallo chuckled as Manny and I left the conference room. As soon as the door closed behind us, I spoke. "Gallo is, or he thinks he is, dying. He's convinced that he has nothing to lose by blackmailing us into certain actions. He's not asking us to break any laws, which in itself is interesting."

"I don't like it, Doc." Manny crossed his arms. "Giving in

to that psychopath's demands can only lead to trouble."

I thought about it. "I'm not so sure about that. He has some connection to the Vernet brothers and feels they betrayed him. They are planning something that might be much worse than allowing two young people to study in France. Gallo wants to use me, use us, to take revenge on Claude and Emad."

"I agree with Jenny." Colin was leaning against the wall, Vinnie next to him. "Why don't you get on the phone, get some document guaranteeing their visas on the condition they don't raise any red flags and their academic achievements warrant it? We give that to Gallo and hear what else he has to say about this threat to the presidents."

"And thousands of people," Vinnie said. "The arsehole said a few times now that thousands of people's lives are in danger."

Manny rubbed both hands over his face. "Fine. Let me speak to Privott about this. I'll see what I can do."

We watched as Manny walked towards the reception area, his smartphone already against his ear. Colin stepped closer and took my hand. "How're you feeling?"

"I'm fine."

"How are your ribs?" With his index finger he drew a diagonal line across my chest.

"Fine." I hadn't taken the time to think about or even feel any bruising the seatbelt might have caused. "I don't want to talk about this now."

Vinnie chuckled and started talking to Colin about GIPN's protocol for breaching a closed building with hostages inside. I appreciated the distraction and listened as they continued a conversation that seemed to have started before Manny and I left the conference room.

Twenty minutes later, Manny came back. His eyebrows were drawn tightly together and his lips in a thin line. He waved a piece of paper at me. "Gallo better bloody accept this or I'm throwing him in a dungeon where he can spend his last few days."

"What is that?" Colin reached for the page, but Manny pulled it out of reach.

"It's the document you suggested we get for Gallo." Manny rolled his head as if to remove some tension from his neck muscles. "It took a lot of shouting to get this so quickly, but those kids will have their visas if they have sparkling clean records. Gallo better give us intel worthy of all this bloody hassle."

He opened the door and we returned to our previous seats. Manny put the piece of paper on the table and rested his hand on it. "This is a document guaranteeing student visas for those two children on the condition that there is nothing suspicious in their background checks."

Gallo's eyebrows lifted in surprise and he held out his cuffed hands. "May I?"

"One phone call and this document is useless." Manny handed the page to Gallo. "I'm not Doctor Lenard. I don't play games. This will be the only act of kindness you'll see from me. If you don't deliver and give us actionable information about the Vernet brothers, I will be making that phone call."

Gallo read through the document twice, then put it on the table. He looked at me. "After you destroyed my family and froze all my assets, I needed money. You already know that we had the diamonds from the 2013 heist. They were in a safe in a storage unit I rented, just sitting there. We never planned to do anything with them. Maybe use them one day when we retired. But they were there and I needed to turn them into cash.

"I'd heard about the smuggling duo and asked around. Imagine my joy when I found out they were in Brazil. I managed to get them to come to Rio and they agreed to give me cash for the diamonds. It was daylight robbery, but I was desperate enough to agree to take twenty percent of the real value of those stones."

I recalled what Vinnie had said earlier. "Did they smuggle you into Europe?"

"Ah, Genevieve. It gives me such pleasure to talk to *you*." His smile was genuine. "Apparently, the two brothers don't only smuggle articles. They were really good with finding me safe and, I must add, quite comfortable passage into Europe." He shrugged. "Of course, the cost was high, but here I am."

I couldn't let that micro-expression go unchallenged. "What was the cost?"

"Two million euros." He wasn't successful in sounding blasé.

"There's more. They wanted more from you. What?"

Manny grabbed the piece of paper and held it up as if to tear it. "Start spilling, Gallo."

Gallo looked at the paper and shook his head. "Those kids are the reason the Vernet brothers betrayed me. When I sold them the diamonds, they didn't show any interest in me. Just the diamonds. But when I asked about getting into Europe, they did a search on me and became very interested in me. Well, not really me.

"They wanted Vitor's contacts at the Department of Defence. With all the security work we'd done in the past, Vitor had built a good relationship with the DoD. They had a job that required an insider in the DoD and asked me to arrange it. I refused."

"Why?"

"I don't care about anything or anyone." His tone was unapologetic. "I used to care about my brothers, but you took them away from me. The only people left are Davi and Alda. I never had a good relationship with them, but they are my brother's children and getting into bed with the Vernet brothers would've put their lives in danger."

"How so?" Manny asked.

Gallo looked at me for a few seconds. "All Vitor's, all of *our*, contacts are saved on a micro SD card. The police have looked everywhere for it, but never found it."

"Where is it?" I asked.

"Sewn into Alda's teddy bear. I gave that toy to her when she turned three and she still has it. I've offered to replace it many times, but she has some silly sentimental value for that ugly thing."

"It's in her room?" Manny asked.

Gallo nodded. "And that is why I couldn't give Emad and Claude the contacts. It would bring them too close to the kids."

"And they took revenge by making you fatally ill." My eyes narrowed at his reaction. He'd been unmoved by my statement. Until I mentioned him being fatally ill. Gallo was dying. But who or what had made him this ill?

He blinked a few times, then straightened. "N523AX7291ZP328G. I'm really tired. You can leave now. I need to rest on my horribly uncomfortable bed."

I took my time studying his ill-looking pallor and got up. He was not going to say anything else and I needed to find out what that string of numbers and letters could reveal.

Chapter THIRTEEN

"Have you found a use for those numbers, Doc?" Manny added another heaped spoon of lasagne to his plate. He hadn't even attempted to hide his pleasure when Vinnie had announced he'd brought lunch and we had to take a break. We were at the round table, the aroma of Vinnie's cooking filling the air.

"Not yet." I looked around the table. Francine was paying more attention to her tablet than the food on her plate. Vinnie and Colin were both glaring at Lucien Privott, who had joined us minutes after Vinnie had come in with the food. The director of public relations had not received a warm welcome from them. As long as Privott's presence didn't interfere with my search into the numbers and letters Gallo had given me, I didn't care that he was here. "Francine and I have looked at IP addresses, GPS co-ordinates, possible website addresses—"

"Bank account numbers, safety deposit box numbers and a bunch more," Francine continued. "Nothing. Nada. Bupkis. I honestly don't know where else to try to squeeze those numbers and letters in."

"Could it be a case file?" Privott asked. Despite his strong reaction yesterday, he'd been surprisingly non-confrontational. He'd ignored Vinnie's aggressive body language and had shown an intelligent interest in our discoveries so far. He had not been able to hide his concern over the leak of the top-secret leaders' meeting. "Maybe a police case file number or another agency's?"

"Hmm. Look at you being helpful." Francine tapped on her tablet while absently lifting her fork to her mouth. When her lips closed around an empty fork, she rolled her eyes and focused on scooping lasagne on her fork. "It will take a minute to check for that."

Manny turned his full attention to Privott. "Where is this meeting that's taking place tomorrow?"

"I don't know." Privott faced me, allowing me to read his expression. "I really don't know. The location is being kept top-secret to prevent it from getting into the wrong hands. I had a look at that dark web site and that is exactly the information I have. The president's head of security and two other people are the only ones who know where this meeting will take place. All eleven other leaders agreed to this. The fact that the information about the meeting is on that site is enough proof that we need to take extreme security measures."

"These are volatile times we live in." Francine didn't look up from her tablet.

"Hmm." It was clear that Manny had also seen the truth in Privott's statement. He put his knife and fork down. I was always amazed at how quickly he ate. "I've heard back from the police department. They've been questioning the gallery owner, Monsieur Bissette, and he's been very co-operative. He's confessed to selling those diamonds, but is adamant that he never sold any forgeries. Apparently, selling stolen diamonds is okay, but selling forged paintings is a bloody crime. He's given the police the names of all the people who bought the thirty-four diamonds." Manny's smile wasn't kind. "Some rich people are about to spend a lot of money on lawyers."

"Didn't Monsieur Bissette give us phone numbers for Emad and Claude?" Colin asked. "Did anyone check those numbers?"

"Pink and I did." Francine took a sip of her water. "Monsieur Bissette gave us two numbers and both are turned off. Just like the numbers we got from Gallo's computer. That made me think and I did a little check. The phones for those two numbers were sold at the same store and at the same time as the numbers from Gallo's computer."

"Have any of those phones been turned on again?" Manny asked.

"Nope. As soon as one of those phones is turned on, I'll know and believe me, I'll let you know." She looked at Privott. "It was a good idea, but my search into all the agencies' databases shows that the number Gallo gave us is not a case number."

"Pity." Privott pushed his plate away and looked at Vinnie. "This was really good. Thank you. I needed that."

Vinnie's eyes narrowed and he nodded. He didn't trust Privott's friendliness and I understood it. Privott hadn't been an easy person to work with. He would need to prove himself as more than just a trusted member of the president's inner circle before my team would trust him.

"Jenny, did you ask Gallo about Norbert Sartre's stolen Vecellios and diamond ring?" Colin leaned back in his chair.

"We're so busy looking into Emad and Claude that we're forgetting about the paintings. They might give us more clues."

"I didn't." And now I regretted it. Could Colin be right? Could the persons Gallo had hired to steal the paintings and diamond ring lead us to information that could help us close this case?

"I don't think you'll get anything out of Gallo now in any case." Francine nodded towards her computer station. "I checked the video feed of the conference room and he's sleeping so hard, it looks like he's in a coma."

"Are you sure he's only sleeping?" I asked.

"Um, not really." She shrugged. "I just assume that people in a coma don't snore louder than Vin."

"I don't snore." Vinnie pulled the serving dish with the lasagne towards him. "And this is the last time I'm giving you any of my Auntie Teresa's food."

We still had far too many open-ended elements to this case. It was most disconcerting. I looked at Francine. "What did you find in Gallo's CatchDunk account?"

"Bloody hell. I'd forgotten about that thing with Gallo's entire phone history." Manny turned to Francine. "Did *you* remember?"

She leaned away from him. "With that lack of faith, you're not allowed close to me."

"Supermodel."

She gave him another fake irritated look. "CatchDunk was a bust for anything new. It pretty much just confirmed all Gallo's whereabouts. His smartphone and computer were set to sync, so the only new info I found was his exact locations.

There's nothing actionable or useful there."

"Bugger." Manny pushed his hands in his trouser pockets. "I hoped we'd get a decent break there."

"Sorry, handsome." Francine's regret was genuine. "I'm still working on that one-gigabyte encrypted file on Gallo's computer. I really want to know what's there."

"Hallo? Anyone? Hallo?" Timothée drew out the last syllable in a singing tone. I looked at Francine's computer, then at my viewing room. His face was on one of my monitors. "Yoohoo? Somebody speak to me."

Francine laughed softly as she swiped her tablet screen. Tim's face appeared on her computer monitor facing the round table. She waved at the monitor. "Hi, Tim. What's up?"

Tim fiddled with his necktie. "A Monsieur Alain Vernet is here to see Doctor Lenard and Mister Millard."

"We'll be there in five minutes." Manny pointed at the food still on my plate. "You going to finish that or can we go, Doc?"

I looked at my plate and shook my head. "No. I've had enough."

"I'm joining you." Privott pushed his chair back and got up. He looked at Manny's face and smiled. "I'm not going to steal your interview, Manny. I think it might be a good idea that I represent the president in there. Especially if Vernet has done something to put the president's life in danger."

Manny lowered his chin and looked at Privott from under his brows. "No shenanigans."

Privott lifted both hands, palms out. "No shenanigans."

I didn't want to ask about the tricks or pranks Manny and

Privott were talking about. It was too distracting. I needed to mentally prepare myself for interviewing a man who had won the world's respect with the many noble causes he had initiated and supported.

Francine had found a few interviews with Alain Vernet and I'd watched them while she continued looking into the clue Gallo had given us. He was in his mid-sixties, a highly intelligent man and someone I could easily call Phillip's peer. He had the same bearing, the same soft-spoken yet uncompromising manner in conveying his opinion. He was the kind of person one immediately respected without knowing why.

In the interviews I'd watched, Alain Vernet had shown distress when talking about human trafficking, starvation, child soldiers and other difficult topics. He had addressed those with passion and sincerity that was consistent throughout the four interviews I'd watched. We were about to speak to a man who had spent his life trying to implement sustainable changes in societies that frequently preyed on the weak.

Manny and Privott used the elevator to Rousseau & Rousseau while Vinnie, Colin and I waited. Francine ignored Vinnie's order to clear the table and returned to her desk. Pink had left to do something with his team and Daniel was talking to the two GIPN officers who were guarding Gallo.

The elevator returned and three minutes later I was standing in front of the smaller conference room. This one was in a different hallway than the large room where Gallo was currently sleeping. Again I wondered how close to death he really was. Those thoughts left my mind when Manny nodded at me and opened the door to the conference room. Vinnie stood to one side of the door and Colin closed the door behind me, leaving them in the hallway.

Phillip was sitting next to Alain Vernet, both drinking tea from a china tea set Phillip had received as a gift from an eighty-year-old client. Of the three conference rooms in Rousseau & Rousseau, this was my preferred room. The large windows allowed in natural light and even though the round table could seat twelve people, it didn't take up as much space in the room as the conference tables in the other rooms. It was a spacious and well-lit room.

Phillip stood up and held out his hand towards us. "Monsieur Vernet, I would like you to meet my very good friend, Colonel Manfred Millard."

Alain Vernet also got up and shook Manny's hand. "Pleased to meet you, Colonel."

Manny shook his hand while studying him through narrowed eyes. His hand dropped to his side and his muscle tension relaxed marginally. "Call me Manny, please."

"Then I insist you call me Alain." He turned to me. "Doctor Lenard, I presume?"

"The most amazing person you'll ever have the pleasure to meet, Alain." Phillip's smile was genuine. And proud.

Alain lifted his hand to shake mine, then pulled it back with a smile. "It is truly an honour to meet you, Doctor Lenard. I've heard a lot about you before I came and Phillip hasn't stopped singing your praises."

"Why would Phillip sing?" I closed my eyes and winced. I should've recognised the expression as such and ignored it. Now the older gentleman was looking at me with wide eyes and a smile tugging on the corners of his mouth. I chose to change the topic before he could answer. "Call me Genevieve and please sit down. We have questions."

Phillip lifted one eyebrow in a look that I recognised. I seldom received that warning gaze, but in this situation, I supposed I deserved to be reminded to put into practice my best social skills. I nodded and sat down next to Manny, watching Alain closely as Phillip introduced Privott and invited both men to take a seat.

The public image Alain Vernet had portrayed in the interviews I'd watched wasn't a pretence. Even though this was not a personal and relaxed situation, he didn't exhibit any calculating cues. His responses and micro-expressions revealed the same dignified gentleman I'd seen onscreen. I could imagine him and Phillip becoming good friends.

"Phillip didn't want to tell me what this was about." Alain first looked at Manny, then at me. "This is about my sons, isn't it?"

"I'm afraid so." Manny didn't expand.

Alain's reaction was immediate. He put his one hand over his eyes in a gesture we so often employed when we wanted to block out unfavourable news or images. When he lowered his hand, the muscles around his eyes were tight and he looked tired. "I've been waiting for this day. For the last ten, twelve years, I've been waiting for this day."

"What day?" I asked.

"The day my sons would finally be caught and put in a place where they are no longer a threat to society."

"You know about their activities?" Manny's tone was no longer respectful or friendly.

"No. Yes. Oh, God, I don't know how to answer this." He sighed heavily, his shoulders dropping. "Claude lost his way when he was a teenager. To this day, I don't know what made him turn his back on all the values I taught him. It was shortly after his fifteenth birthday that he was caught beating up a boy in his school. This boy had been bullying Emad and I would've approved of Claude protecting his younger brother if he hadn't put that boy in a three-week coma.

"Everything went from bad to worse after that. Nothing I tried worked. I told him that I was going to wash my hands of him if he didn't change the direction his life was going in. He didn't. When he turned twenty-one, I stopped trying to help…" Alain's voice broke and he took a deep breath. "I stopped trying to help my child. Instead I put all my energy into trying to keep Emad on a good path. Throughout his childhood and teenage years, Emad had been such a great child. He did everything I expected of him and excelled in sport, academics, even music."

The pain of failure was clear on his face. "I didn't see it. I just didn't. Not until after he joined the Directorate-General for External Security. He was away for several months and came home for a few days. He was having a shower when he received a text message. I shouldn't have looked, but I did. It was from Claude. By then Claude and I hadn't been on speaking terms for some years already."

"What did the message say?" Manny asked when Alain didn't continue.

"'Got the package. Had to get rid of the help.'" He pressed his hand over his eyes again for a few seconds. "It didn't make sense, so I looked at their messaging history. Sadly, it wasn't hard to reach the conclusion that they had been smuggling things for a few years already. It was all there in the messages. They used a lot of vague terms, but it was easy to come to the conclusion that Emad was opening all the doors with his spy contacts and Claude was doing a lot of the planning and making those plans reality."

"Why didn't you report this to the police? Or to his bosses at the DGSE?" Manny asked.

Alain swallowed. "I'm not proud of it, Manny. But you have to understand, these are my sons. I can't tell you how many times I regretted picking up that phone and reading those messages. I wish I'd never known they were criminals. I wish they'd grown up to be men I could be proud of."

I thought about everything he'd said. "Do you have irrefutable proof that your sons are criminals? That they are involved in smuggling?"

"Not irrefutable, no." His smile was sad. "If you're trying to make me feel better, it's not going to work. If I'd reported those messages, the authorities would've investigated and maybe they would've found enough proof to stop my boys."

"But you couldn't do that to your own children," Phillip said softly.

Alain shook his head. "I just couldn't. I put Emad's phone back where he'd left it before his shower and pretended I didn't know anything. He left a few days later and I didn't see him again for a year. Since then I've seen my youngest son four times. Four times in twelve years."

"Have you seen either of your sons recently?" Manny asked.

"No." He inhaled deeply as if to brace himself. "They're

involved in something really bad, aren't they? Monsieur Privott is on the president's staff. And I know that your team works for the president. You guys have a highly regarded reputation, so I know you wouldn't look into something petty. Is it terrorism? Children? Oh, God. Please tell me it isn't children. I would prefer terrorism."

"We don't yet know the extent of their involvement and can't give any specifics," Manny said. "But I *can* tell you that so far we haven't found anything that points to children being involved."

"Good. Good." He swallowed a few times, glanced at Phillip and looked at me. "Please stop them. I wasn't—I am not—strong enough to do that, but they need to be stopped."

I didn't know what to say. This man's openness and full disclosure about his children and the hurt they'd caused him was overwhelming my senses. There had been no deception cues visible when he'd talked about his sons, only emotional turmoil.

"We are doing everything we can to find out exactly what's going on." Manny leaned forward. "And we'll put an end to their criminal activities."

"Thank you." His relief was genuine. He swallowed again and pulled his shoulders back. "What can I do to help?"

"Give us permission to monitor your calls and emails in case one of them contacts you."

"I'll give you full access to my private phones and emails. Unfortunately, my work phone and emails contain classified information. I can't share that." Alain placed both hands on the table. "But I give you my word that I'll contact you the moment I hear from either of them on my work email or phone. I've been carrying this around for far too long. This has to end."

Manny turned to me. "Doc?"

"He's being truthful." I studied Alain's micro-expressions. "He's also very sad."

Alain exhaled a puff of air and pressed his fist against his mouth. It took him a few seconds to gain control over his emotions. "It's a sad day for any father to ask that his sons be imprisoned because they are a menace to society. And not just one child. Both."

Phillip rested his hand on Alain's shoulder. "You'll get through this, Alain. We're here for you."

It took another five minutes for Alain to give us access to his home phone, his private smartphone and three private email addresses. Phillip offered to walk him to the elevator and soon Manny and I were alone in the conference room.

Manny slumped back in his chair. "I really feel sorry for that man."

"Bad seed, old man." Vinnie walked into the room and sat on the chair closest to the door. "Some people are just born bad."

This was a complex discussion with so many variables to take into consideration. I was still compiling my arguments when Francine rushed into the room, followed by Colin. Francine fell into the chair next to Vinnie, her eyes wide with excitement. "You will *not* believe what I found. Ooh, it's too delicious for words."

"Spill it, supermodel."

"So I was running a search for more hacked cars and

possible hacked machinery like Genevieve asked when I got a few hits."

"Please don't tell me some nuclear plant was hacked." Manny leaned away from Francine as if to physically prevent the news from reaching him.

Colin sat down next to me and took my hand. I didn't take my eyes off Francine. I'd come to recognise different types of excitement in her. There was a type when she discovered a political scandal, a type when she found a complex IT challenge and a type when she discovered something that would shock us. It was the latter that I saw in her nonverbal cues at the moment.

"Nope. No nukes at the moment, handsome." She wiggled in her chair. "I found two possible car hackings. In both cases, the owners were very confused about how they'd lost control over their cars. The first one happened three days ago."

"In Strasbourg?" Colin leaned forward. "Were both hackings in Strasbourg?"

"They were. But you're jumping ahead in my delivery of the delicious news." She tapped her silver index fingernail on the table. "There's so much more. The second vehicle was a small delivery truck. The driver was transporting bottled water to the city centre when he lost control of his truck. He reported the same as the first guy. No crazy driving or robbery like with Norbert Sartre. Just driving around the city for about forty minutes and then the truck stopped and he had control back. He thought he'd felt some movement in the back of the truck, but when he checked, everything was fine, his delivery undisturbed."

"But it's the first one that has you excited." Vinnie rolled his eyes. "Did they transport a consignment of handbags?"

"I wish!" She sat straighter. "This one would not have been reported if it weren't for people getting worried about the man sleeping in his car. The driver insisted that his car wasn't hacked and that he drove a bit erratic because he was tired. The police gave him a breathalyser test and he tested clean, but the cops were suspicious enough to write this up.

"I got Pink to speak to the cops and they confirmed that the driver looked very spooked when they spoke to him. Unlike the others, the police found him and his car in a remote location after someone phoned the emergency line. When they got there, this guy was standing next to his car as white as a sheet."

"What sheet?" I grunted. "Ignore my question. Why is this driver different from the others?"

"Because of who he is and what he does. This is so delicious." She rubbed her hands. "Franck Reiss was Émile Roche's transporter for many years before Émile decided to go legit."

"Bloody hellfire." Manny sat up. "Émile Roche, the bloody mafia boss who kidnapped Doc?"

"He didn't kidnap me." Even though Émile had surprised me by waiting for me in my car, I had gone willingly with him to meet his peers. They were a group of men who had been involved in organised crime for many years until they'd decided to reform.

"We need to get that bloody criminal in here now."

I shrank away from Manny's glare. "Why are you looking at me?"

"Take a deep breath, Millard." Colin got up and took his smartphone from his trouser pocket. "I'll call Émile and ask him to join us as soon as possible."

Manny continued to glare at me when Colin disappeared into the hallway. "Why the hell does Frey have Roche's number?"

Chapter FOURTEEN

"My dearest Genevieve." Émile Roche ignored the hostile glares from Manny and walked straight to me. He stopped in front of me, rare gentleness in his expression. "It's really good to see you again."

"Hello, Émile." I took a moment to analyse my feelings. "I'm happy to see you."

"Aw." He pressed both his palms against his chest. "You just made this old man's heart smile."

I frowned. "A heart cannot smile."

"I know." The smile lifting Émile's cheeks and causing wrinkles in the corners of his eyes was strong and genuine. "I had an hour-long debate about this with my granddaughter."

"Émile." Colin held out his hand.

Émile took Colin's hand in both his and shook it warmly. "My precious boy. Are you well?"

"Very well, thank you." Colin's expression also revealed his pleasure at seeing the sixty-nine-year-old man. "You're looking snazzy."

Émile laughed and dusted invisible particles off his expensive suit jacket. "This old thing? I had to do something to look better than Vinnie." He turned to Vinnie, his smile wide. "How are you, son?"

"What the bleeding hell is this?" Manny pushed himself between Vinnie and Émile, preventing Vinnie from shaking Émile's hand. "Is this some kind of reunion?"

Émile ignored Manny and turned to me. "Are we still on for brunch on Sunday? Just like the last time."

"Holy hell." Manny threw his hands in the air and sat down hard on his chair. "When did you all become best friends?"

Colin and Vinnie chuckled and I gave Émile a look that I hoped communicated my censure. "You're being malicious."

"But it's funny, Jen-girl." Vinnie sat down next to Manny and slapped him hard on his back. "The old man has his knickers in a tight knot."

I hated that expression and turned to Manny before I gave in to the urge to start yet another debate about men wearing female underwear. I waited until Manny finished swearing at Vinnie and turned his scowl on me. "Émile invited me for brunch five months ago. Colin and Vinnie joined me. Despite the appearance Émile is trying to create, we only had brunch twice in the last five months."

"Please sit down, everyone." Phillip made a sweeping gesture with his hand and walked to his previous seat. "Tim is bringing coffee."

"Forgive me for seeming ignorant, but why are we entertaining a known criminal?" Lucien Privott sat down and looked at Émile. "No offence."

"None taken." Émile sat down and pulled at his cuffs. "I used to be a criminal. Not anymore. Genevieve can attest to the life changes I've made."

I sat down. "Émile provided us with sufficient information

to arrest several criminals. He also helped us prevent more people being murdered by a crazed opera singer."

"And he checked out." Francine winked when Émile looked at her. "All our searches proved that he has not been involved in any illegal activity for a long time."

I flinched when I saw Émile's expression. "What have you done?"

"Not me, Genevieve." Émile waited for me to study his expression. "I didn't do anything. It's someone I know."

"Coffee!" Tim walked into the room, carrying a large tray with coffee mugs. I was surprised that he didn't serve coffee from the more formal coffee cups and saucers. Émile didn't seem to mind. He gratefully took a mug and inhaled the aroma with appreciation on his face. It took Tim less than a minute to serve the coffee.

The moment the door closed behind him, Manny knocked on the table. "Start talking, Roche."

Again Émile turned to me, opening his expression for me to read. Before he could say anything, I pointed at his face. "You're concerned. And angry. But the concern is stronger."

"I need you to believe that I had nothing to do with this." From the moment Émile had introduced himself to me, he'd treated me as a valued friend or even member of his family. I didn't understand why a man as sceptical as he would immediately include me in his inner circle of trust. The truth of the need I saw on his face confirmed that he cared about my opinion. About me.

I considered everything I knew about him as well as the nonverbal cues I'd observed since he'd entered the conference room. "I believe you."

"Oh, thank God." He exhaled loudly. "I can't tell you how fucking angry I am that Reiss pulled me into this insanity."

"What insanity?" Impatience was clear in Manny's tone.

Émile glanced at Manny and looked back at me. "I heard you had some car problems a few hours ago. Are you okay?"

"I'm well." I narrowed my eyes. "How did you know we had car problems?"

"You know my IT guy is good." He nodded towards Francine. "She's much better, but my guy is good enough to know that your car was hacked this morning. Not really a great discovery since these things can be overheard by just listening in on police radio chatter."

"I thought you were no longer breaking the law, Roche." Manny took a sip of his milky tea.

Émile turned to face Manny. "I'm not. If Colin hadn't phoned me, I would've visited Genevieve later this afternoon. Especially after I found out she was in a hacked car. Four days ago, Reiss' car was also hacked. I know that you've read the police reports and everything you saw there is true."

"But there's more," Privott said.

"What there is is a mystery." Émile hesitated. "Reiss came to me after the police finished with him. At first, I didn't believe him, but now I don't know any more. He claims that he lost three hours."

"What does that mean?" I asked.

"I think it might be better if you ask him yourself. He's in my car with two of my associates. I thought it best that you speak to him. You can see if he's telling the truth or whether he's making all this shit up."

"Why don't you believe him?" The scepticism was clear on his face.

Émile sighed. "He's been trying really hard to straighten out his life, but it's a struggle for him. He's also never been the most reliable person. If you want something transported, he's the right person for the job. Then he's reliable, discreet, fast and honest. But anything else? From experience I've learned not to believe anything he says."

Manny pushed his hands in his trouser pockets. "Bring him in. What's another criminal at the table?"

Émile took his phone from the inner pocket of his jacket and tapped out a short message. "They'll be here in two minutes."

An awkward silence settled in the room while we waited. Lucien Privott tried twice to engage Émile in conversation, but was completely ignored. Émile did answer Phillip when asked about his granddaughter's progress at school. He was still talking about her successful violin performance at a school concert when there was a knock on the conference room door.

Tim opened the door, his face pale. "Monsieur Muller and Monsieur Reiss are here."

A lanky man walked past Tim, nervously glancing around the room. Behind him, a dark-haired man entered the room, his aggressive body language relaxing slightly when he saw Émile. He nodded at Émile and stepped out of the room. "I'll wait in reception."

Tim winced, but hid it quickly behind the professional expression he'd started using more often. He closed the door while offering the dark-haired man decaffeinated coffee.

The lanky man stood by the door, his unease growing as he looked around the room. "I didn't do anything wrong. I swear."

"Sit down, Reiss." Émile pointed at an empty chair. "Sit down and tell them exactly what you told me. Exactly."

Reiss flinched at Émile's cold tone. He pulled out the chair, sat down and immediately rubbed his arms a few times before he settled with his arms crossed. He cleared his throat. "I have a small coffee company. I import exclusive coffees from Africa, Central and South America. On Sunday evening, I received a panicked call from a customer that his company was in desperate need of Jamaican Blue Mountain coffee and they needed it first thing Monday morning. I had three kilograms of the coffee in stock, which was not as much as he'd ordered, but he said it would do. So Monday morning early, I got in my car and drove to deliver the three kilograms."

This man's micro-expressions fascinated me. He was one of those people who tried so hard to create an image of competence and success that even his truthful statements came across as boastful and pretentious. I understood why Émile found it difficult to believe this man.

"Do you always deliver small orders like this personally?" Privott asked.

Reiss snorted and uncrossed his arms. "Never. I don't even accept such small orders. But this is one of my best clients and it is always a good idea to keep one's clients happy. Going the extra mile and all, you know?"

I closed my eyes and took three deep breaths to prevent myself from asking what mile he was talking about. I had another, more pressing, question. "How did you lose three hours?"

He looked at me. "First, my car developed a mind of its own, driving me all over the city. Then it stopped in the middle of nowhere. For a few minutes, I couldn't get out of the car because all the doors were locked and wouldn't unlock. Then they unlocked. I got out and next thing I know, I'm back in my car, it's three hours later and the police are knocking on my window."

"You have no memory of how you got back in your car?" Manny's tone conveyed his disbelief.

Reiss' lips thinned. "Look, I know you have no reason to believe me. But I also have no reason to lie. I wasn't transporting anything illegal—"

Manny held up his hand to stop Reiss and looked at me. "Doc?"

"He's being truthful."

"At last!" The relief on his face was sincere. "Someone believes me. Then you must also believe that I don't know what happened between seven and ten o'clock Monday morning. By the time I convinced the police that I was okay and my car was okay, my client was ready to cancel our contract. He was livid. He thought I had lied about having the coffee and that I was going to leave him in the lurch. It took a lot of fast talking to convince him that I had the coffee and this kind of thing would never happen again."

I thought of everything he had just told us as well as what the police report had said. "Was anything stolen from your car?"

"Not you too." He shook his head and sighed in frustration.

"I told the police that nothing was stolen. They didn't believe me. Émile doesn't believe me." He leaned forward and stared at me. "Nothing was stolen from my car. There was nothing illegal in my car. I did nothing wrong."

"Doc?"

I nodded. "He's being truthful."

Reiss' shoulders relaxed and he leaned back in his chair. "Thank God. Someone is listening to me."

"Who is your client?" I was hoping to find a connection between all these loose pieces of information.

"Francis Rodet." He glanced at Émile before addressing me again. "Look, I've worked really hard to build a reputable business. And I had to work even harder to get larger contracts. Some of them are giving me a tiny profit margin, but it's giving me credibility. Francis was one of the few big guys willing to take a chance on me. He did nothing wrong. I did nothing wrong. Please don't drag us into some police investigation that will destroy my company and break Francis' trust in me."

I turned to Manny. "Have the crime scene investigators looked at his car?"

"What?" Reiss jerked away from me. "No. Nobody is going to touch my car."

"Ah." Manny's smile wasn't friendly. "That kind of reaction makes me very curious to know what we'll find in your car." He glanced at me. "And since the crime scene guys haven't looked at your car, I think it will be a great idea for them to do so now."

Reiss closed his eyes and sighed. "You won't find anything illegal in my car. I just don't want anyone touching my Porsche."

Manny's top lip curled. "I'll make sure to tell them to take good care of your precious little car."

Reiss' lips thinned as he threw a key on the table. "I will use every last cent I have to sue you if my car has as much as a scratch on it."

"Doc, do you have any more questions?" Manny lowered his brow in a warning look when I inhaled. "Any more questions for Reiss."

"Oh. No. Not now." I did have a lot of other questions though. The room was quiet while Phillip offered to walk Reiss out. The older man's confidence had an immediate effect on Reiss and he left the room already calmer and only glancing once at his keys on the table before disappearing into the hallway.

"Can you tell me what is going on here?" Émile paused for a second. "When I found out that your car was hacked this morning, I thought it was a simple crime, but this is obviously much more than that."

I studied Émile. He had been consistent in his help and honesty during the opera singer case. The two brunches Colin, Vinnie and I had enjoyed with him had confirmed that his concern and offers to help had been sincere every time. Without thinking about Manny's reaction, I decided to take the risk. "Do you know Claude and Emad Vernet?"

Émile's eyes widened then narrowed. "Those are two men you should stay away from, Genevieve."

"You know them."

"Unfortunately." He looked up and thought for a while. "Okay, it's been nine years, so I can no longer be arrested for this."

Manny straightened in his chair. "Oh, please. Give me something to arrest you on."

Émile ignored the baiting. "I was still involved in some less legal activities when I needed a shipment brought in from the Middle East. And no, I'm not telling you what or exactly from where. But I'd heard about these two men who were exceptional at moving things across borders. I only met with the one." He frowned. "Claude. Yes. That was his name. I found it strange that he would so freely share his name with me, especially since it made it easier to look into him. And find out who his father is. I still don't know why he did that.

"But I met with him, gave him half the fee in cash and that was it. Two weeks later, my shipment arrived without any problems and I paid the last fifty percent into an offshore bank account. Those days, they were quite expensive, but they were building a reputation for being extremely reliable and were never caught."

"Have you heard from or about them since then?" I asked.

"A few times, yes. I heard about them, not from them. The last I heard was... hmm... about a year ago, I guess. Someone said that these two were becoming more and more political and that some of their clients were looking elsewhere." He shrugged. "Sometimes, criminals just want to sell drugs or guns or art without getting all high and mighty about religion or politics."

"How noble." Manny slumped in his chair.

Again Émile ignored Manny. "Please be careful, Genevieve. The Vernet brothers have built a reputation for being reliable, but they've also built a reputation for being brutal when crossed. No one ever orders their services without knowing one hundred percent that they can pay. There have been too many stories about slow and painful deaths when someone didn't pay. Hearing these stories, I wondered if these brothers even care about the money. I mean, it doesn't make sense to kill someone when they owe you money. Break a few bones, maybe, but not kill. Dead men can't pay."

I saw Manny's scowl and spoke before he had the chance. "If you hear anything, let us know. As soon as you can."

"I'll do that for you." Émile got up and looked at Vinnie. "Walk me out, son."

Vinnie raised an eyebrow, but also got up. There were a few terse goodbye nods and a warm goodbye for me before Émile walked out of the room with confidence that made him appear as if he owned this building.

"I don't like that man." Manny rested his fists on his hips. "And I don't like that you're spending time with him."

"Aw, Millard." Colin's expression of affection was fake as he pressed his fist against his chest. "You should know by now that no one will ever be our grumpy Millard. You really don't need to be jealous."

"Bugger off, Frey."

"Seriously?" Privott tapped his fingers on the table. "I cannot believe that you're trusting Émile Roche. That man ruled the streets of Strasbourg thirty years ago. Even the police feared him. Hell, even the president feared him. What kind of team are you running here? Sharing all kinds of confidential information to the likes of Roche?"

"Be very careful what you say next, Privott." Manny's voice was low. "Our methods might not be conventional, but have we ever put the president, this country or anyone else in danger? We get better and faster results because we know we have the best of the best on this team."

Privott put his hands up as if to surrender. "I know. This is just... I don't know if I can work like this."

"Then don't." Manny pointed at the hallway. "Don't let the bloody door hit you on the way out."

"Can you find out where the leaders' meeting is being held?" I wanted to know this as soon as possible. This information might help us narrow the possibilities for what Claude and Emad were planning.

"I'll try." Privott's expression could easily be mistaken for anger.

"Why is this frustrating you?" I asked.

"Because I can't do my job." Privott winced. "That is not really true. My job is not the president's security and that is why I'm not privy to any details regarding the location of this meeting. I can try to find out, but I wouldn't hold my breath if I were you."

"Try." Manny pointed at the hallway again, this time without any aggression. "I suggest you get onto that as soon as possible."

Privott got up and left after a few more warnings that we needed to find out what the Vernet brothers were planning for tomorrow's meeting. I looked at my watch and was surprised to see it was three minutes past six. I hadn't expected it to be this late.

"I agree, Doc." Manny was also looking at my watch. "I think it's time we take a break from this. Let's all eat and rest. We can start again early tomorrow morning when we're fresh and rested."

I didn't want to go home. There were still those encrypted files on Gallo's computer that we needed to find a way to access. But from experience I knew that Manny was right. Taking a break from the intensity of this case and resting might bring connections forth that were currently getting lost in the constant influx of new information.

And I would have the opportunity to speak to Nikki and find out what was ailing her.

Chapter FIFTEEN

"Where's Nikki?" Manny looked around the living area of my apartment, then towards Nikki's room. "Is she joining us for dinner?"

"She's with friends." I had been greatly disappointed when I'd phoned her. "They're studying for an art history test next week."

Manny grunted and walked towards the dining room table. Vinnie had started cooking as soon as we'd arrived home. Since we'd had a substantial lunch, he'd decided to make lentil soup and serve it with fresh bread. The appetizing smells coming from the kitchen were making me hungry even though I hadn't been hungry when we came home.

I frowned when the muted sounds of my smartphone's ringtone came from my handbag. I'd spoken to Nikki ten minutes ago, so she wouldn't need to phone me. Everyone else who usually phoned me was either in the kitchen or impatiently standing next to the dining room table.

I took my phone from its designated place in my handbag and blinked. I did not expect to see the first lady of France's number flash on the screen. I swiped the screen and lifted the phone to my ear. "Hello?"

"Genevieve." Isabelle Godard sounded happy. "Isabelle here. How are you?"

"Well." I hated phone conversations and had to remind myself to be courteous. "How are you?"

Her laughter was light and genuine. "I'm very well, thanks. I just wanted to check up on you. It's been ages since we talked."

"No, it hasn't. We talked five weeks ago." I remembered then also being surprised that she had invited me for lunch. Just to chat. She'd done it a few times and the last time I had been much more comfortable socialising with her. Despite her success as a neurosurgeon and the uncredited work she'd been doing as the president's wife, she remained humble and easy to converse with.

"Well, five weeks feel like ages to me. I think it's time that we meet for lunch again."

I thought about Gallo, the Vernet brothers and the meeting her husband was hosting. "Now is not a good time."

"Now as in tonight or now as in this week? I also can't meet for lunch right now, because I've just had dinner. But I was thinking maybe we could meet next week. I'll be busy the next two days in any case. Hey, did I tell you that I'm getting back into medicine?"

"No." It was hard to follow her when she jumped from one topic to the next. "Your voice changed when you said this. Are you excited?"

"Am I ever. As much as I love the work Raymond and I are doing, I really miss my work. So when a hospital invited me to give three guest lectures and spend two days in the hospital doing rounds with the other doctors, I said yes."

"What about security?" I had to listen at each lunch to her complaining about constantly being followed by a security detail that was discreet, but still stood out in the restaurants. Not many other patrons had weapons forming bulges under their suit jackets.

She hesitated. "It took a lot of convincing to get those guys down to the minimum. Fortunately, the hospital I'm going to has excellent security." There was something in her voice that indicated there was more to the security that she couldn't share with me. I wouldn't have been surprised. As the first lady of France, Isabelle had to keep a lot of secrets. "I will tell you all about my short visit at the hospital when we have lunch. Is next week Thursday good for you?"

"I don't know." I didn't. I was hoping we would find Claude and stop whatever he and Emad were planning for tomorrow, but there was no guarantee.

"Oh. Okay." She tried to, but wasn't successful in hiding her disappointment.

I sat down on my usual chair at the dining room table and took a moment to organise my thoughts. "I want to meet you for lunch, but am working on a case at the moment and I don't know if I will have time next Thursday. It is possible that we'll solve this case, but I don't want to make promises I can't keep."

"Tell her you'll make a tentative arrangement for Thursday and confirm on Wednesday," Colin whispered next to me. I hadn't seen him sit down at the table.

"Um." I didn't like making appointments when there was no certainty, but I trusted Colin's advice. "Can I confirm on Wednesday?"

"That's a perfect plan." Isabelle's tone conveyed her pleasure. "I'll pencil you in for lunch on Thursday. If you're still busy with the case, it won't be a problem. We'll just pencil in another date. Oh, and bring Francine if you want to. We'll make it a ladies' lunch."

"I'll tell her."

"Okay then." The smile in her voice alleviated any concerns I had that my telephone skills had offended her. "Give my regards to everyone at home and I hope to see you next week."

I lowered the phone and ended the call. Colin put his hand on my forearm. I looked up and was surprised by the laughter on his face. "You should say goodbye, love. Not just end the call."

I winced. "Our conversation was at an end. It didn't seem necessary to say goodbye."

"Maybe not. But it is polite."

I nodded. I disliked phone conversations for many reasons, including the exaggerated need for social niceties. With only tone of voice and words to communicate one's message, it was even more important to understand and use socially acceptable behaviour. These changed with time and technological advancement which made it harder to know how to be inoffensive when speaking on the phone.

"It's really good to know there is someone with worse phone manners than me." Manny picked up his spoon and tapped it against his soup bowl. "Where's my food, big guy?"

"You'll get it faster if you remove this woman from my kitchen." Vinnie flared his elbows wider to prevent Francine from reaching the pot on the stove. She was holding a spice shaker and trying to get around Vinnie. "Take her away now or you're not getting anything, old man!"

Francine giggled and walked to the table. "I thought some cinnamon and rosemary would go well with the soup."

"It's clear you've never served in the armed forces." Manny shook his head sadly. "Because then you would know to never get on the cook's bad side."

"Oh, no." She shuddered. "Please don't tell me another one of your diarrhoea-in-the-barracks stories. Last time I couldn't eat for two days. Put a bunch of men together and you get a whole load of disgusting."

Vinnie brought a basket of bread to the table and chuckled. "Please tell us one of your stories. Please. Anything to get back at her for always being such a kitchen hazard."

Their banter was calming. The topic not. "I would prefer to not hear anything that could affect my appetite."

"Thank you!" Francine leaned across the table and held out her hand. When I just looked at it, she shook her hand and held it closer. "High-five me, girlfriend."

"No." I put my hands on my lap. "I washed my hands for dinner."

She sat back. "And then you touched your phone."

"Oh, my." I jumped up and went to the bathroom connected to my bedroom. Francine was shouting an apology and that she'd only been joking, but she was right. A study had shown that the average smartphone contained eight thousand more colony-forming units of bacteria than a toilet door handle. I took my time washing my hands.

A large soup bowl was on the table when I returned. Manny and Vinnie were arguing about who to serve first. Francine huffed and took the ladle from Vinnie. "Ladies first."

"Then you'd better serve Jen-girl, because no lady would suggest rosemary for my lentil soup."

Manny and Colin laughed at Francine's expression and the next hour was filled with teasing, eating and a conscious avoidance of the case. As usual, I didn't join in the banter. My mind was torn between wanting the connections in my subconscious to come forward and wanting to speak to Nikki. The latter would have to wait. Nikki usually came home in the early hours of the mornings when she was studying with her friends.

Manny, Vinnie and Colin were discussing football and I mentally called up Mozart's Concerto for Flute, Harp and Orchestra in C. There were so many unconnected pieces of information that I didn't know where to start. I didn't even know if all those bits floating around my brain, screaming for analysis, were even important or relevant. But something had clicked into place in my mind and I needed to access it. It had happened after I'd spoken to Gallo this morning. After he'd given us the string of numbers and letters.

I listened to another three lines before it came to me. I gasped and opened my eyes. I sighed inwardly when I saw that I'd pulled my legs up and was hugging my knees tightly against my chest. The groan that escaped when I lowered my legs got everyone's attention. They were still around the table, but only coffee mugs and a plate of cookies remained in the centre.

I looked at Francine. "The numbers and letters Gallo gave us could be the key to that one-gigabyte encrypted file on Gallo's computer."

"Oh, my God." Francine grabbed her tablet and started

tapping and swiping. It didn't take long. "I'm in! You were right. I've just accessed... hmm... five hundred and sixty-one folders. It's going to take forever to go through all of them."

"Then let's do it at the office." I got up. "We can divide the files and work through them."

Francine tilted her head, not looking away from her tablet screen. "I don't know if that will be a good use of time. There seems to be a lot of crap here. I will have to... then maybe we could... but first—"

"Supermodel!" Manny slapped his hand on the table next to her tablet. "Speak in full sentences."

She looked up from her tablet. "I think it would be better if I go through these first and sort out what could be useful or not. Some are just empty folders. And this folder I just opened has three hundred files. Let me sort through this first and you rest."

"It will go faster if I help." I was nowhere near Francine's level when it came to computer skills, but I was quite capable of seeing if the folders and files held important information.

"Not if I write a programme that will sort through this for us." Francine tapped a few more times on her tablet screen, then looked at me. "Really. It makes more sense if you look at the stuff I found in the morning when you are rested and fresh. You can even look at it really early if you want to, but after the day you've had, I think it might be good if you rest a bit."

I wavered. Even though I had been suppressing it, the exhaustion from this morning's event, the conversation with Gallo and then Émile's visit felt like a heavy weight on my shoulders. "Only if you promise that you will phone the moment you find something of real importance. No matter what time it is."

"Done." She got up and pulled at Manny's sleeve. "Come on, handsome. You can calm me with snoring sounds while I work."

Manny pulled his arm out of her reach and got up. "I do not snore."

I heard them arguing even after Colin closed and locked the front door behind them. He walked towards me and I realised how thankful I was that he didn't find the same pleasure as Francine and Manny in constant bickering. I would've found that most upsetting and arduous.

"What?" Colin slowed down until he stopped in front of me. "Something wrong, love?"

"You don't argue."

Vinnie's laughter was loud and immediate. He put two plates in the dishwasher and leaned against the counter, still chuckling.

Colin lowered his head, a smile tugging at the corners of his mouth. "And this is wrong?"

"No. I spoke without thinking. I like that we don't argue. It's not productive."

He straightened. "Ah. You're talking about Millard and Francine. Yeah, that would drive me up the wa... it would frustrate me a lot. I just agree with everything you say and life is easy."

"You're teasing me. Why?"

He leaned forward and kissed me on my forehead. "Because you make me happy. And just so you know, it's not hard to agree with you. Most of the time you're right."

I thought about this. And then I thought some more. "You're mistaken. You often disagree with me. You just don't present it as an argument. You were a successful criminal because you are exceptionally good at manipulating people."

"Whoa." Colin sat down next to me, his eyes wide. "You think I manipulate you?"

"In a sense, yes." I waved my hand at his face. "Don't look so alarmed. Motivating or helping people find their own answers are different, more positive forms of manipulation. You know how to phrase your disagreement so I can understand your sentiment and we can reach a compromise."

He looked at me for a long time. "I love you too, Jenny."

"You guys crack me up." Vinnie hung the dishtowel over the oven door handle. "I don't know anyone who has the conversations you two have."

"Go away." Colin didn't look at Vinnie.

"Yeah, I love you too, dude." Vinnie chuckled and walked to his side of the apartment. "Sweet dreams, y'all. I'll see ya bright and early."

I watched him leave and waited until I heard his bedroom door close. "He's distressed."

"Why do you say that?"

"When he's not actively involved in conversation, the anger and emotional turmoil surfaces."

"I hope we find Claude and find enough evidence to lock both him and his brother up for life. Maybe then Vin can find some closure for what happened with Becks." Colin sighed. "It really did a lot of permanent damage to him."

"Let's go sleep." It was before my usual bedtime, but if I went to sleep now, I could get up much earlier and help Francine. Maybe we'd find the evidence Colin was talking about. Maybe I could do something to help Vinnie find a way to heal.

Despite going through my usual night-time routine, then lying in bed and listening to Colin's deep breathing, I couldn't fall asleep. The earlier bedtime was breaking my routine and not even mentally writing Mozart's Requiem Mass in D minor helped my mind slow down. Eventually, I reached for my book and read until eleven o'clock, the time my mind was comfortable letting go of its obsessive analysing.

It felt like I'd just fallen asleep when a sound woke me up. I glanced at the digital clock on my bedside table and frowned. It was thirteen minutes past two. I closed my eyes, slowed my breathing and listened. The relief I felt when I heard Nikki move around her room was overwhelming. It lasted only eleven seconds.

The sound of retching had me up and grabbing my robe. Nikki had told me she wasn't ill, yet she was throwing up just after two in the morning. This was not normal.

I opened her bedroom door without knocking and went to her bathroom. She'd left the door open, but I stopped at the threshold. She was sitting on the floor, her arms on the toilet seat. She was breathing loudly and sounded like she was trying to control the heaving. I didn't go in. Not only did I want to give her some privacy, I simply couldn't bring myself to be that close to anything that unsanitary.

I waited until some of her heaving stopped. "What is wrong with you?"

Nikki jerked and looked around. Her face was pale, her eyes wide and watery. "Doc G. You nearly gave me a heart attack."

"What is wrong with you?" I didn't like the sound of desperation in my voice. Or the tightness squeezing my chest.

"I'm not sick." She closed her eyes and breathed a few times before she slowly pushed herself up. "Okay, I think I'm good for now."

She rinsed her mouth with mint mouthwash, washed her face and hands, then drank a few sips of water from a bottle standing next to the basin. Still she didn't look at me. She put the bottle down and winced at her reflection in the mirror. "Throwing up is so not sexy."

"Nikki." My voice was a whisper. In a very short time, this young woman had become extremely important to me. Her happiness, her health, her dreams. I even tolerated watching banal 'chick flicks' because it made her so happy to eat popcorn and watch movies with me. The mere idea of anything threatening her health brought darkness pushing at my consciousness.

She walked to me and pointed at her bed. "Let's sit there and talk."

I nodded and carefully stepped over two pairs of jeans, a t-shirt and three sweaters to reach her bed. She scrambled to the centre of the bed and sat with her legs crossed. I sat down on the side of the bed and studied her face. "Did you really meet your friends last night?"

"Yes." She put her hands on her lap. "But we met late afternoon and finished at around eight."

"And you didn't come home because you didn't want to talk to me." I didn't know why my chest tightened even more.

"No. Yes. No. Ah, shit!" She grabbed a pillow and put it on her lap, placing a barrier between us. She saw me looking at the pillow and threw it across the room. "I'm scared to tell you."

I was at a loss how to respond to that. I couldn't promise her that I wouldn't say anything hurtful or that I would always understand. It wouldn't be true. So I just watched her.

"Ah, Doc G. It's coming out all wrong." She pressed her fingers against her mouth for a few seconds. When she lowered her hand to her lap, tears filled her eyes. "If I'm really honest, I'm not scared to tell you. I'm scared because I don't know what to do."

"I used to scoff at the way Manny insisted that we speculate, but I've found that brainstorming a problem often helps find solutions one cannot reach on one's own."

She stared at me for almost a minute, a few tears making it down her cheeks. I gave her the time to gather her strength or organise her thoughts or do whatever she needed to before talking to me. Eventually, she took a shaky breath and wiped her cheeks with the backs of her hands. She rested her hands on her lap and straightened her shoulders. "I'm pregnant."

I froze. Of all the things Nikki could've told me, this was not something I'd been prepared for. I swallowed and mentally wrote another two lines of Mozart's Requiem Mass with a desperation I'd never experienced before. Nikki needed me. I was the one she came to for comfort, advice and sometimes even entertainment. I'd realised early on how highly she valued my opinion of her and how fragile her ego still was at this age.

I held up my index finger and wrote another two lines while hunting for an appropriate response. None came to me, so I gave her my honesty. "Why didn't you use the condoms Francine bought you? She gave you four packs. With twelve condoms in each pack."

Nikki laughed. Then tears flowed down her face and she laughed again. "Seriously? That's your reaction?"

"I don't know what else to say." I lifted both shoulders. "I have a lot to say, but I don't know if it would be good or bad."

"Do you still love me?" Her question was asked in jest, but I saw the truth behind it. Her eyes were desperately seeking mine.

This was all I needed to organise my thoughts. I put my hand on her bed, reaching out to her. "Look at me. After all this time, you know me and you also know how to read the truth in someone's face. Look at my face when I say this." I waited a heartbeat. "I love you."

She burst out crying and scooted over to me. It took all my control to keep the panic at bay when she threw her arms around me and cried on my shoulder. I patted her twice on her back, took a deep breath and put my arms around her. Most of the tension in her muscles immediately left and she relaxed in my embrace. It was a long ninety seconds until I simply couldn't take it anymore. "Nikki."

She hiccoughed and took three shaky breaths before she pulled away from me. She dried her cheeks on her shoulders. The expression on her face when she looked at me was something I would treasure for a long time. Her trust, love and relief was overwhelming. "Thanks, Doc G. I needed that."

"I don't know much about pregnancy, but I do know that there is a great change in a woman's hormones. You might experience frequent bouts of emotional outbursts." I swallowed. "I will have to buy books. I need to read more about this."

"You and me both." She sat back and rubbed her thighs. "I don't know what to do."

"What exactly are you referring to?"

She chewed her bottom lip, then said in an almost whisper, "I don't know if I should keep the baby."

I blinked. This was a part of life I'd never spent much time thinking about. I had known at a young age that I never wanted children of my own and therefore never wasted time researching the options, the long-term effects or anything related to children.

"Let's start with some facts." I could handle that. "Are you one hundred percent sure you're pregnant?"

"Yes. I first did the home test, but wanted to make sure. The doctor phoned me three days ago when the blood test results came in. I'm definitely knocked up."

"Does that mean pregnant?"

She giggled. "Yes."

"How far along are you?"

"The doctor and I did some calculations and we think I'm nine weeks pregnant."

I thought about our conversations in the last few weeks. "Is Martin the father?"

"Yes." She leaned forward. "Please don't tell Vinnie or Manny. They'll kill him. I don't want Marty dead. He's a really nice guy."

"Does he know that you're pregnant?"

"Yes. He went with me to the doctor." She blinked a few times. "But we're not getting married or something stupid like that. We're too young. We had fun for a while, but we both agree that we're not a good romantic match. I want what you have with Colin. We didn't have that."

I resisted asking about what I had with Colin. "Will he play an active role in your pregnancy, in the baby's life?"

"He said that he would respect my decision. If I didn't want to keep the baby, he would be with me the whole time. If I wanted to keep him or her, Marty wants to be a part of it. He said that we were both stupid and we both should take responsibility."

My eyebrows rose. "That's very mature thinking for a man so young."

"Like I said, he's a really, really, really nice guy."

I had so many questions, so many concerns that I fought again to keep the panic away. We sat in silence for a few minutes. I didn't know what was going through Nikki's mind. I was too busy obsessing about the possibility of having a small human in my life. Having the constant fear for Nikki's wellbeing weighing on me was one thing. She was a young adult with the ability to make reasonably intelligent decisions. Having the wellbeing of a helpless and fragile baby weighing on me might be my undoing.

It took a lot of willpower to move my obsessive thoughts away from my own panic. This wasn't about my life. This was about Nikki's. About the decision that she had to make and the consequences she would have to live with. I put my hand on the bed again. "What do I always tell you?"

She frowned at my question, then snorted. "Observe, analyse, assess, then act."

"This is a decision you're going to have to make on your own, but you won't be alone. I will help you find as much information as I can about all your options. We'll assess and analyse together." I put my hand a bit closer to her. "I don't know how to handle this situation, but together we'll find a way. No matter what you decide, I'll learn how to support you."

Chapter SIXTEEN

"Are you okay, love?" Colin started the new SUV and pulled into the street. I didn't know when he'd found the time, but yesterday he'd ordered a vehicle exactly the same as his last. I also didn't know when the car dealer had delivered the SUV, but it had been there this morning when Colin and I had gone downstairs to go to the team room. Colin turned into another street and glanced at me. "Jenny?"

"I'm worried and distracted." I hated that I couldn't be honest with him about the cause of my concern and distraction. Nikki had begged me not to tell anyone until she was ready. She'd promised that she would do this today or tomorrow. She knew my honesty was something I didn't always have under full control. I hated deception.

"Are we talking about Gallo and the Vernet brothers or something else?" He glanced at me again.

"I don't want to talk about it," I said quickly before pressing my lips tightly together. Apart from the overwhelming urge to tell the truth, I also needed Colin's advice. He would know better what to say to Nikki, how to support her, how to make her feel less scared. I had seen her fear last night and it had kept me from falling asleep again.

I had lain in bed for two hours, listening to Colin sleeping and obsessing over this new development. When Francine had phoned at eleven minutes past five, I had been relieved to get up. She had separated the files that she considered worth exploring and needed me to look at them. I was happy that I could find something different that required my focus.

The sound of a ringtone filled the interior of the SUV. Colin took the phone from his winter coat's pocket and handed it to me. "Answer it, please."

I didn't like handling anyone else's phone. Too many hygiene issues to distract me. But this was Colin's phone and for some irrational reason, I wasn't as put off by it. I took the phone and swiped the screen. "Hello?"

"Oh. Doctor Lenard." Timothée's tone conveyed his surprise and disappointment. "Where is Colin?"

"He's driving. What do you want, Tim?" I frowned when Colin chuckled.

"Um, you might want to drive to Guédon-Leroy Hospital. Monsieur Gallo got really sick and we had to call an ambulance." He hesitated for a second. "I think he's dying."

"When did this happen?"

"The ambulance left with him about thirty minutes ago. He wasn't happy to leave. He asked for you. A lot. And he kept saying that he's not finished. And that he's not finished with you."

I frowned. Those were odd statements, but consistent with Gallo's unexpected appearance at Rousseau & Rousseau as well as his peculiar behaviour. "We'll go to the hospital now." I remembered what Colin had told me last night and quickly added, "Goodbye," before I ended the call.

"Which hospital?" Colin slowed down and looked at me.

"Guédon-Leroy."

He nodded and turned right into the next street. "Who's there? Gallo?"

"Yes."

"Hmm. That's an interesting choice for a hospital."

"Why?" I loathed hospitals. As a child, I'd been subjected to far too many tests in my parents' attempts to find a cure and make me 'normal'. I didn't spend much time thinking about hospitals or that they could be interesting.

"For starters, it's one of the most modern hospitals in France. It also has some of the best doctors in the country. They have a unit dedicated to tropical diseases and I know that their burn unit is one of the top units in Europe."

I wondered if it was coincidence that Gallo had been taken to that hospital or if he had asked specifically for it. Colin's phone played a ringtone that sounded like the theme music of one of Vinnie's favourite wrestling shows. I swiped the screen after Vinnie's name flashed on it. "Hello?"

"Where are we going, Jen-girl?"

"You're not in the car with us. Why are you saying 'we'?"

Vinnie laughed. "I'm right behind ya. Franny phoned me too. Thanks for not waking me up, by the way. I really didn't want to know about any new developments."

"I don't know if you're sarcastic or sincere."

"Joking, Jen-girl. Joking." He cleared his throat. "So, where are we going?"

"To Guédon-Leroy Hospital. Gallo became very sick and was taken there a short while ago."

"So that bastard is really dying. Huh. Okey-dokey. I'll see you at the hospital."

I ended the call and had just put the phone on my lap

when it rang again. This time the ringtone sounded like a troop of monkeys. I frowned at the screen when I saw it was Manny calling. Colin had the strangest sense of humour. I swiped the screen. "Yes?"

"Good morning to you too, Doc." Manny sounded irritated. "Are you on your way to the hospital?"

"Yes. Are you?"

"Of course I am." He was silent for a moment and I wondered if he was taking calming breaths. "I'm so pissed off with that bloody Tim for not letting me know the moment Gallo got sick."

"How did Timothée know?" Phillip's assistant worked normal office hours and would have had no reason to be in the office at such an early hour.

"Apparently the little twit had become pals with one of the GIPN guys who decided to phone Tim and Daniel and not me. Supermodel and I were right next door. Bloody hell!"

"You've been in the team room the whole night?"

"Yes. We came here after dinner and supermodel has been working the whole time on Gallo's computer. I hope to hell you got some sleep in because I feel like death warmed up."

"That's a very disturbing expression." I shifted in my seat. "Do you know what Francine found?"

"Not all the details. She wanted you to be there when she showed her discoveries, but she went on and on about hitting the jackpot. It seems like she found a lot of evidence about Gallo's crimes as well as information implicating a few other people."

"Did she or didn't she find evidence?" I hated vagueness.

"She wouldn't say." Manny grunted. "I'm pulling in at the

hospital. I'll wait for you at the main entrance."

He didn't say goodbye before ending the call and I wondered why everyone else thought it to be so important. It hadn't offended me.

"What did Francine find?" Colin asked.

"Manny is not sure. He's speculating."

Colin smiled and turned into the parking area for the hospital. "Next time put the calls on speakerphone. Then I can irritate him some more."

"No." I pulled his phone closer to me, then realised what I was doing and put the phone on his lap. "You can phone him if you want to irritate him."

There had been almost no traffic on the streets and only a few cars were in the parking area. I supposed the only people at the hospital at quarter to six in the morning were medical staff and family members of emergency cases. Colin parked the car and Vinnie parked his vehicle next to us. He was driving a truck that looked the same as his previous one, but was dark green. He joined us with a happy smile and we walked to the well-lit main entrance.

The hospitals my parents used to take me to were mostly situated in old buildings. I remembered visiting only one modern building, but my parents hadn't approved of the open-mindedness of the staff. We'd gone back to the old buildings and the old doctors who'd agreed that I'd needed to be 'fixed'.

Colin had a doctor friend who worked at a hospital on the other side of the city. That hospital was also in a newer building, their technology advanced, but it didn't have the modern appearance of this building. Most of the walls facing the street and the parking area were glass, the lights from the interior spilling onto the snow-covered garden separating the building from the cars.

"About time you got here." Manny rubbed his hands, then blew into his fists. "This bloody cold front is pissing me off."

"You could've waited inside." I walked past him and waited for the automatic doors to slide open. A blast of hot air flowed over me from above the door as I entered. The reception area looked like that of a hotel. Large marble pillars along the length of the area added even more elegance to it. Clusters of chairs were arranged in a way that made me wonder if the designers had indeed taken their inspiration from five-star hotels.

Colin and Manny followed me to the reception desk where we were greeted by a bright-eyed and friendly young woman. "Good morning. How may I help you?"

Manny pulled out a small leather folder, opened it and showed it to the receptionist. "Interpol. We're here to visit Marcos Gallo."

"Oh, yes. He came in about half an hour ago." She looked at Manny's identification. "May I confirm this before I give you any more information?"

Manny's eyes widened in surprise, but he nodded. The receptionist tapped on her tablet and put a Bluetooth headset in her ear. She aimed the tablet's camera at Manny's identification and had a short conversation with the person on the other side. It took her less than a minute to confirm Manny's identity. Her smile was wide but professional when she handed it back to him. "Thank you for your patience, Colonel Millard. Would you like to speak to Monsieur Gallo's physician?"

"We would like to speak to Gallo."

"Oh, let me call his physician and she can take you to him." Again she tapped on the tablet and had another short conversation. She ended the call and pointed at the chairs behind us. "Please take a seat. Doctor Ferreira will be here in a minute."

We didn't sit down, but we did move a few feet away from the reception desk. Vinnie looked around the area and stared at the marble pillars. "This looks far too fancy to be a hospital. It doesn't even smell like one."

"There are quite a few private clinics that are adopting a different approach to hospitalisation." Colin pointed at the potted palm tree closest to us. "Having many plants around has been proven to improve patients' moods and speed up their healing process. These hospitals and clinics also have very few shared rooms. Studies have shown that patients feel constantly tired while in hospital. They are woken up at all hours of the night and never given the rest they need to recover. These types of hospitals try to make patients feel cared for and as relaxed as possible. Interestingly enough, patients spend fewer days and show shorter recovery periods than in traditional hospitals."

"That's a very good summary of what we're trying to do here."

I turned around to see who the rich alto voice belonged to. The first thing I noticed was the thirty-something woman's dark hair. It was out of control. It appeared that at one point she'd tied it back, but the natural curls had escaped and framed her round face and fell down her back. She was slightly overweight, but moved with an energy that made me nervous. She was the kind of person who seldom sat in one place for long.

The African heritage in her bloodline was clear in her darker skin tone, but her light brown eyes and the softer curls in her hair indicated Caucasian ancestors. She held her hand out to Manny. "I'm Doctor Roxanne Ferreira, but please call me Roxy."

"Manfred Millard." Manny shook her hand.

"But you can call him Old Man." Vinnie laughed when Manny aimed a most hostile look at him.

"I don't think I'll be doing that." Roxy's smile was wide and genuine when she held her hand out to Vinnie. "And you are?"

"Vinnie."

"Vinnie?" She shook his hand and took a step back. "Like Madonna or Bono? Just one name?"

"This is Doctor Genevieve Lenard and that is…" Manny paused and waited for Colin to introduce himself. I would've given Colin's real name, but Manny had clearly remembered that Colin used many aliases.

"Colin Frey." Colin held his hand out to Roxy, his eyes friendly, but assessing. "Pleased to meet you."

Roxy looked at me and I took a step back. "I don't shake hands."

Her eyes widened. "Okay then. Well, let's talk about Monsieur Gallo."

"How is he?" I asked. "Is he conscious?"

"Oh, he is conscious all right." She rolled her eyes and puffed out air in a most unprofessional manner. "And he wouldn't stop talking. He's been asking for you since the moment he arrived."

I pointed at her face. "Your expression changed when you said he's talking. What's wrong with his speech?"

"He's not always making sense. Sometimes his speech is clearer than other times. It's definitely one of the symptoms."

Her micro-expressions concerned me. "Symptoms of what?"

"You don't know?" She shifted from one foot to the other and tucked a wayward curl behind one ear. "I wasn't surprised when the others didn't know what was wrong with him, but from what I understand he's been under your care for a few days now."

"Two days," I corrected.

She scratched her head and a few more curls came loose. "Huh. He seems so desperate to talk to you, I thought you would know."

"Know what?" Manny's impatience made his voice sound even louder in the empty reception area. "What is wrong with him?"

"Well, we are still doing our own tests, but he brought his own test results from his doctor in Amsterdam. Why they didn't detain him or hospitalise him and why it isn't public is beyond me. Something this big should be controlled by a supervisory body."

Manny took a step closer to her and lowered his chin to glare at her. "What is wrong with Gallo?"

Roxy blinked a few times at Manny's aggression, but didn't flinch or step back. "He's been poisoned with polonium-210."

"What the fuck?" Vinnie took a step away from the doctor as if she was contagious. "That shit is deadly. Why isn't he dead already?"

"He isn't far from it." She frowned. "You didn't know about this? For reals?"

I was momentarily distracted by wondering why a well-educated woman of her age would use language Nikki frequently used. Then I thought of Nikki and panic rushed at me so fast, I could barely focus on my breathing. I forced Mozart's Symphony No.41 to mentally play at top volume.

"Jenny?" Colin pulled me under his arm and hugged me close to him.

"She doesn't look well. Let me look at her." Roxy's voice came closer, but she didn't reach me.

Colin turned us away from her. "She'll be fine. Just give her a moment."

"Tell me more about this pollynonsense ten." Manny's incorrect recall of the radioactive isotope brought some feeling of normality to me and I took a deep breath.

"It's polonium-210. And one-name Vinnie is right, it's deadly. A few years ago, someone was poisoned with it in London and he died soon after. It was the first such recorded case in history. It's a rare and highly radioactive isotope that is extremely hard to detect. It was identified in this man only a few hours before his death."

I had read two articles about that case, but had never researched the isotope any further. Now I wished I had. I took a few more deep breaths and turned to face Roxy. "How is it absorbed into one's system?"

"Bloody hell!" Manny rubbed his palms against his hips. "Have we been exposed?"

"The only way polonium-210 will poison you is if it is ingested or inhaled. Did Monsieur Gallo offer you anything to drink? Did he work with your food?"

"No."

"Then you should be fine. I suggest we test everyone just as a precaution, but if you're not vomiting, losing your hair or having severe headaches, I doubt you've been poisoned."

"Could it affect a pregnant woman?" I had to force my mouth to form the words. Even though I'd read the two articles, I needed confirmation. And reassurance.

Roxy didn't have the opportunity to answer me. Manny and Vinnie's reactions were immediate, loud and overwhelming. "Bloody hell, Doc! Are you pregnant?"

"Dude!" Vinnie slapped Colin hard on his back. "Why didn't you tell me?"

"Jenny?" Colin pulled slightly away from me to fully face me.

"I'm not pregnant." I needed an answer from Roxy more than I needed to answer the men's questions. I looked at her, my eyes wide. "Could I have absorbed some of it and transferred it to a pregnant woman?"

"No." She pushed Vinnie and Manny away from me and stood in front of me. "Polonium-210 does not emit gamma particles, which can even travel through thick walls. It only does its damage if ingested. Since Monsieur Gallo must have ingested the polonium-210, the damage will look like the end stages of cancer. If you're worried about your friend, I suggest you bring her in so we can also test her." She raised both eyebrows, her expression serious. "But I highly doubt that there would be any problems."

She was being truthful and the relief I felt was vast. Manny put his phone to his ear and waited, his expression tight. His nostrils flared slightly when his call was answered. "Are you pregnant?... I'm not joking, supermodel. Are you or aren't you pregnant?" The tension in his face and his shoulders decreased significantly with the answer he received. "I don't know... I don't have time for this now, supermodel. Get back to work."

Roxy stared with wide eyes as Manny put his phone back in his pocket and turned to me. "If you and supermodel aren't pregnant, that leaves only one other female."

"Motherfuckers!" Vinnie threw his hands in the air then put his fists on his hips. "Nikki? Nikki! That little punk is pregnant?"

"Vin, calm down." Colin stepped away from me, but didn't let go of my hand. "Jenny, please tell us everything you know."

"I promised to wait until she could tell you." I was disappointed that I hadn't been able to succeed. "I found out this morning when I heard Nikki vomit."

"Morning sickness." Roxy nodded. "Normal for the first trimester."

"Who did this to her?" Vinnie's *masseter* muscles flexed as his jaw tightened. "Who did this?"

"Vin." Colin's tone was strong and a warning. "Calm down. You're not thinking straight. You know Nikki would never let anyone 'do this to her'. Right, Jenny?"

"She wasn't raped. This was consensual."

"Blood hell, Doc. She's just a kid. She shouldn't be doing any consensual anything."

"How old is this Nikki?" Roxy asked.

"Twenty." Vinnie crossed his arms. "And too frigging young."

Roxy patted him on his bulging arm. "She's an adult."

"Bloody hell." Manny walked away from us, rubbing his face, his head and again his face. He stopped at the front door and returned to us. "We'll deal with this later. Now we need to speak to Gallo."

"I'm afraid that won't be possible." She shifted on her feet, a movement that seemed to be a habit rather than a nonverbal cue. "I gave him a light sedative. He was becoming very agitated about not being in touch with Genevieve." She looked at me. "Can I call you Genevieve?"

"Yes. Did he say why he wanted to be in touch with me?"

"Not specifically. He just went on and on about needing to speak to you. That he wasn't finished, he hadn't given you everything and it was too soon."

"Too soon for what?" I shook my head when Roxy inhaled. "I know you don't know the answer. I was thinking aloud."

"Oh, cool. I do that a lot." She leaned towards me. "My colleagues think I'm cuckoo."

I leaned away from her. "If that's their professional opinion, you might consider finding treatment."

Her laughter echoed through the reception area. "I sometimes think I should find treatment for working in this place."

"Why?" Colin asked.

She started to speak, but stopped herself. A false smile lifted the corners of her mouth. "This is a wonderful hospital with state-of-the-art equipment and security."

"You're truthful about the quality of the hospital, but you don't like the security." It was easy to read this woman's nonverbal cues. She was not good at deception.

She tilted her head and stared at me. "What kind of doctor are you?"

"The kind who will know when you're lying." Vinnie stepped closer and straightened to tower over her. "What's the problem with the security here?"

She pushed against Vinnie's chest. "You don't scare me, Vinnie-bear. I have five brothers and all of them have tried to intimidate me. I made them beg for mercy while I laughed and laughed and laughed."

The more she spoke, the more Vinnie's eyebrows pulled closer in a perplexed frown. He glared at her hand against his chest, then leaned down until their noses almost touched. "You're cute. Cute and harmless." He straightened. "Now answer my question. What's wrong with the security?"

Vinnie must have picked up on the same combination of alarm and dislike I'd seen in Roxy's expression. I was also curious about her answer.

She patted his chest and took her time to look at each of us individually. I saw the moment she decided to trust us. "This is one of the most secure hospitals in the city. Hah, maybe even the whole country. There are cameras everywhere, codes for doors, eye scans for some doors, fingerprints for other doors and other kinds of security measures. I really don't like feeling like I'm being watched all the time. But I suppose that is why we have quite a lot of celebrities and other public figures coming here." She shrugged. "That and of course the brilliant doctors working here."

"You are one of them," Colin said. "What is your specialisation?"

"Tropical diseases and poisons." She shifted again. This

time her feet turned towards the side doors. "It was lucky that I was on duty when they brought Monsieur Gallo in. Not that I can really do anything for him except make sure he's comfortable."

"What is your prognosis?" I asked.

"I don't know if I can believe him, but he told me that he was poisoned a week ago. Apparently, he'd been on a ship, so when it happened he thought at first that it was delayed motion sickness or something like that. But when his vomiting became uncontrolled, he went to that doctor in Amsterdam. I really need to find out who that idiot is. He should've put Gallo in a hospital immediately."

"Gallo wouldn't have allowed it," I said. "He needed to see me."

Roxy tilted her head and looked at me for a few seconds. "Clearly, this is some top-secret stuff you guys are working with. But if you know anything that could help me treat Gallo, I would appreciate if you could tell me."

"Can you really still treat him? Cure him?"

She shook her head and more curls fell around her face. "No. He pretty much only has another day or two at most to live. The polonium has done far too much irreversible damage by now."

"And you are sure Nikki will be fine?" I was going to insist that Nikki had tests done immediately.

"Ninety-nine percent sure." She took a step towards the doors. "Send her in and I'll make sure of it. You guys should also get tested. Just to be safe."

I really didn't want to be subjected to more tests, but reason far outweighed my dislike. We followed Roxy to the side doors while she happily chatted about the strange cold front we were experiencing so close to spring. I stopped listening when she went onto a full weather analysis of the tropical countries favoured by tourists where they picked up strange diseases or were bitten by insects.

I wanted the tests done so I could go to the team room and find out what Francine had discovered. And phone Nikki and order her to have herself tested.

Chapter SEVENTEEN

"You're pregnant?" Vinnie stormed from the elevator and stopped in front of Nikki. "What the fuck, little punk?"

Nikki looked at me. "You told them."

"It's more complicated than that, Nix." Colin pulled Nikki away from Vinnie and pointed at the round table. "Let's all sit down. Vin, I'm sure we can all do with some coffee."

"Not her." Vinnie shook his index finger angrily at Nikki. "She's not getting any caffeine for the next nine months. Not even decaf."

"Wait. What?" Francine jumped up from her chair and ran over to Nikki. "You're pregnant? Ooh! Oh, wow. That's so... Ooh!" She clapped her hands. "I'm going to be an auntie." Then she sobered and her hands fell to her sides. "Wait, is this a good thing? Are we happy?"

I had been surprised to find Nikki in the team room when we arrived. She'd been talking to Phillip while Francine was working on her computer. Phillip was now standing next to Nikki, shock clear on his face.

I had considered phoning her while we were driving here, but I'd had a hard time finding the right way to tell her she needed to be tested for polonium-210 poisoning. I had just put my handbag in its designated place in one of my antique-looking filing cabinets when Vinnie and Manny arrived. I had feared their reaction. Rightly so.

"No, supermodel. We are not bloody happy." Manny sat down hard in his usual chair and glared at Nikki. "What are you doing having sex? You should be studying."

"Oh, pooh." Francine slapped Manny's shoulder. "Like you're a virgin. You shouldn't be shouting at Nix. Can't you see how close to tears she is?"

Phillip walked to the far end of the table and sat down slowly, his eyes watchful. I sat down and was surprised when Colin put Nikki in his seat. He sat next to her and took her hands, his expression tender. "Ignore Millard. We're all here to support you." He glared at Manny. "Not judge."

"I'm not judging." Manny rubbed both his hands over his face. "I'm just… Bloody hell!" He looked at Nikki. "You're like my bloody daughter and I can't tolerate the thought of you doing… that."

Nikki didn't react to his last proclamation. Her eyes filled with tears and she wiped at them with the back of her hand. "Thanks, Manny. That's really sweet."

Manny slapped both hands on the table. "It's not bloody sweet. You're bloody pregnant. Have you—"

"Enough." My tone conveyed my anger. "I implore everyone to carefully consider what you say. My reaction wasn't perfect, but it is completely unproductive to talk about past actions. Nikki is an adult—"

"Who can speak for herself." Nikki exhaled loudly and straightened in her chair. "Marty and I weren't careful enough." She held up both hands to stop Manny and Vinnie from talking. "No, you don't get to shout at or about Marty either. We both know that we shouldn't have been so careless. We are both taking responsibility for what happened and what will happen."

Vinnie put a tray with our coffee on the table and sat down without distributing the coffee. He leaned his elbows on the table. "What do you plan to happen, little punk?"

Nikki's confident posture deflated a bit. "I don't know. Doc G said she'll help me get all the info I need to make the right decision. I haven't thought of anything else since I found out."

"When did you find out?" Francine asked.

"Three days ago." Nikki pulled her shoulders back and looked at everyone at the table. "You're my family and this will affect us all. I'm sorry that I'm causing trouble, but I'm going to need your help and advice to get through this."

"You've got my total support, Nix." Francine was trying to hide her excitement, but was failing greatly. "I'll go shopping with you. For maternity clothes or even just retail therapy, I'm your girl."

"Bloody hell, Nikki." Manny pushed his hands in his trouser pockets. He was quiet for a few seconds, then looked at her. "You make sure you listen to what Doc says. She'll help you make the right decision."

I jerked back. Surely Manny couldn't expect me to have wisdom in a situation like this.

Nikki leaned closer to me until our shoulders touched. She pushed slightly. "Doc G's the best."

"I need to punch something." Vinnie got up, but didn't walk away. He looked at Nikki. "You sure you don't want me to go put some hurt on this Marty?"

Nikki giggled. "He did nothing wrong, Vin. He's being quite amazing about all of this."

"What's his take on this?" Colin had been listening quietly, but I'd seen the deep concern pulling at his eyes and mouth. Nikki told them everything she had told me about the mature manner in which Martin was handling this situation. Colin nodded. "He's a good man. I'll make sure you'll both be okay."

"*We'll* make sure." The look Phillip gave Colin was just as loaded as Colin's statement. I wondered what he was going to do to ensure Martin would be okay. I wouldn't be surprised if Colin and Phillip secured employment for Martin, the type of employment that would provide him not only with a good income, but also opportunities for advancement and development.

Nikki bumped my shoulder again and moved away. "So why did Colin say it was complicated when I asked you about telling them?"

My eyes widened and I caught myself just as my hand pressed against my suprasternal notch, the hollow just above my breastbone. I lowered my hand. "Gallo has polonium-210 poisoning. The doctor said it should not have transferred from him to me and then to you at all, but I want you to be tested."

"Oh, my God." Nikki wrapped both her arms around her stomach. "Is that doctor sure there will be no problem? Is he a specialist?"

"*She* knows what she's talking about, punk." Vinnie sat down again. "Jen-girl asked her a few times and she explained very carefully that everything will be fine. But she also agreed that you should be tested. Just for peace of mind."

Francine's eyes narrowed. "What's that doctor's name?"

"Roxanne Ferreira," Vinnie said. "Why?"

Francine was already tapping on her tablet. "I'm checking her out, that's why. Oh, my. She's quite pretty. Right, Vin?"

"She's pretty?" Nikki leaned across me and held her hand out to Francine's tablet. "Lemme see."

Francine turned her tablet for Nikki to see. The image of Roxy appeared to be a professional photo taken for the hospital's website. Even then she hadn't been able to control her hair. A wayward curl fell across her right cheek, a few others down the back. Her light brown eyes were accentuated by the lighting, the extra weight making her face look soft. Looking at her static photo, I had to agree with Francine. Roxy was beautiful.

"Ooh, she's gorgeous." Nikki sat back in her chair. "So, big punk, did you flirt with her?"

"We're talking about you, not me." Vinnie crossed his arms and looked at Francine's tablet. "She told us she's a specialist in tropical diseases and poisonings. Is that true?"

Francine snorted. "And then some. Her bio is impressive. This woman has not only the education, but also the experience to treat patients with chronic and acute infections acquired in continental Europe and international patients who need specialist diagnosis and treatment. She's also written an article about radiation poisoning for one of those lah-di-dah medical journals. She seems to be a bit more than she told you."

I looked at Manny. "Do you know if Gallo asked to be taken to that hospital or if the ambulance just took him there?"

"He asked." Manny scratched his stubbly chin. "You said he does nothing without a reason, Doc. What would be his reason to go there other than he knew this was the best place to get treatment for his poisoning?"

Nikki leaned back even more in her chair. She was trying to make herself less noticeable. The lessening of the tension in her muscles indicated that she was glad that she was no longer the topic of discussion.

I thought about what Manny had said. "Could there be another reason? Maybe the security?"

"I'm thinking he knew that he would be in our custody and that he wouldn't need extra security, not with GIPN standing guard at his door." Manny's lips tightened. "Is he up to something, Doc?"

"If you're asking me whether Gallo has plans other than taking revenge on the Vernet brothers, I don't know. I can't read his mind." I recalled my observation when I'd last spoken to Gallo. "Gallo's micro-expressions confirmed my statement when I told him that he was fatally ill. But he didn't react when I'd said it was the Vernet brothers who'd poisoned him. It would seem reasonable to deduce that they poisoned him with polonium-210 when he refused to give them the list of contacts."

"Who else would poison him?" Manny asked. "Would he poison himself?"

I thought about this. "It's possible, but not probable. Gallo has shown no symptoms of depression or anything that could hint at suicide. And since he can't infect anyone with his polonium-210 poisoning, a suicide attack is not a viable option."

"What exactly is polonium-210?" Nikki winced when everyone looked at her. "I'm an art student, not a scientist."

I recalled everything I'd read in those two articles. "It's an isotope that emits pure alpha particles."

"I didn't understand a word you just said." Nikki wrinkled her nose. "Can you, like, make it simpler?"

"It's a radioactive isotope that can be stopped with a sheet of paper outside the body. Alpha particles are…" I closed my eyes when I saw Nikki's blank expression and thought how to simplify this even more. "Polonium-210 is two hundred and fifty thousand times more poisonous than hydrogen cyanide. When ingested or inhaled, it causes significant biological damage to living cells. But it cannot penetrate skin and is only dangerous when ingested."

"I've got more here." Francine waved her tablet in the air. "For a long time scientists and other important people considered polonium-210 unfeasible as a murder weapon. That is until the Alexander Litvinenko case."

This was the case Roxy had referred to. "There has been a lot of speculation about who poisoned him."

"Speculation, schmeculation." Francine made a rude noise. "It was totally the Russians. Litvinenko was given asylum in the UK and started working for MI5 and MI6. Russian President Andreyev and the FSB didn't like it, so they sent someone to put some polonium-210 in his tea. He died three weeks later."

"How and where can someone buy polonium-210?" Manny looked at Vinnie. "Would one of your contacts have it in stock?"

"No way, old man. I don't know anyone willing to mess

around with stuff that could get them killed just by being close to it."

"That doesn't make sense," I said. "You've told me you know people who sell explosives. That would kill them if they stood close to it."

"Yeah, okay. I didn't say it right, but the others got my meaning."

"So where would I go to buy enough polonium-210 to kill someone?" Manny asked.

Francine tapped on her tablet and stopped for a moment to read. "Okay, this says that polonium-210 has a very short half-life. Only a hundred and thirty-eight days."

"What's a half-life?" Nikki asked.

"A half-life is the time needed for the amount of polonium-210 to halve its initial value." As a child, I'd spent three months absorbed by learning about the half-lives in biology and pharmacology. "It means that polonium-210 will have half its strength in a hundred and thirty-eight days and half that strength in another hundred and thirty-eight days."

"Hey, this is interesting." Francine pointed at her tablet. "Marie Curie discovered polonium and it was named after her homeland, Poland. Not really useful, but interesting. Anyhoo, nowadays polonium is obtained by irradiating bismuth with high-energy neutrons or protons. Getting it from nature is far too tedious."

"Okay, so who can irradiate bismark with stuff?"

"Bismuth, handsome." Francine swiped her tablet screen a few times. "Hmm. Apparently, it's not even used in industry anymore because of its short half-life. In the Litvinenko case, the scientists think the polonium-210 had to be about a year old. You'd need a nuclear reactor to generate larger amounts of the stuff. Huh. Apparently, Russia exports about eight grams per month to the United States. Oh, my God. One gram of this sells for two million dollars."

"All this would point fingers to Russia," Colin said. "They've been implicated in using this before to get rid of someone they didn't like. They also have the facilities to produce more."

"Bloody hell. Could this be the weapon they intend to use at this afternoon's meeting?" Manny frowned. "Wait. This doesn't make sense. Russia has a lot to lose if the talks do not go in their favour today. Why would they do something like this at such a crucial moment?"

"This is wasting time." I put my hands on the armrests of my chair. "You are speculating that Russia is being set up for a crime we don't even know will happen and if it will, how. Francine, what did you find in Gallo's encrypted files?"

"Ooh! I completely forgot about that with all the excitement." She tapped on her tablet a few times, but stopped to look towards the elevator when the doors opened.

"Good morning, early birds." Pink walked in, carrying a large pink box. Daniel followed behind him, looking as if he hadn't slept in a few days. Pink put the box in the centre of the table. "We brought breakfast."

"You're the man, Pink." Vinnie pulled the box closer and opened it. "Pastries. Perfect."

He got up and walked towards the small kitchen area. Pink and Daniel sat down. I looked at Daniel's face to see past the tiredness. "Something is causing you great concern."

"I don't like any kind of radiation poisoning in my city." Daniel nodded his thanks when Vinnie put a small plate and a mug of coffee in front of him. "Have you found anything that links Gallo's poisoning to the meeting between the leaders?"

"Nothing concrete." I didn't consider the circumstantial evidence of Gallo's threat and his poisoning to be solid proof. "It would be wise, however, not to dismiss it as a possibility."

"I think it's more than a possibility, Doc." Manny put two pastries on his plate and looked at Francine. "You were about to tell us what you found."

"There were tonnes of dummy folders. The programme I wrote eliminated most of them, but I still have to check all the others." She clapped her hands. "But I found scandals, darlings! Delicious scandals."

Manny rolled his eyes and slumped in his chair.

Daniel laughed. "What scandals?"

Francine sobered. "It's a delicious political scandal, but it's actually horrible. Gallo has a very detailed folder on Cesare Lucetti."

"Wait." Pink scratched his chin. "Why does that name sound so familiar?"

"Because he's the Italian vice president of the Chamber of Deputies. That's why." Francine rubbed her hands. "And he's going straight to prison with the stuff I have on him. And hopefully after that, he'll go straight to hell."

"What is in his file, supermodel?"

"Irrefutable proof of his involvement with a Russian human trafficking ring. The photos, correspondence and finances go back as far as nine years." The corners of her mouth turned down. "The sick bastard has been getting rich selling Russian girls to rich Italian men."

"That's going to cause major upheaval in Italy." Colin took a sip of coffee. "Already their politics are all over the place because they have a newly chosen female president. The old boys' network is not handling that so well."

Francine looked at Colin. "There's even a folder in Gallo's computer for you. One with a lot of stolen artworks."

"Works that you verified?" Colin put his coffee mug down. "Are there any more Vecellios?"

"There are a lot of works here. The list is on the system, so you can check it out from your computer. He's even marked the ones that are original and the artworks which are forgeries."

"Shit." Colin looked at my viewing room with longing in his eyes. I knew he would much rather be looking at all the different paintings, making sure that the marked ones were indeed authentic. But locating Claude and finding out what they were planning for this afternoon's meeting was top priority. Colin picked up his mug and sank back in his chair.

"Gallo might've given us the key to his encrypted files, but he didn't make it easy to find the good stuff." Francine gathered her long hair at the back of her head, then dropped it. She only did this when she was tired. "Apart from the folder with all the artworks, there are also files detailing some of his business contracts. From what I saw, these were the contracts that weren't all above board. For example, there's this one construction deal which has details about supplies that are listed as bought, but cheaper and lower-quality materials were used. I'm pretty sure these lists never made it to any authority or inspector."

"Anything relevant to this case?" At the moment, Gallo's past crimes didn't concern me.

Francine scrunched up her nose. "Sorry, no. I only got as far as scanning the art files and a few business files. There are about eighty other folders that I thought we could split up."

I got up. "I'll take the first forty folders."

"And I'll help." Colin took his coffee and also got up.

Nikki looked at us and pushed her chair back. "I'll—"

"Stay here until we know what is going on." Manny leaned forward, his expression serious. "Gallo is not above hurting innocents, Nikki. I don't want you out there today."

"I agree with the old man." Vinnie crossed his arms. "You're staying here."

Nikki's shoulders sagged. "I wanted to go shopping today."

"I promise to take you shopping when this is over, Nix." Francine walked to her desk, but winked at Nikki over her shoulder. "I'll take handsome's credit card and we'll go visit a few of my favourite stores."

I didn't want to listen to Manny's outrage and walked to my viewing room. Once settled in front of my monitors, Colin and I divided the forty folders between us and got to work. There was a lot of detailed information that I couldn't afford to spend adequate time on. With only eight hours until the meeting, we were on a deadline and I had to force myself to open the next folder each time I didn't find anything related to the Vernet brothers, the president of France or my team.

It still took most of the morning to go through seventeen

folders. I had found enough concrete evidence to convict Gallo of numerous crimes if he wasn't a few hours away from death. There was also sufficient evidence to prosecute five businessmen for crimes ranging from fraud and market manipulation to extortion and more.

The eighteenth folder's name was 'Travel Pics and Drawings'. When I opened it, I wasn't surprised to find thirty-three photos of exotic-looking locations and fourteen colourful sketches. I opened each photo and carefully inspected it. Nothing seemed amiss. The sketches looked like scans of the originals. Each sketch was of a nature scene, some much more realistic than others. There were three sketches that looked like the artist had attempted an abstract style, but it didn't appeal to me.

The second of those sketches looked like it was supposed to be an abstract rendition of a farmhouse with a barn and a few animals in the foreground. I wasn't able to identify the animals, so distorted were their proportions. There was something about the house and the barn, the seemingly random blue and red dots that bothered me. I stared at it for a few minutes, but didn't know whether it was the lack of artistic skill that troubled me or if it was something more noteworthy.

I decided to leave this sketch for later inspection and opened the nineteenth folder. "Oh, my."

"What?" Colin looked up from his laptop. He was sitting next to me instead of working at his desk behind us. "Did you find something?"

"I think so." I pointed at the names of the seven files. "The files are named with only a few letters, but AV could stand for Alain Vernet, EV for Emad Vernet, CV for Claude Vernet, GL for Genevieve Lenard, MM for Manfred Millard."

"Take a breath, Jenny." Colin put his hand on my forearm and I followed his advice. He must have heard the growing panic in my voice. "Let's have a look at these files."

I opened the folder I thought might be for Manny. My breath caught in my throat.

"Millard!" Colin's tone conveyed his concern as well. "You might want to see this."

"What?" Manny stepped into my viewing room, looking at the monitors. "What the bloody hell is that?"

"It appears to be every single detail of your life." Colin looked at me. "Open the other files on the monitors so we can see what Gallo got on Millard."

Colin's request jerked me out of my frozen state. I took a deep breath and did as he asked. Francine joined us and pointed Daniel and Pink to the back of my viewing room. Vinnie took up his usual place, leaning against the doorframe. I glanced back, grateful that the two GIPN officers didn't ask any questions, but quietly stood next to Nikki. She was sitting on the floor between two of my antique-looking cabinets, pencils and paper scattered around her. She was staring at the monitors as well, a pencil hanging loosely in her hand.

"Hellfire." Manny leaned forward. "He's got my secondary school teachers in there. I don't even remember some of them."

We stared at the monitors for a few minutes. Colin might have been hyperbolic when he'd said that every detail of

Manny's life was here, but it was indeed a very comprehensive history of Manny's childhood, secondary school, his early career in the British military, his later career in the EDA and his current career in Interpol.

The more recent information was not as thorough as the earlier parts of Manny's life. The photos and newspaper clippings must all have been public record whereas the last ten years or so of Manny's career had been much more guarded with very little news coverage of his work.

"There's a folder for Jenny as well," Colin said.

I ignored Francine's request to open that folder and made sure that I inspected every detail in Manny's folder. "It looks like there's only information here. No current information about your routines, restaurants or places you favour. I don't think he compiled this to find when best to attack you."

"Then why the bloody hell would he find out who my frigging secondary-school English teacher was?"

"To get to know you." That was the only reason I could think of.

"Better see if there's anything in your folder that could indicate an attack, Doc."

I realised how irrational it was that I didn't want everyone to see details of my life. All of them had the ability and access to find out everything about my life. I swallowed a few times and opened the folder with my initials. There were sixteen files and I put fifteen of those on the monitors. It was very similar to Manny's folder.

I went through each file and winced at the photos of the newspaper article about my graduation from university at a young age. I saw the wild panic in my eyes as I stood alone, clutching my handbag close to my chest. I was no longer alone and I no longer felt like I was in a constant battle with the world around me. But I still experienced that panic every single day.

Not even the sixteenth file gave any indication that Gallo had been following me to establish my routine. It was merely a record of my life history. Nowhere did I find any mention of Colin or Nikki. It was a relief.

And it was perplexing. If he'd done a thorough investigation of my life, surely he would've discovered I shared a home with Colin, Vinnie and Nikki. It made me wonder about the true purpose of these files.

Nikki and Francine complained when I closed the files and opened the 'CV' folder. If they really wanted to read about my life, they could do it later. We needed to find Claude. I ignored everyone's comments and carefully went through every file. There were photos of him as a child, his high-school graduation photo, but there were more photos of him soon after he was arrested. Gallo had to have hacked police records to find these photos.

"What's that?" Francine pointed at the second middle monitor from the left. "Can you zoom in?"

I enlarged the text file and stared at it. I had above average computer skills, but I could not write code. And it looked like code to me.

"That's a virus." Pink sounded intrigued. "And it's for a specific website. Huh. It looks like Gallo wanted to infect a website."

"Shall we?" Francine waved Manny from the chair he'd taken to my right and sat down. She waited until I pushed my keyboard and mouse towards her. Her fingers flew over the keys for a while. "It's a pretty harmless virus as viruses go. This is only to follow everyone that visited this site."

"Is it one of those underweb sites?" Manny asked.

"Dark net or dark web, handsome. And no, it's not." She typed again. "This website is on the surface net, available to all."

"Is it safe to open?" I didn't want to infect our system with a virus Gallo had written.

"This virus will be squashed by our antivirus system, girlfriend." She clicked twice with the mouse and sat back. "There you go. That's the website."

I flinched at the face glaring at me from the monitor. The man's jaw was clenched, his brows lowered and drawn together, his lower eyelids tensed. His rage was real and dangerous. I read the headline. "This is an extremist website."

"Yup." Francine scrolled down. "See all this vitriol? Urgh. This dude really hates France. Listen to this: 'The French have the mistaken belief that their socio-political model is the absolute ideal, the ultimate end of political development. They are architects of delusion, spreading this rhetoric and seeing all others as innately offensive, ignorant and contradictory.'"

"Look, I'm not a nationalist, but this crap is not right." Daniel rested his hand on his holstered weapon. "This is when I wish freedom of speech could be more controlled. No one should incite this much hatred."

"Ooh, there's more." Francine highlighted another sentence. "'This country filled with pretentious egomaniacs is still benefiting from an era of occupation, colonisation and abuse. And yet these rude, effete bastards lean towards undeserved ethnocentrism.'"

On an academic level I understood the need humans had to assert their superiority. In a Darwinian manner it created an appearance of the strongest who would survive. But such displays were seldom productive. It attracted weak-minded individuals who were easily influenced or people who were angry with life and needed some way to release that anger. Unfortunately, it often ended violently.

I looked at the website design. "Click on the blog tab."

Francine did and Manny swore. "I've got to tell Privott about this. Bloody hell."

I read the short blog post while Manny left the viewing room, his smartphone pressed against his ear. It was a hateful two paragraphs against President Godard and Isabelle, his wife. There were two photos of them—one had crudely drawn targets over their faces, the other looked like the author had used a design programme to put oversized bullet holes on the foreheads of the president and his wife.

"This isn't telling us anything." Colin leaned back in his chair. "Only that the president's reign will end today."

I agreed. It was too generic to be meaningful or useful. Before I could analyse the text further, it moved down and was replaced by a new post. Francine grabbed my keyboard. "He's posting right now. He's online. Let's see where you are, you slimy lowlife son of a fatherless tramp."

"Do you think this is Claude's site?" Vinnie's question was quiet, but his tone was filled with animosity.

"I think so, Vin." Colin pointed at the other monitors.

"Gallo had detailed and correct information about Millard and Jenny. I can't imagine why he would have this website, or at least the virus for this website, in Claude's folder if Claude wasn't somehow connected to or even running this site."

"Find him, Francine," Vinnie said through clenched teeth. The tension in his body and the deep hatred on his face concerned me. I didn't know if Vinnie would be able to control his anger if he were to be face to face with Claude Vernet.

A ping sounded from Francine's lap and she glanced down. "Pink, grab my tablet. Someone just turned on one of those burner phones."

Pink glanced at me as he rushed over and grabbed Francine's tablet. He stepped to the side and leaned against the far wall as he tapped on her tablet. "This is one of the phones we put a trace on, one of the phones we got from Gallo's decrypted computer files. And the bastard is using it."

"Got you!" Francine pointed both index fingers at the website, her top lip curled. "I got you!"

"So have I." Pink lowered the tablet. "I have a location for the phone. He's on Rue Leblanc."

"What?" Francine swung around to look at Pink. "I've got the same address."

"It's in the industrial area." Daniel narrowed his eyes. "If I'm not mistaken, there are only warehouses on that street."

"It sounds like a setup to me." Nikki's comment drew everyone's attention to her. She shrugged. "Hey, I don't know everything, but it sounds like you've been looking for this guy for two days. And suddenly, out of the blue, you've got his phone and blog location? Nah, sounds fishy to me."

"She's got a point." Manny stood next to Vinnie. "But that's working on the assumption that Claude knows that we have Gallo's computer, that Gallo led us to this website and gave us the phone numbers."

I thought about this. "Gallo is exceptionally adept at deception. I've not been completely convinced with his reasons for hacking Norbert Sartre's car or for surrendering himself to me. He's the type of person whose every action is calculated and strategic."

Manny turned to Daniel. "So we know it might be a trap. What do we do?"

"We go in."

Chapter EIGHTEEN

"ETA, thirty seconds." Pink's voice came over the system in my viewing room and I searched the monitors to find a body camera aimed at him.

It had taken fifteen minutes for Daniel's team to be on their way to Rue Leblanc. Vinnie had left with Daniel after giving his word that he would only detain Claude, not kill him. His promise had been sincere, but I didn't know if he would be able to control his emotions when confronted with the man who'd played a role in Becks' death.

As soon as they'd left, Francine had connected our system to their body cameras as well as the cameras on the operational truck and Daniel's SUV. She was sitting on my right, while Colin was in his chair to my left. Manny was pacing in and out of my viewing room and Nikki was still on the floor.

I watched as Daniel's team turned into Rue Leblanc and raced past a large warehouse flanked by an empty lot. They passed another two medium-sized warehouses before stopping in front of a building that looked like it had not been in use for a while. The paving in front was overgrown with weeds, half-hidden by the snow.

Daniel and his team left the vehicles and I resisted the urge to draw my knees up to my chest. Nikki had been correct when she'd said the sudden discovery of a location for both the website and one of the phones was too convenient. But the present distress I experienced was more than just my concern for Vinnie's wellbeing as well as that of Daniel and his team.

I thought back on what I'd observed during their drive to the warehouse. "Oh, no! Francine, go back on the footage to the last two warehouses they passed."

Without questioning me, Francine did as I asked. She paused the footage with a view of the alley between the two buildings. "Should I play it?"

"No." I stared at the monitor in horror.

"What's he doing there?" Colin must also have recognised the two deep blue Mercedes Benz SUVs parked between two medium-sized warehouses.

"Who?" Manny stormed into my viewing room and stopped behind Colin's chair. "Who's there?"

"Émile." Colin took his phone from the desk and swiped the screen.

On one of the monitors, Vinnie touched the Bluetooth headset in his ear. "Whassup?"

"Émile is there, Vin." Colin held his hand up to stop Manny's loud swearing behind us. "I reckon he brought some muscle with him. Two of his blue SUVs are parked between the warehouses to your west. Make sure you don't take Émile's guys out."

"Shit. Thanks, dude." Vinnie jogged over to Daniel and told him.

"What is that bloody criminal doing there?" Manny walked

to the door and returned. "And how the hell did he know to go to that warehouse?"

I intended to ask Émile that very question. He must have decided to look further into the car hackings and had uncovered evidence that had pointed him to this warehouse. I would have liked to know what evidence he had. It might help us stop whatever Claude, Emad and Gallo had planned for the meeting that was going to take place in three hours.

Colin was speaking into his phone again. "Émile, pull your men back. GIPN is there... Yes, at the warehouse... Pull your guys out now. If they get in GIPN's way, they'll get arrested."

"Bloody hell!" Manny pushed his fists into his trouser pockets and watched the monitors. Daniel's team had spread out. Pink and another team member moved along the left of the building and stopped on either side of a closed steel door. Two other GIPN officers were at the back of the warehouse, their weapons trained at the three rows of double-glazed windows. Two others had their weapons aimed at a door on the right of the building.

Daniel and Vinnie were about four metres from the front door, two other team members guarding their backs. Pink and one of the men at the back of the warehouse announced that they were ready and Daniel nodded. "We'll go in on my count. Three... two..."

The front door burst open and two men came running out, their eyes wide, their mouths open in silent screams. The tallest man noticed the law enforcement officers and ran straight to them just as another two men came rushing out. "Get down! Get down! This place is going to blow!"

His last word was swallowed in an explosion that lit up all fifteen monitors in front of me.

Immediate blackness pushed into my peripheral vision and I was tempted to just give in to its safe warmth. The hand grabbing my arm didn't allow me. "Jenny. Fight it. Look. Vinnie's okay."

I tried to follow his finger pointing at a monitor in the centre, but couldn't get my eyes to focus.

"Vin." Francine's voice was strong, without panic. "Speak to us."

If Colin and Francine weren't panicking, it meant that they could see Vinnie. I blinked a few times and looked at the monitor Colin was still pointing at. Vinnie was pushing himself up from the snow-covered ground, his jaw tense, his brows lowered and pulled together. "That motherfucker! I'll fucking kill him!"

"Sitrep." Daniel's order was loud and urgent.

"We've got a few scratches, but we're both fine." Pink and his teammate were also picking themselves up from the ground, the other man looking at a piece of metal embedded in his thigh, away from any major arteries. "Meslot needs medical, but it's not urgent."

"Priou and Vautrin both good." The men at the back of the building looked up at all the broken windows. "The blast wasn't too bad back here."

"I'm good." Claudette, the petite woman who frequently drove the operational truck, pressed her hand on the other man's shoulder. "Roman's also going to need medical. Not critical."

"So you say." Roman looked at his shoulder. "If that cut

destroys my tattoo, I'm going to be pissed. I just got it last month."

"Franny, find out where Claude is." Vinnie stared into Daniel's body camera. "I want him. I want him now."

"Already on it, big guy." Francine was working at a frantic speed on her laptop placed next to my keyboard. I didn't know where she was searching for Claude that she hadn't already looked.

Back on the monitors, three of the four men who had run from the building were standing, staring at the large hole where the front door used to be. The fourth man was lying still, blood colouring the snow around his head.

One of the other three looked down and saw their friend. "Bruno!" He rushed over and fell on his knees next to Bruno's head.

Daniel was talking into his comm set, ordering a bomb squad, paramedics as well as crime scene technicians. He walked over to Bruno and got down on his haunches. "We have one with a ten-centimetre laceration to his skull. He's unconscious… nope, he's gaining consciousness."

"Stay down, Bruno. We've got help coming." The other man pushed Bruno's shoulder gently to hold him down.

"What the fuck, Émile?" Vinnie stormed towards Émile as the older man entered the property.

Émile stared at the all the debris covering the ground, the damaged building and Bruno lying on the ground, talking to his friend. He turned to Manny, his nostrils flared and his clenched fists rested on his hips. "We were ambushed."

"You?" Vinnie sounded surprised. I wished I could see his expressions, but there were no body cameras aimed at him.

"How did you even know to get here?"

Émile pointed at Bruno's friend. "Gil got a call from a source that told us where we could find the lowlifes who've been hacking cars."

"A call from who?"

"Whom," I said.

Émile stared at Gil. "I would like to know that too."

Vinnie and Émile walked over to Gil and Bruno. Pink and the others were staying in their positions to secure the perimeter until backup arrived. Daniel didn't react when Émile grabbed Gil by the collar and pulled him up until their noses were almost touching. "Who told you we should come here?"

"Boss, I didn't know this was going to happen."

"Who?"

"Reiss." Gil grabbed Émile's wrists. "No, wait. Before you punch me, just listen. Reiss was feeling really bad that you were disappointed in him. He phoned some people and some guy with an accent said this might be the place where you could find the douche who'd hacked his car."

"Why didn't he tell me himself?"

"Um, he's scared of you?" Gil blinked a few times.

"Doc?" Manny asked from behind me. "Is this the truth?"

"Yes." I nodded. "The only nonverbal cues on Gil's face are his fear of Émile and his concern over his friend on the ground. He's not lying."

Émile pushed Gil away from him and turned to Vinnie. He pointed at the body camera on Vinnie's bulletproof vest. "Is Genevieve watching this?"

"Yes."

Émile looked straight into the camera. "Gil is telling the truth. I know you know, but I just thought I'd say. He's lost too many poker games with that expressive face of his. I will find out where Reiss got his information from and I'll let you know. You just make sure you stay inside and stay safe."

"She heard, Vin." Francine glanced at me and smiled. "Tell Émile Genevieve says thank you."

Vinnie snorted, but conveyed the message. Émile looked into the camera again. "Thank you, IT girl."

The sounds of sirens became louder and soon the street in front of the warehouse was blocked off with emergency vehicles. I knew it would take time for the bomb squad to clear the building before Daniel and his team could go in to look for any useful evidence.

"We have three hours until that bloody meeting," Manny said.

I glanced at the clock on one of the monitors. "Two hours and forty-six minutes."

"And that's not a lot of time to stop this thing that could be so disastrous." Manny rubbed both hands over his face. "We're going on the rantings of a lunatic here, Doc. Are we sure there even is a threat?"

I thought about all the information we had learned in the last three days. "There is a threat. What it is and where it is, I don't know."

"There are way too many things pointing in that direction, handsome." Francine didn't look up from her computer. "Gallo gave us the Vernet brothers, told us that he—and they—know about a meeting that was supposed to be super-secret and he's in hospital with radiation poisoning. I think we should treat this seriously."

"I *am* treating this seriously." He exhaled loudly. "It just feels like we're chasing our tails."

I didn't want to spend time trying to understand chasing tails. I had something more important pressing on my mind. I looked over my shoulder at Manny. "Can you find out if the crime scene technicians found anything in Franck Reiss' car?"

Manny nodded and took out his phone. I turned back to my computer and followed up on a piece of the puzzle that was niggling in the back of my head. When Manny ended the call, I was completely absorbed in my search and ignored him. I also ignored the three times he ordered me to explain what I was doing.

There were people with Autistic Spectrum Disorder who were nonverbal. Some people's brains simply couldn't translate the complex reasoning and conclusions their brains had reached into mere words. No neuropaths existed to transform an intricate, multifaceted idea into language. I had no problem speaking, but frequently found it challenging to simplify my thoughts into sentences neurotypicals would understand.

Such was the case now. I was working through my suspicions at an incredible speed. Finding the right words and presenting them in an easy-to-understand sequence would take far too much time. Ignoring Manny was easier. It took me seven minutes to find what I was looking for. I displayed it on three of the bottom monitors.

"What are we looking at, Doc?"

"What did the crime scene technicians find?"

"Traces of polonium-210." Manny nodded when I turned to look at him. "Daniel asked them to check for it after we found out Gallo had been poisoned. They found the traces in the back of Reiss' Porsche. They didn't find anything else worth mentioning."

"Did they find these traces where Reiss had kept the coffee he was going to deliver?"

"Hmm. Let me check." Manny took out his phone and swiped the screen a few times. "The police report says that Reiss had the coffee in the back. Where they found the traces. What does this mean, Doc?"

I took a few moments to organise my thoughts. Then I pointed at the bottom monitors. "Reiss told us he was delivering the coffee to his friend, Francis Rodet. What he didn't mention is that Monsieur Rodet owns a catering company, Délicieux et Rapide." I glanced at Francine when she grabbed her laptop and started typing. She might find more than I had. "The small delivery truck that had been hacked was delivering water to the city centre. What they didn't tell us was that the delivery was also meant for Monsieur Rodet's catering company."

"Oh, my God." Francine moved away from her laptop as if was dangerous. "Délicieux et Rapide is one of the few companies approved to cater for events the president attends. They went through crazy security, health and service checks before they got approval."

"Bloody hellfire." Manny leaned down to look at me. "Has the president's food and water been poisoned, Doc?"

"That's my hypothesis." I swallowed. "I posit that Reiss was drugged to give Claude or whomever the opportunity to lace the coffee with polonium-210. The delivery truck driver said he'd felt some movement at the back of his truck, but everything had been in order when he checked. I think that they somehow gained access to the back of the truck and laced the water as well while the truck was being driven around town. As soon as they finished, the hacker gave control back to the driver."

Francine nodded. "Even though the location is nowhere to be found, it won't be hard to find out who would be catering this afternoon's event."

"Holy mother of all." Manny lifted his phone. "I have to tell Privott to cancel all their catering and confiscate all that water and coffee."

Manny left my viewing room, his voice terse, his words clipped. I looked at Francine. "Have you found Claude yet?"

She lifted both shoulders. "I don't know where else to look, girlfriend. I've got facial recognition running on every camera in this city. No hits so far. It's not very hard to avoid being picked up like this. Push some cotton wool between your gums and cheeks, wear large glasses and a hat and you're hidden from even the best systems. If I knew where this meeting was going to be held, I could set up surveillance there, but that's also a no go."

"Have you looked?" Colin's tone indicated his question had a nuanced meaning.

"I did. I got into the email of Lieutenant-Colonel Christophe Gosselin, head of the GSPR."

"You did what?" Manny walked back into the team room. "Bloody hell, supermodel. That's the bleeding head of the security unit in charge of the president's personal safety."

She rolled her eyes. "I didn't find any mention of a meeting, never mind a mention of where it is to be held. I've got nothing."

I ignored the ensuing argument and turned my attention back to the unconnected bits of information. I brought up the two files I hadn't had time to go through. The file Gallo had compiled on Alain Vernet didn't offer me any useful information. It had the same appearance as the files he'd had on me and Manny. Filled with facts about our childhoods, academic and professional achievements.

Emad's file had all the same information, but had an additional file with photos. I scrutinised each photo, but didn't see anything useful apart from the subtle changes to his appearance that I assumed went with his many identities.

Looking at these photos reminded me of a file in Claude's folder I hadn't looked at. I opened Claude's folder and clicked on the file with photos. They appeared insignificant until I reached the last seven photos.

Unlike any of the other photos in the folders, these appeared to have been taken while Claude had been under surveillance. He was seated at an outside table in front of a café. On the table were two cups and saucers and two small plates with half-eaten croissants. Claude was facing the camera, the other man had his back to the photographer.

It was quiet in my viewing room as I put each of the seven photos on a separate monitor. I studied Claude in every photo to see what his nonverbal cues revealed about his relationship with the dark blond man.

"Doc, please don't make me ask you every single bloody time what you're looking at."

"I'm not making you do anything." I looked at the third photo and tilted my head. "Why does Gallo have these photos about Claude? He has nothing like this on any of the other people he created folders for."

"That looks like Paris." Francine reached for my keyboard and mouse. She waited until I nodded, then took my equipment and zoomed in on a newspaper stand two shops down from the café. "This photo was taken last week."

"It was taken last Sunday," I corrected. "Six days ago."

Francine pushed my keyboard and mouse away and started working on her laptop. It took less than a minute before she sat up in her chair. "I got video, people. God, I love Big Brother."

"Just show us, supermodel."

The footage she put up on one of the top monitors looked like it came from a city CCTV camera. The camera had a wide angle, its focus on the side of the street where Claude and the other man were having an animated conversation. Both had their hands under the table—an unconscious way to hide our true intentions, our true feelings. The aggression on their faces was not aimed at each other, but rather at the focus of their conversation.

It was only during the second minute that the other man turned to give us a full view of his face. Francine took a screenshot of his face and loaded it into her system. "Let's see if we can find out who this is."

From the corner of my eye I noticed the sudden stillness in Colin's body. I turned to him and blinked in surprise. His eyes were riveted to the monitor, his face pale. "That's Fradkov. Ivan Fradkov."

"The political assassin who's best pals with Russia and North Korea." Manny glared at the photo on the monitor. "Russia again."

I looked at Francine. "Have you found anything else about the meeting?"

"No. Just what I told you." She typed on her laptop and read for nine seconds. "Wait. There's new information on that website. Not a lot here extra, but it says that they will try to find a solution for Russia's annexation of Crimea, its military involvement in eastern Ukraine as well as their backing of Syrian pro-Assad forces."

"The West feels that Russia is giving them the finger with every peacekeeping effort in war-torn countries." Colin shook his head. "Nobody is innocent in the bloodshed in Crimea, Ukraine and Syria. But Russia is not doing anything to endear itself to the western world."

"Ooh!" Francine clapped her hands. "A conspiracy against Russia. How delicious."

"No." I didn't share the same intense interest in politics as Colin, but knew enough to be concerned. "If Russia is implicated in an action against world leaders, especially while they're discussing Russia…"

"It will have catastrophic results," Colin continued. "The West is getting tired of Russia's strong-arm tactics. Something like this might result in a war. Even a world war."

"Then how the hell does Gallo fit into this? And the Vernet brothers?" Manny pushed his hands in his trouser pockets. "Doc, does Gallo have any political passions?"

"Definitely not." I thought about this. "I don't know enough about Emad and Claude to have an informed opinion. One would think that if Emad was working as a spy for France, he would have a strong sense of patriotism. When you spoke to him at the GIPN offices, I didn't get the impression that he is loyal to anyone. One has to keep in mind that he's a trained spy and therefore a trained liar."

"Let's get him here." Manny took his smartphone from his pocket. "Maybe we can get something useful from him with a few more questions."

His phone conversation was short. He shoved the device back in his trouser pocket and breathed deeply a few times, the artery on his forehead pronounced.

"What happened, handsome?"

Manny cleared his throat and took a few more breaths. "Somehow, the DGSE tracked Emad to the GIPN office. Emad now has a lawyer there threatening to sue GIPN for unlawful arrest."

"Can one government agency even sue another agency?" Francine raised both eyebrows. "I mean, this is not the US where everybody sues everybody."

"When it comes to authority, we will be hard-pushed to win against the Directorate-General for External Security, supermodel. They function on levels that even the president doesn't always know about."

"The only thing that binds all this together is Fradkov." Colin leaned back and looked at the ceiling. "I'm willing to bet all my investments that someone paid Fradkov to set Russia up. To create a situation so dire that the West will be forced to take aggressive action."

Manny nodded. "He might have a good relationship with Russia, but his loyalty has always been to his bank account.

He would easily betray his friends and family for money."

"I'm still not sure"—Colin straightened—"but from my memory of the time I had with Fradkov, I want to say that it was his voice on the last recording."

"The Russian voice that told Claude he must stand by and that he would be contacted this week?" Francine asked.

"Yes." Colin shrugged. "And it fits. Fradkov has always been behind political disasters."

The muffled ringtone of my smartphone came from the bottom drawer in one of my cabinets. I was about to get up when Nikki opened the drawer and brought my handbag over to me. She'd been so quiet at the back of my room that I'd forgotten about her presence. She held out my bag and gave me an exaggerated haughty look. "See? I didn't go into your bag this time." The last time she had done that, I'd been most displeased.

The ringing ended, but started immediately again. I took my phone from its designated place and frowned when I saw an unfamiliar number. I swiped the screen and lifted the phone to my ear. "Hello?"

"Oh, at last!" The woman's voice sounded familiar, but her annoyance was too distracting to try to place her name. "You people are impossible to get hold of. I've been phoning Vinnie for hours."

I pulled the phone away from my ear and glared at it. I put it on speakerphone. "Who are you?"

"Sorry, Genevieve." She didn't sound sorry. "It's Roxy. Um, Doctor Roxanne Ferreira."

"Hi, Roxy." Francine leaned closer to my phone. "I'm Francine and you're on speakerphone."

"Hi, Francine. Where's Genevieve?"

"I'm here." I was still frowning. "Why did you phone? Is Gallo dead?"

"Hah. Oh, wait. Are you serious?" She seemed to shift between emotions faster than the typical person. "He's not dead. As a matter of fact, he woke up and wants to talk to you."

"How is he?" Manny asked.

"He's… without sounding indelicate, the man is dying fast. I suggest you get here as soon as possible."

Chapter **NINETEEN**

"Genevieve." With effort, Gallo turned his head to look at me. "You're here."

"You asked for me." I didn't want to be in the hospital. I didn't want to speak to Gallo. But I knew that despite being close to death, he was not finished playing his game. I didn't know how the medication would affect his cognition and hoped that he might reveal more than he intended.

"So I did." He closed his eyes and for a moment I thought he'd fallen asleep. His breathing was shallow and looked pained. He opened his eyes and glanced at the door. "Did you bring all your puppets with you?"

"I don't have puppets."

"I disagree." He stopped to catch his breath and I considered his words.

Colin and Manny were outside Gallo's room, ready to intervene the moment I called for them. When we'd arrived at the hospital, Gallo had insisted on speaking to me alone behind closed doors. Since we were running out of time, I'd reluctantly agreed. Colin and Manny hadn't been pleased either, but had agreed that it could give us what we needed. Vinnie had phoned to say that he was on his way to the hospital and Francine had stayed behind in the team room to continue her online search for Claude.

None of them had bowed to my wishes not to come to the hospital and speak to Gallo. They supported me in ways that I had never imagined friends could support someone, but these people were not blindly following my directions.

I didn't tell Gallo that. He was trying to bait me and I wasn't going to give him the pleasure of a reaction. I waited for him to slow down his breathing enough to talk again.

It took a few more seconds. "Have you found Claude?"

"No." I studied his micro-expressions and tried to find the truth behind the pain and deception contorting his face. "Why is it important that we find Claude?"

"Not you plural. You singular." He pointed a shaky index finger at me. "You must find him."

"Why?"

He blinked a few times and looked around the room as if it was moving. "He'll take you to the barn. No, I mean the house."

"What house?" Was he acting? Was this the pain medication influencing his thoughts to the point of hallucinations?

"The door." He glanced at the door behind me. "Are the animals coming? We have to get those cows back in the barn. They have a smartphone. They're going to use it."

I stared at him. Sweat covered his face and it looked like his whole body was trembling. His fingers twitched above the covers and his eyes appeared unfocused. This was a man who had once had the respect of the elite in Rio de Janeiro. Ministers had dined in his house and influential businessmen had heeded his advice. No psychopath would take kindly to a fall as great as his.

That was why I found it hard to believe that his ramblings

were hallucinations. There was no mistaking the micro-expressions of pain—they overshadowed his other nonverbal cues. Spies were taught to insert a thumbtack in their shoe or stick a pin in their thigh while being interrogated or measured with a polygraph. The constant pain they experienced would alter the baseline formed when they were telling the truth, which in turn would make the lies believable.

Gallo's eyes fluttered closed and his breathing slowed. I didn't want to spend another minute in the same space as him and turned to leave. Two steps from the door, his whisper stopped me. "This was fun, Genevieve."

I turned around, but Gallo's eyes were closed and he seemed to be in a deep sleep. I walked out the room and didn't stop until I reached the end of the hallway. Colin followed me immediately, Vinnie and Manny slowly making their way to us.

"Did you get anything useful from that bastard, Doc?" Manny stopped in front of me and lifted one eyebrow. "Anything?"

"I need to talk to Roxy."

"I'm right here." Roxy pushed between Vinnie and Manny. She tucked a few loose curls behind her ear. "What do you want to know?"

Vinnie's reaction when Roxy had pushed his arm caught my attention and I looked at him. His lips thinned and he pulled his shoulders back when he saw me studying him. Then he sighed and rolled his eyes. "I'm fine, Jen-girl."

I pointed at his sleeve. "You're not. You're bleeding."

"A teensy little cut." He scowled when Roxy took his

elbow and turned his arm to inspect a dark, wet patch on his black long-sleeved shirt.

"This much blood didn't come from a teensy cut, Vinnie-with-no-surname. Come, let me see." She pulled his elbow and giggled when he didn't move. "It's like pulling a wall. Only you're much sexier." She pulled again. "Stop being such a ninny and come with me. We'll go to one of the large private rooms, I'll patch you up and Genevieve can ask her questions."

"How large is the room?" I didn't want to be crammed into a space the size of Gallo's room with Manny, Vinnie, Colin and Roxy.

She pointed at the third door from us. "If the sexy wall will move with me, I'll show you how large the room is."

Vinnie shook his head and allowed Roxy to pull him to the door. Her smile was genuine when she winked at him and opened the door. "Enter, said the spider to the fly."

Vinnie snorted and walked into the room. Manny and Roxy followed. I stopped at the threshold and raised my eyebrows. The bed was higher than a hotel bed, but looked of similar quality. Two wingback chairs were next to the bed with more than sufficient space for doctors to move around without bumping into the people sitting in the chairs. On the other side of the room were another two chairs, a desk and a closed door that I assumed led to the bathroom. This room was easily twice the size of my viewing room. Five of us in this space did not make it feel crowded at all. "This is for one person?"

"Like I said before, we have quite a few VIPs come here and they just love to be treated like princesses." Roxy walked to a wooden cabinet above an expensive-looking chest of drawers. She swiped her security card over the lock and the door swung open to reveal a fully stocked first-aid kit. "Personally, I think these kits are superfluous in a hospital, but someone thought it was a great idea to have even more medicine inside each room." Roxy walked back to Vinnie and pointed to the bed. "Get undressed and on the bed."

Vinnie's eyes widened and he burst out laughing. "You do know how completely unprofessional that sounds, right?"

She shrugged. "Professionalism is overrated. Now take off your shirt."

Vinnie chuckled and started unbuttoning his shirt. He winced when the sleeve slid over his cut, then bundled his shirt in his hand and sat down on the bed. His white undershirt did nothing to hide his muscular torso. Or the scar tissue on his chest. "I'm all yours, Doctor Roxy."

"Yay me." She let the gloves dramatically snap when she put them on. Her outrageous behaviour and Vinnie's favourable reaction had been enough to distract me from the five-centimetre-long cut down his biceps. It didn't appear deep, but it was ragged. Roxy cleaned the dried blood around the cut and reached for a bottle of disinfectant. "Not too bad. Do you want stitches? One of our cosmetic surgeons will stitch this so it will heal with almost no scar."

"Just clean it up." Vinnie turned his face so she could see the large scar running down his left cheek. "One more scar isn't going to make me any uglier."

Roxy grabbed Vinnie's ear and pulled him closer until they were staring in each other's eyes. "Don't you ever say anything like that to me again. You are an extremely handsome man and that scar tells me that you've lived an interesting life. It does not make you ugly. It makes you strong. It makes you a survivor."

The surprise on Vinnie's face was mirrored in both Manny and Colin's. Roxy's complete lack of fear around Vinnie was in itself uncommon. But the unorthodox and irreverent manner in which she was displaying compassion fascinated me. Especially because it had such an effect on Vinnie. He took the hand that had grabbed his ear and kissed her gloved knuckles. "Cute *and* feisty. Yay me."

She laughed. "Touché."

"Would you two like the room to yourselves or can we get back to business?" Manny failed to infuse enough annoyance in his tone. The shock of what had just taken place was still in his expression as he watched Roxy clean and dress Vinnie's wound.

Roxy glanced at Manny, but immediately dismissed him and turned to me. "Genevieve, you had some questions for me."

"Will Gallo's medication cause hallucinations?"

"Hallucinations? No. It will make him loopy though."

"What is loopy?"

She frowned at me. "You're very literal, aren't you?"

"Yes. What is loopy?"

"He will appear as if he is under the influence of alcohol. Why?"

"Yes. Why, Doc?" Manny took a step towards me.

I held up a finger. "Give me a moment." I needed to process what Roxy had told me and add that to my observations when I'd spoken to Gallo.

Roxy smoothed her hand over the dressing on Vinnie's arm. "Good as new. Well, almost."

"Thanks."

"Doc?" Manny took another step to place him in my line of view. "What did Gallo say?"

"He talked as if he was delusional, but it was hard to determine whether it was genuine." I looked at Roxy. "Is he receiving pain medication?"

"Of course. That's what will make him loopy."

"Enough medication to take away all his pain?"

"Sadly, no." She rearranged the first-aid kit and closed the cabinet door. "His pain is so severe that he needs something much stronger than what we're giving him."

"Why aren't you giving him the stronger medication?"

"He insisted on staying alert. He was furious when he came to after I had sedated him. He said that he wanted to die knowing about it."

I looked at Manny. "He's in a lot of pain and it masks his other expressions, but a few did come through strong enough to read. One of those was smugness. He thinks that he's winning this game he's playing."

"Have you been able to figure out his endgame, Doc?"

"No." I organised my thoughts and told them what Gallo had said.

"Barn? House?" Manny scratched his jaw. "What do you make of that?"

"I don't think he made a mistake by first mentioning the barn. I think it was intentional. What I don't know is if the barn could refer to the warehouse."

Everyone looked at Vinnie. He widened his eyes and

nodded at Roxy. She must have seen his exaggerated gesture and smiled. "I suppose that's my cue to leave. Not that I want to. This stuff is fascinating."

"And classified," Manny said.

"And since one-name Vinnie is my patient, I'm bound to doctor-patient confidentiality." She tapped her mouth. "My lips are sealed. If you need me for anything, I'm not leaving this hallway, so you'll just have to hang out the door and yell for me."

We watched as she left the room and closed the door behind her. Colin looked at Vinnie, his eyes narrowed, but he didn't say anything. I planned to ask Colin about the hope I'd noticed on his face as he'd watched Vinnie interact with Roxy and the way she had tended Vinnie. I was also going to ask him why he was looking at Vinnie with undisguised happiness.

Vinnie saw Colin's expression and jumped off the bed. "Don't even go there, dude. This is so not the time."

"Whatever you say, Vin." Colin laughed when Vinnie swore.

"I'm not talking about it." Vinnie shrugged back into his wrinkled and bloody shirt. "Let's talk about how we didn't find anything at the warehouse."

"Nothing?" Manny sat down on one of the chairs next to the bed. "Was the warehouse empty?"

"Not completely. The bomb squad went in to secure the place and didn't find any more explosives, but they found a computer and a mobile phone."

"In working order?" Colin asked.

"Fried to a crisp. Pink said there was almost no chance of getting anything from the hard drive of the computer and the phone was melted into a twisted bit of plastic." Vinnie shook his head. "There was nothing and nobody else there."

"What about Bruno?" I remembered Émile's rage when he'd seen his associate on the ground.

"The paramedics said he should be okay. Some shrapnel gave him a bad cut on his head, but they didn't think it cracked his skull. It was enough to knock him out for a few seconds, but they will only know after x-rays and tests if there's any serious damage."

I thought of Francine's findings before Roxy had called us to the hospital. "Vinnie, what else do you know about Ivan Fradkov?"

All good humour on Vinnie's face disappeared. "Did that fucker's name come up again? Where?"

"One of Gallo's files on Claude." I put my handbag on the desk. "There were surveillance photos of Gallo having lunch or coffee with someone six days ago. Francine was able to get a clear image of this man's face and Colin confirmed his identity."

"Oh, this is not good. That man has far too many friends in bad political places."

"Do you know where he is now?" Manny asked.

"No." Vinnie took his smartphone from one of the side pockets of his cargo pants. "Maybe I can find out." He dialled a number and lowered his phone. "I'm putting this on speakerphone."

No sooner had he said that than a soft female voice answered the call. "As I live and breathe! Vinnie, how are you?"

"Well, thank you, Justine. Are you still as beautiful?"

"Such a charming young man." She coughed. "Sorry about that. I might still be beautiful, but I'm recovering from a horrid chest cold."

"Sorry to hear that. Do you need anything?"

"Oh, Vinnie. The world needs more men like you." She coughed again. "Thank you so much, but I have three of my grandchildren looking after me. They're supposed to be studying for their university exams, but are using the Granny-is-sick excuse to watch movies with me. But you didn't phone to hear about my chest cold and my grandchildren. What can I do for you?"

Vinnie's voice lowered to an almost whisper. "Ivan Fradkov."

Justine cleared her throat and it sounded like she was walking to another room. A door clicked. "Why are you asking about a man so evil?"

"Because I know you're keeping tabs on him."

"You would too if he was the reason you lost both your sons and their wives and had to raise four grandchildren on your own." She took a deep breath. "Why are you asking?"

"I've got a situation I can't talk about, but I would really like to know where that motherfu... where he is."

"No need to be polite around me, son. Ivan Fradkov is a motherfucker if there ever was one." The rustling of paper came over the phone. "I tell you where he is and you kill him for me, okay?"

Vinnie chuckled. "I can't make that promise, but I will do my best to find him and make him pay."

"You do that. I'm getting too old for this now." She sighed. "Fradkov was in Turkey last week and was making his way to France. Of this I'm pretty sure. The rumour that he's going to your valley is just that—a rumour. But now I'm thinking that there might be more to it if you're phoning me about him."

"Do you have any idea what he's up to?"

"Vinnie"—her tone was much more concerned—"how serious is this?"

"Serious."

"Are my little ones safe?"

"Nothing so far has pointed in your direction. Or in the direction of your grandchildren."

"I think I'll take them on a little holiday nevertheless." She cleared her throat. "He's in bed with Crimea. There are some big people in the on- and offshore natural gas industry who would like Russia to leave. This is all I know. I've been fishing for more information, but I don't want to risk the lives of my informants. You know what a brutal... motherfucker that man is."

"I know." Vinnie looked worried. "If you think of anything else, please let me know. And Justine?"

"Yes?"

"You need me, you phone me."

"You're a good man, Vinnie." The sound of knocking came over the phone. "That's my grandkids calling me for their movie. I'll speak to you soon."

The call ended and we were silent. Then Manny rubbed both his hands over his face. "Bloody holy hell!"

Chapter TWENTY

"Why not, Doc?" Manny's brow wasn't pulled into an angry scowl. His frown was curious. "There's no reason for us to stay here. Gallo is in a coma and Roxy said he's got maybe a few hours left. We need to get back to the team room."

"No." I crossed my arms. "Gallo said or did something that makes me want to stay. No. That's irrational. My mind must have registered some nonverbal cues that it needs to process."

"Because God forbid you be irrational." Manny sighed. "Well then, do your Mozart thing. We don't have much time."

"We have very little time." I glanced at my watch. "There are only eighty-two minutes left until the meeting starts."

"Let me try Privott again." Manny pointed at the desk. "Go do your Mozart thing."

I walked to the desk, but didn't pull out the chair to sit down. Instead, I stared at the painting above it. I didn't know the artist, but it appeared to be an original painting, not a print like most hospitals had. It was a beautiful pastoral scene with a large colonial farmhouse in the background. Three cows and two calves were grazing in the foreground, trees to their right lining a narrow road leading to the house. It didn't look like a typical European farm.

I didn't know how long I stared at the painting, but when I turned around, Roxy was back in the room. She was arguing with Vinnie about a man called Styles being the best pro wrestler. "Put Styles and Jericho in a smackdown and Styles will make mincemeat of ol' Jericho."

Colin and Manny were sitting in the two wingback chairs by the bed watching Vinnie and Roxy. It surprised me to see the same hope I'd seen in Colin's micro-expressions mirrored in Manny's. I cleared my throat. "Roxy, who else was in the room with Gallo?"

She turned away from Vinnie. "Oh, hi there. Hmm, let me think. Your GIPN guys didn't let many people through, so it was me, obviously, Doctor Janquin, Nurse Génisson, Nurse Lorgeoux, and—"

"Can you get us the security tapes?" Manny asked.

"Of course. That would make it easier to see who came and went." She walked to the door. "I won't be long."

I glanced at my watch. I had not lost a lot of time. We still had seventy minutes before the meeting.

Roxy's disappearing footsteps were drowned out by the loud clicking of high-heeled shoes coming towards us. Two seconds later, Francine walked into the room carrying her computer bag. "Here you are! I've been looking all over this fabulous hospital for my favourite peeps."

"What are you doing here, supermodel?" Manny got up and glared at her.

"I know how you men always gang up on poor Genevieve, so I came as moral and if necessary physical support."

I frowned. "I'm not sure what you're implying, but it doesn't sound positive towards the men. They always support me.

You're not here because of that."

"Pah!" She waved her free hand and walked over to the desk. "I don't want you to have all the fun."

I narrowed my eyes and studied her face. "You're scared something's going to happen to us. But there's more."

She rolled her eyes and gave me a belligerent look. "I wasn't going to sit on my sexy behind and watch another car hacking, all right?"

"We're not in a car." I registered her expression. "You really are worried. Did you find something?"

"You might say that." She sat down at the desk and took her laptop and tablet from the computer bag. "And before you ask, Nikki and Phillip are playing poker in the team room. Nikki is winning and Phillip is jumping between being proud of her and angry with me for teaching her a few tricks."

I was relieved that Nikki was still in the team room. She would be safe there. And happy. She always enjoyed Phillip's company and he hers. I watched as Francine turned her devices on. "Did you locate Claude?"

"No. That man is really good at staying under the radar. He's not showing up on any of the city cameras, or if he is, our facial recognition software is not catching him. He must be wearing a disguise of sorts. Or he's gone underground."

"What did you find, supermodel?"

She pointed at her laptop monitor. "I looked a bit deeper into that anti-France website and I found a few interesting titbits. Firstly, this site was created four and half years ago and there have been weekly posts on the blog part of the site. I really believe this is Claude's site more than Emad's and will tell you why in a sec. This being Claude's site, he's really well versed in French history, especially all the not-so-nice things France has done to other countries since the beginning of time.

"What caught my eye was that a few of the posts were much more passionate and personal in tone than the others. Look at this one." She highlighted a few lines on screen. "This is why I think Claude is behind this site. This article is all about Alain and how he pretends to be doing noble things, but by interfering with local governments, he's the reason those economies can't recover and corrupt politicians are still in power.

"He goes as far as accusing his own father of paying off those politicians to give him the access he needs to do his good deeds. This whole article is about Alain Vernet bribing his way through all the aid he's given and all the mediation he's done."

I thought about this. "It would make sense for Claude to feel betrayed by his father when Alain stopped coming to his rescue after his twenty-first birthday."

"And look at this post." Francine opened another post and highlighted two sentences. "See how he's saying that life teaches us that we can't even rely on our own fathers and mothers and that only brothers are the ones who will never let us down?"

Manny walked closer and read over her shoulder. "Scroll down. Bloody hell, look at all the comments."

"Don't get me started." Francine gave an exaggerated shudder. "These people are vile, angry and dangerous. In this post, it looks like they understood Claude to say that they were his brothers and they responded very positively to this."

"If threats to kill all the politicians are positive." Manny shook his head. "We'll have to hand this over to the General Directorate for Internal Security for further investigation. These extremist groups can mobilise a certain demographic to do some very stupid and deadly things."

"This still doesn't give us a clear motivation for Claude to take action against the leaders having this meeting today." And that caused me great concern. If the motivation was clear, it was easier to find and stop the suspect.

"If he planned to do something against France, against his father, it would make more sense."

"Hmm, I don't know about that." Francine glanced at her laptop. "The tone of his posts has changed over the last two years. I don't have your super-duper psychology skills, but when I scanned the posts, it seemed like he became angry with the entire world, not just France."

She opened a post and highlighted a paragraph. "He posted this a few months ago, blaming Western media, especially television with huge focus on reality shows, for the breakdown in morals, ethics and values."

Vinnie swore. "He's one to talk. Morals, ethics, my ass. He killed Becks."

I studied Vinnie to reassure myself that he was still okay. This case had to be very hard on him. "You said it was Emad who'd killed Becks."

Vinnie crossed his arms. "Emad or Claude. In my opinion, they're both responsible."

"And I honestly don't know which one is more dangerous." Francine rubbed her upper arms. "Claude's site scares me.

Someone with this much hatred is a bomb waiting to blow. But Emad? He gave me the total creeps when I watched you guys interview him. He's the kind of sicko who would torture puppies just as an experiment. He wouldn't even get pleasure from it, just more sick info that he would consider useful." Her hands tightened around her arms in a full-body hug. "They're both freaks."

"I've got it!" Roxy rushed into the room, holding a tablet up. Her steps faltered when she saw Francine. "Hello?"

"You must be Roxy." Francine tried to sound as if she didn't know, but wasn't successful. She'd done thorough research on the doctor. "I'm Francine."

"Oh, hi!" Roxy held the tablet out to Francine. "Vinnie told me you're the computer genius, so you can do your thing."

"What is this?" Francine took the tablet.

"It's a tablet." The moment everyone started laughing, I realised that was not the answer Francine had been looking for. "It has the security footage of everyone who's been in Gallo's hospital room."

"Oh, goodie. Wanna watch it now?" Francine sat down and tapped on Roxy's tablet and then her own laptop. "I'll put it on my laptop monitor."

"Or you could put it on the TV." Roxy pointed at the large flat screen television attached to the wall. "Do you need the security passcode?"

"Nope." Francine tapped a few more times and leaned back to look at the television. I stepped closer to have a better view of the footage from the camera aimed at Gallo's door. We spent the next ten minutes in silence while

Francine fast-forwarded through hours of footage, only slowing down when people went into and left Gallo's room.

I counted five people who'd had access to Gallo. I dismissed Roxy as a suspect since nothing she'd done, said or revealed with her nonverbal communication had given any indication of deceit or ulterior motives. The doctor she mentioned also displayed no suspicious body language as he entered and left the room. Neither did the two female nurses.

"Stop." I pointed at the screen as a young male nurse left Gallo's room. "Look at his posture. His shoulders are back, his spine straight and his fists are held up as if in victory. Go back to when he entered the room." I waited until Francine stopped the footage a second before the young man walked into Gallo's room. "There he's nervous. He's looking over his shoulder to see if there's anyone else in the hallway. His arms are close to his sides, his shoulders hunched. People have this posture, trying to make themselves look less visible when they intend to steal something."

"That asswipe Gallo has nothing to steal," Vinnie said.

I shook my head. "It was only an example. People also use this when they try to get away with something. I don't know if he stole something from Gallo, but something definitely transpired in that room in the ninety-three seconds he was there."

Roxy put her hands on her hips, her thumbs facing back. It was the first time in our short acquaintance that I'd seen her show any other emotion than friendliness. She was angry. She didn't tuck her wayward curls behind her ear or shift from one foot to the other. She was focused. "This is unacceptable. I've been told ad nauseam how secure this hospital is and that they only hire people who pass a stringent background check."

I wondered why she would need to work at a safe hospital, but decided it was not of importance now. "I need to speak to that young nurse."

"Oh, I'll get him for you." Roxy swung around and marched to the door, but Vinnie grabbed her arm.

"Slow down, tiger." He looked at Manny. "I'm going with her."

"Go." Manny didn't wait for a reaction, but turned to me. "What are you thinking, Doc?"

"You have to be more specific." I didn't know if he was interested in my thoughts about how Vinnie's body language changed subtly every time Roxy was around. Or that Roxy's pupils dilated every time she spoke to Vinnie and that she only twirled a curl around her finger when talking to him.

"Bloody hell." Manny glared at me. "What are you thinking about Gallo? About his role in all of this?"

I thought about Gallo's words and behaviour before he'd gone into the coma. "Taking Gallo's history and the profile I created for him into consideration, I find it really hard to believe that he was poisoned by accident. Or that Claude and Emad are really in control of whatever this is. I don't know how, but I'm convinced Gallo has orchestrated everything."

"Including his own poisoning?" Surprise raised Colin's voice a pitch.

Again, I spent a few seconds mulling over this. I hated speculating, but no other alternative made sense. "I think so, yes."

"Holy saints, Doc. Why on God's green earth would he do

that to himself?"

"I don't think he saw it as doing it to himself. It would be part of a larger strategy."

"For what?"

"Gallo reacted strongly every time he talked about revenge."

"You think he's using Claude and Emad to take revenge on us?" Colin asked.

"By making Claude and Emad believe they're taking revenge on their daddy?" Francine added.

"It's a hypothesis that makes sense to me, taking their characters and histories into account." I glanced at Francine and my eye caught the painting again. I wondered what it was about the painting that drew me into it, but didn't have time to follow that line of thinking.

Roxy walked into the room first, followed by Vinnie pulling a young man by his elbow into the room. The young man tried to jerk his arm out of Vinnie's grip, but it didn't work. His eyes widened in fear and he swallowed a few times. He was an average-looking young man with short dark hair and the skinny appearance of a youth whose body hadn't filled out yet.

Vinnie pulled him to the centre of the room and shook his arm. "Tell them what you told me."

"My mother is sick and needs medication." The words rushed out of his mouth as his eyes flicked between all of us. "I'm the only one in our family with a full-time job and still we don't get by. When that man offered me five thousand euros cash for a smartphone, I thought it was a gift from the angels."

"Did he give you the cash?" Vinnie asked the question that also troubled me. Where would Gallo get that amount of cash when he'd been in police custody at Rousseau & Rousseau and then the hospital, stripped of all his belongings?

"No." The young nurse was wringing his hands. "He gave me a number to call. That man asked for my bank account details and the money was deposited a few minutes later."

"Do you still have the number?" Francine's fingers were hovering above her laptop keyboard.

"Yes." He took his smartphone from his trouser pocket and gave Francine a number.

Her eyes widened a few seconds after she entered the number. She looked at me. "It's one of the numbers we found on Gallo's computer."

"It must've been Claude." I studied the nervous young man. "Did he say anything to you?"

"No. I phoned the number, he answered by asking for my bank account details. I gave it to him and he ended the call by saying it would be in my account within five minutes. That was all he said. The money was in my account five minutes later."

"Would you recognise his voice again if you heard it?" I looked at Francine and saw the moment she realised where I was going with my question.

"I think so." His eyes were wide. "Can I keep the money? My mom really needs it."

"You can worry about that later." Francine snapped her fingers to get his attention. "Listen to this. Tell me if one of these is the man you talked to."

She played the second recording we'd found on Gallo's computer. Emad and Gallo's voices filled the room with their short and cryptic telephone conversation. The recording ended and the young nurse pointed at Francine's laptop. "The first voice. The man who said, 'Is it there?' and, 'It will go down this week.' That's the man I spoke to."

Claude. The nurse had just confirmed that Claude and Gallo were working together. Manny and Vinnie asked the young man a few more questions, but he had nothing more to add. They left the room with him to retrieve the phone from Gallo's room. I hoped it was still there.

Again I found myself drawn to the painting above the desk. I walked closer and stared at it, hoping for the connection my mind had made to filter through to my consciousness. Francine was asking Roxy about the technology in the hospital and Roxy enthusiastically described their complicated staff log-in system.

"But seriously, in the beginning I thought the security was totally OTT. Now I'm used to it. All the retina scans, double doors and cameras everywhere."

"Retina scans?" Francine's tone indicated her excitement.

"Yup, can you believe it?" She moved, but I didn't turn to see if she was shifting in her usual manner. "But most of the serious security is downstairs in the VIP area."

"The VIP area?"

"That's where celebrities, politicians and über-rich people are hosted when they come to the hospital. The security down there is really top-notch. The conference room down there is even bulletproof and I was told once the door is locked, it's impenetrable. It's the safest floor in this whole building, but it's creepy. Whenever I walk down those hallways, it always feels like eyes are following me everywhere."

Something clicked in my mind. I swung around to Francine. "I need to see the sketches in Gallo's encrypted folder, 'Travel Pics and Drawings'."

"On it." Francine winked at Roxy and turned to her laptop.

"Should I leave?" Roxy turned her torso towards the door.

"No." I realised my tone was harsh when she flinched. I took a breath and softened my voice. "No. I might need your help."

"There you go, girlfriend." Francine leaned to the side so I could see her laptop monitor. "Any specific sketch you want me to bring up?"

"That one." I pointed to the abstract sketch that had caught my attention a few hours ago. "Oh, my. There's the barn. And the animals."

"Translate your thoughts, please." Francine's face was scrunched up in confusion.

"Gallo told me when he was or pretended to be hallucinating that Claude was going to take me to the barn. Then he corrected himself to say it was the house. He asked if the animals were coming and that we had to get the cows back."

"And you think it has something to do with this sketch?" Roxy squinted at the monitor. "Nah, I don't see it."

"He was giving me a clue so I would look at this sketch." I knew it was there. Somewhere in this sketch was a key. I allowed my eyes to lose its focus on the monitor until everything became a blur. That was when I saw it. I pointed to the sketch. "Isolate the solid lines of the barn, the house, the gates and the red and blue dots."

It took Francine three minutes to do that. As the last of the abstract animals disappeared, Roxy gasped. "Oh. Wow. That's... Oh."

"What is that?" Francine turned around.

"It's a blueprint." I looked at Roxy for confirmation.

She looked at me, her eyes wide with fear. "That is the exact layout of the most secure floor in this building. The red dots are all the cameras and the blue dots are the secure doors. And the space with the cross on it is the VIP conference room."

Chapter **TWENTY-ONE**

"Holy Mary and all the saints." Manny put the smartphone he'd brought from Gallo's room absentmindedly in his trouser pocket. "Gallo had blueprints of this hospital? Are you sure, Doc? Roxy?"

Roxy hadn't taken her eyes off Francine's laptop for longer than a few seconds. She stared at it and chewed her bottom lip. "I'm not one hundred percent sure, but it really looks like the layout of the VIP floor."

"This is my fault." Francine closed her eyes and pressed her lips tightly together. Her anger was clear when she opened her eyes again. "I promised to find footage of the handover of the blueprints and I didn't."

"What are you talking about, supermodel?"

Roxy burst out laughing. "He calls you supermodel? It's... perfect."

I was happy to see some of the severe distress leaving the doctor's face. The intensity of her fear had affected my focus.

Manny glared at Roxy, but it didn't stop her giggles. He turned his attention back to Francine. "Speak."

"Remember the last recording where the guy was going to give Claude the blueprints at Oh-Suh? I said that I was going to look for any kind of security footage in the area that could give us an idea of who that guy was. I forgot." She waved her hands in the air. "How could I forget?"

"I don't know you guys very well, but I imagine you forgot because you were too busy with other things." Roxy had sobered and put her hand on Francine's shoulder. "Seriously, you can't remember everything."

"She does." Francine pointed an accusing finger at me.

"I don't." I crossed my arms. "We don't have time for this ridiculousness. Roxy is right. Now move on. We need to find out if Claude indeed planned something for this hospital and what it is. Manny, give Francine the phone."

"Huh? Oh. Yes." He reached into his pocket and gave Francine a large smartphone with a silver cover. "It was under Gallo's pillow."

"I thought the old man was going to put the pillow over Gallo's face." Vinnie shrugged when Roxy looked at him. "What? It's not like he's going to live much longer."

"It's still a horrible thing to say."

"Can I come in?" Daniel knocked on the doorframe and looked around. "Room for one more?"

Manny looked at me and I nodded. Another person in this room, especially someone I knew and trusted, wasn't going to bring on claustrophobia. Manny waved Daniel in and briefed him on what we'd learned in the last few minutes.

Francine had plugged Gallo's smartphone into her laptop and was running diagnostics and other programmes through it. She was still angry with herself and for the moment, I considered it an asset. It would make her more focused. "Okay, I've downloaded Gallo's call history and he's phoned one of the phone numbers we found on Gallo's computer.

It's a different number than the one the nurse phoned, but it was bought with the same batch."

"Another confirmation they're working together," Manny said.

"Oh, my God." Francine jerked away from her computer. "He accessed the hospital's free Wi-Fi and worked his way into the hospital's database."

"He did what?" Roxy's face paled. "He had access to all the records?"

"Yup." Francine shifted in her chair. "Patients, staff, suppliers and also bookings."

"This is so not good." Roxy rushed to one of the small tables next to the bed and reached for the stationary phone. "I need to tell our security director about this. I have no idea what kind of protocol they have in place for a situation like this. Especially with the rumours floating around."

"What rumours?" Vinnie and Colin asked at the same time.

Her hand paused just before she picked up the phone. "I wasn't really paying attention because I don't have time for gossip around the hospital. But I heard a few times that some VIPs were supposed to be here sometime this week for some kind of something."

"That's very vague." I hated ambiguity.

"Like I said, I wasn't really paying attention. All I know is that it's supposed to be a very important visit for the hospital."

"Get your director to join us." Manny waited until she nodded, then turned to Daniel. "Get your team here. We don't know yet where this is leading."

"Done." Daniel walked to the bathroom door, putting the earpiece of his communication unit into his ear. Vinnie's eyes narrowed as he reached into one of the side pockets of his pants and fitted an identical earpiece to his ear.

Manny had his smartphone against his ear, his gaze fixed on Roxy as she spoke into the hospital phone. He flinched, brought his smartphone down and tapped the screen twice before returning it to his ear. The second time he didn't flinch. His face turned an angry red. For a moment I thought he was going to throw the phone across the room. "Bloody Privott isn't answering his bloody phone."

I watched all the activity around the room, wishing I knew what action to take. "I still don't know who their intended target is."

Manny stopped tapping his phone screen and looked at me. "Explain yourself."

"We've received enough circumstantial evidence to indicate that I am the target of Gallo's actions. But we also have evidence that the Vernet brothers are targeting their father or France as a whole or the president of France or the meeting between the leaders." A realisation struck me and I grabbed my handbag from the desk. Within seconds, I had my smartphone in my hand and was searching for a number.

"Who're you phoning, Doc? Doc! Bloody hell. Speak to her, Frey."

I felt a firm hand on my forearm. "Put it on speakerphone, love."

I did that and exhaled in relief when Isabelle Godard answered her phone. "Genevieve, what a surprise! I can't speak at the moment. I'm just about to…"

"Where are you?" I realised the generic nature of my question. "At which hospital are you?"

"At the Guédon-Leroy hospital. Why? Is there a problem?"

"Madame Godard, this is Manfred Millard speaking. You need to get to safety immediately." Manny looked around the room. "On second thought, get your security detail to take you to"—he walked closer to the door until he could read the number—"room three-oh-nine on the third floor. We're here and you'll be safe."

"Genevieve?" The friendliness in her voice had been replaced with professionalism.

"Do as Manny says. I'm also here." I didn't want to be in a place where an unknown threat was about to take place, but that was where I was at the moment. I had to deal with it. I ended the call with Isabelle and looked at Manny. "Why do you want her to come here? Why not leave the hospital?"

"I don't know what Gallo, Claude or Fradkov is planning, Doc. For all we know, they want to flush us all out so that a sniper can pick us off one by one as we exit the building. For the moment, I think it would be better if she's here with us."

Daniel rested his hand on his holstered weapon. "I agree with Manny."

"What is going on here?" A well-built man walked into the room and I took a step back. He was the first person to enter this room with aggressive body language. "What is this about a threat in my hospital?"

"Colonel Millard." Manny showed the man his credentials. "Who are you?"

"Retired Captain Serge Colot from the Paris Police Prefecture, currently the security director here at the hospital." He looked around the room. "This your team?"

"Yes."

"I've heard about you people." Serge looked at me. "Are you Doctor Lenard?"

I nodded.

"I heard what you did to get Clarisse Rossi's children back when they were taken to Rio." He looked back at Manny. "What are you guys doing here? Can I help with anything?"

"We've uncovered a threat to the hospital. Someone has hacked your system and has gained access to all your confidential data."

"What? No, that's not possible." Serge put his fists on his hips. "We have state-of-the-art antivirus programmes and the best software money can buy."

"It took me nine seconds to get into your system." Francine pointed at her computer.

"What?" Serge stormed to the desk, but stopped when Manny and Vinnie stepped in front of him. He pointed past them at Francine. "She's got my entire security system on her computer. I can't allow that."

"Yes, you can." Manny leaned to cut off Serge's view of Francine's computer.

It took Serge a few moments to control his shock. He nodded. "What can I do?"

"You are expecting VIPs today. Who?"

Serge pinched his bottom lip for a second. "Dammit. It's top-secret information."

"We have clearance."

"I know. I know. Dammit." He looked at Daniel, inspected his uniform, then looked at Roxy. "I don't think she should hear this."

"I've already heard more than I should've, Serge. Kick me

out and I'm telling your wife how many of the cookies I bake for your family you eat before you take them home."

Serge snorted, then became serious. "The president's wife, Doctor Isabelle Godard, is here today. She's visiting patients in the neurology ward with the attending doctors and will give two lectures a bit later."

"Where will she give the lectures?"

"The VIP conference room." His eyes widened and he took a step back. "What? Why are you all looking like that?"

Manny tapped on his smartphone's screen again. "You're not expecting the president?"

"No."

"You're not convinced." I studied his face. "You glanced sideways, hesitated before you answered and your frown confirms your lack of conviction."

"Dammit." He pinched his bottom lip again. "This would not be the first time that the VIP conference room was booked for one thing, but used for another. We're used to it by now. We get a lot of businessmen who book the conference room for a meeting with their doctor, but cancel the meeting at the last minute and ask if they can still use the room. They're willing to pay top dollar for it, so we allow it. A few members of parliament have done something similar. Doctor Godard's visit could be a smokescreen."

I turned to Colin and he smiled. "It could be a ruse."

I nodded. "We can ask Isabelle when she comes."

"Madame Godard is coming here?" Serge looked behind him at the door entrance.

"Yes." I still had many questions. "Did you receive any catering deliveries today?"

"No. It's a bit strange though, since there are usually catering companies delivering for whoever hires the conference room for the day. We had nothing today. Not even coffee or tea or water."

"Good." I was relieved.

Manny's phone started ringing and he frowned when he looked at the screen. He swiped the screen and lifted the device to his ear. "Millard." His eyes widened and he lowered the phone. "Privott, you're on speakerphone. Where the bloody hell are you?"

"Manny! Shit, we need help." The panic in Lucien Privott's tone took my breath away. "We've been compromised and I don't know what to do."

"Where are you?" The calm in Manny's tone belied the alarm around his eyes.

"The basement of the Guédon-Leroy hospital and we're locked in. We can't get out. I was just about to leave the conference room when the doors locked themselves. Everyone tried to phone, but only my phone is working."

"Who's everyone?" I asked.

"The world leaders. I'm the only non-leader in the room."

"Oh, no!" Francine's gasp had every head turning to her. "This is not good."

"What's going on, supermodel?"

Serge pushed past Manny and swore heavily when he saw Francine's laptop monitor. "He's locked *everybody* in, the entire hospital. I was afraid of this happening one day. He's locked all the exits, everything. No one can get in or go out."

"What are you two talking about?" Manny pushed Serge out of the way and looked at Francine. "Explain."

"The hospital has a smart system. Everything in this building is computerised. The doors, the windows, the electricity."

"He has full control?" Roxy's eyes were wide. "That means he also has control of all the medical equipment. He can shut life-support systems off, change the administration of medication that's being sent through a smart system. My God, he could kill all the patients who are dependent on machines."

"Forgive me if I don't care about the hospital at the moment." Privott's tone rose. "I've got twelve of the world's most powerful leaders locked in a room forced to watch a video on replay."

"What video?" If there was footage that could give me insight into the perpetrator's nonverbal cues, it could help us.

"Hold on a second, let me transfer this to a video call and you can see for yourself."

Manny shook his phone at Francine and looked at the television. "Can you get this up there?"

Francine didn't answer him. She turned towards her laptop and a few seconds later a shaky image displayed on the screen. I gasped.

Gallo was facing the camera, looking healthier than he'd been since he'd arrived at Rousseau & Rousseau two days ago. He was wearing the same suit, but it fitted him much better. He paused, his smile smug. "And that is why you are here."

"This is the end of the loop." Privott's voice sounded over the speakers. "It will start again."

It did. The perverse pleasure displayed on Gallo's face

made me feel sick. "Hello, leaders of the world. My name is Marcus Gallo. Hmm... I wonder if the Italian president already knows that. I don't think so. Don't worry, Madame President. You're not the reason you are here, watching me. You can blame your vice-president for that. That son of a bitch. You see, if he hadn't put out a call for my assassination, none of this would have taken place."

He laughed and shrugged. "Maybe it would have. But I would not have been here. You see, an old friend of mine I knew from my youth alerted me to this price on my head. He was approached first because he's been known to eliminate elements causing problems for politicians. Your Vice-President Lucetti wanted me gone because I have evidence of his co-operation with Russian human traffickers. But I'm not going to bore you. Doctor Genevieve Lenard will fill you in on those details, I'm sure."

Dark panic pressed down hard on my chest. Gallo had planned everything. Us discovering his computer and the files implicating the vice-president, his illness sending him to the same hospital where the leaders were. Everything. Colin's hand took mine and I clutched it. I could not afford to give in to the safe shutdown beckoning me.

Onscreen, Gallo straightened his shoulders, all his nonverbal cues communicating confidence. "When my friend told me that my days were numbered, he showed me the evidence and made sure I understood that if he wasn't going to kill me, someone else would come along to do it. But I would be dead soon or looking over my shoulder until I was dead. So he offered me the opportunity to make my death count. What better way to go than to leave a legacy behind?

"What legacy, you might ask? Well, right now, a few of you might begin to feel a bit sick. You see, the stomach is the most sensitive to radiation poisoning. But this is only phase one. Even though we planned everything down to the finest detail, we wanted to make sure that there was a failsafe. If my favourite doctor was able to stop the polonium-210 from reaching you, we have another little surprise in store for you."

Gallo gave a dramatic pause and leaned forward. "You think you are all so well-protected. Well, you aren't. You have pissed off many of your closest allies with your decisions and it really wasn't hard to find a traitor. Especially when we offered him a healthy bonus. You and your secrets. Hah! If you are watching this, it means that we were successful in penetrating even your closest circles and finding out where this meeting was held despite your numerous attempts to feed us misinformation.

"This will be my legacy. One person was responsible for destroying my business, my family and my peaceful life. *I* will be responsible for destroying the leadership of the most powerful countries in the world and showing the world how vulnerable their leaders are. And how volatile any peace agreement is."

He leaned back, the smug smile at the end of the video pulling at the corners of his mouth. "Can you imagine the chaos the world economy will be dumped into with your deaths? Or the aggressive action your countries will take to reassert their power?" He laughed. "Oh, by dying today, you are giving me the gift of going down in history as the man who changed post-9/11 history." He gave the final pause. "And that is why you are here."

"Holy mother of all the saints!" Manny rubbed his hands hard over his face. "Privott, where are the presidents' security details?"

"Not here. Once the leaders were settled in the conference room, they were sent to another room to wait. If you're saying that we are locked in, then they must also be locked in."

I turned to Francine. "Can you access the security ca…"

She already had the feeds of the cameras in the lower level up on the television screen. Manny pointed at one. "There. Bring that one up."

Francine did as he asked and Serge swore. "Are they dead?"

I counted fifteen men on the ground, not moving. Roxy stepped closer to the screen and stared at it. Curls flew around her face when she shook her head. "They're breathing. They're not dead."

"Not yet." Vinnie walked right up to the screen and pointed to cables lying on the ground. He looked at Serge. "Should those be there?"

"No."

"Manny, what are you talking about? I can't see what you see." Privott paused. "I'm putting you on speakerphone. The presidents would like to be kept informed."

Vinnie and Serge leaned away from the phone, but Manny didn't flinch. "All the men are unconscious in a room two doors down from you. They're not dead, but they are surrounded by some kind of cables."

"What cables?" The voice coming over the phone had a strong American accent.

Manny looked at Vinnie. "Well?"

Vinnie glared at the phone in Manny's hand, then shrugged and turned his attention back to the television screen. "I can't see what they are. But you see that?" He pointed at an empty box lying close to the door. "That's for a detonator."

"A detonator?" President Godard's voice was easy to recognise. "Can you see if there are any explosive devices in that room or anywhere else on this floor?"

Manny and Serge stood closer to the screen, searching every corner of that room. Manny turned to Francine. "Show us the hallway."

She put the footage from the four cameras in the hallway on the screen. Vinnie's muscles tightened and with his index finger he drew a line along the wall. "That cable is running from the room with the bodyguards to the conference room. Franny, do we have cameras in the conference room?"

"No."

"That room is the only one on the lower level without cameras." Serge stared with wide eyes at the screen. "We did that for confidentiality reasons."

Manny lifted the phone towards him. "Privott, show us the room."

"Do it." President Godard's tone allowed for no disagreement.

Francine changed the view on the television back to Manny's phone. Privott first aimed his phone at the twelve leaders. The eleven men and one woman all looked concerned, but I didn't see any panic on their faces. These were people who'd had to deal with numerous emergency situations, making hard decisions on a moment's notice. I didn't want their jobs.

The view shifted to the left and slowly Privott moved around the room showing us every space. I saw it first. "Stop. There. What is that?"

"What's what, Doc?"

I pointed at the serving station close to the door. It was a beautiful wooden buffet table with crystal glass plates holding a large variety of snacks. None of those were healthy. It appeared as if someone had gone to the local corner store and bought bags of chips, chocolates and other plastic-wrapped foods. To the left were rows of water bottles and cans of soft drinks. There was no coffee, tea or any fresh foods.

But that wasn't what had caught my attention. "There are a few cables running from the door to behind the table."

"Bloody hell." Manny turned to Vinnie. "What do you think?"

Vinnie leaned towards the phone. "Privott, don't move anything at all, but see if you can give me a view behind that fancy table."

"Um… I don't…"

"I'll do it." The male voice with the Russian accent had to belong to the Russian president.

The image shook for a few seconds, then was pointed at the back of the table. It was too dark to see the cables. At first I thought it could be my imagination, but the second time the red light flickered against the white wall, my grip on Colin's hand tightened. "What is that light?"

"I also saw it," the Russian president said. "Do you want me to have a closer look?"

"No." Daniel stepped closer to the phone. "Don't touch

anything. Slowly and carefully step away from that table. I suggest everyone move to the opposite wall and barricade yourselves behind as many tables as you can put between you and that buffet table."

The sound of retching came over the phone and the image swung towards the leaders. The Italian president, the only woman in the group, was leaning against the wall, heaving.

"Is this the radiation poisoning that Gallo person has been talking about?" The British prime minister glanced at the television showing Gallo repeating his gleeful monologue.

"I can't be sure." I frowned. "Did anyone drink or eat anything from the buffet table?"

"I did," the Italian president said as she slowly straightened. "I had water."

"So did I." The German chancellor pulled at his collar. "Have I also been poisoned?"

"There is no way to be sure now." Daniel's tone was filled with authority. "Our priority now is to get away from the bomb. I'm working on getting everyone out of there as soon as possible. Right now, I want everyone to go to the other wall, behind as many tables as possible."

"I'm going to disconnect to save battery power." Privott appeared on screen as he held his hand out to take his phone from the Russian president. "I only have one bar left and my charger is in the other room."

"Text me as soon as everyone is safe behind the tables."

"Will do."

The call disconnected and Manny turned to Vinnie. "You know Fradkov and you know Claude. Are they going to blow this place up?"

Vinnie scratched his chest where his scar was hidden by his shirt. "That's Claude's style. As far as I know Fradkov is usually more subtle."

"What should we do about the patients?" Serge asked. "We don't know how much damage that bomb is going to cause to the structure of the building."

"We can't evacuate," Vinnie said. "Not while we're locked inside."

"Holy hell!" Manny rubbed his hands over his face. "Daniel, order the bomb squad here."

"They're already en route." Daniel put his phone back in one of the side pockets in his uniform. "But they will need to get into the hospital."

Manny grunted. "Supermodel, do you have control of the hospital yet?"

Everyone looked at Francine as she worked furiously on her laptop. She shook her head. "Not yet. Just give me a few more minutes."

"We don't have that much time."

Urgent beeping sounded from outside the room. Roxy swung around. "That's an alarm. It only goes off when life-support equipment malfunctions."

More alarms sounded and running footsteps filled the hallway. Doctors and nurses yelled out orders, the sounds of panic triggering my own. I took a deep breath and exhaled in surprise when Isabelle Godard and her personal bodyguard Luc entered the room.

"Genevieve." Isabelle walked deeper into the room and I took a step back. There were too many people in the room. Luc was Isabelle's childhood friend and I'd met him a few times while I had lunch with the first lady. That didn't make me more comfortable with his presence in the room.

The panicked sounds of doctors and nurses trying to keep their patients alive without the help of medical equipment pushed at me. I took another step back, unable to focus on how to stop the bomb from exploding in the downstairs room with twelve world leaders. I couldn't pull my mind back to anticipate Gallo's next step or how Claude would finish what Gallo had started or how Fradkov might fit into this.

Everything went dark.

I blinked when I realised the darkness wasn't my brain blocking out the looming danger. The large room we were in had been plunged into darkness, a lone red emergency exit light above the door flickering on and off. My heart rate increased exponentially and I didn't know if the darkness around me was from the lack of electrical lights or my shutdown enveloping me.

Chapter TWENTY-TWO

"We've gotta move." Luc grabbed Isabelle's arm and pulled her behind him. "We can't stay here."

"I agree." Daniel looked around the room and focused on me. "Are you good to go?"

I shook my head. I didn't want to go anywhere. I could hardly control my breathing.

"Which is the fastest way out of here?" Daniel asked and I assumed he was talking to Serge.

"The stairwell is to our right, but it is also controlled by the smart system," Serge answered. "It would also be locked."

"Bloody hell." Manny's pause gave me two seconds to focus on Colin's arms holding me tightly against his chest.

It took another second to unclench my fists and grab his arms. This grounded me enough to look around the room. It was not as dark as I'd thought. The eerie emergency light threw the entire room in a red glow, the light from Francine's laptop screen adding to it. Not once had she stopped working.

"Supermodel." Manny touched Francine's shoulder.

"Working on it, handsome."

"Work faster, Franny." Only Vinnie's silhouette was visible where he was standing. He was battle-ready.

Manny stepped away from Francine. "We've been working

on the assumption that if Claude was to make his move, it would be in another thirty minutes. Somehow he knew the leaders were meeting earlier and he's got a ticking bomb in there with them. *And* we have two poisoned presidents. We need to get our people in here. Now."

"We need to move." Luc was at the door, Isabelle's face looking even paler in the red glow.

Manny took a deep breath and I caught a glimpse of inner conflict on his face. "We're going to have to split up. Supermodel can't do her work on the move. Daniel, you, Frey and Luc can take Doc, Roxy and Madame Godard to the closest emergency exit. Serge, the big guy and I will stay with supermodel."

"I'm not leaving my patients." Roxy crossed her arms.

"We have Serge to help us here with the hospital layout. You're the only other person who can help Doc and Madame Godard find the exit."

Roxy dropped her arms. "Fine, I'll do it."

"Jenny?" Colin relaxed his arms around me and panic immediately rushed at me.

I focused on my breathing and forced my legs to move towards the door. I hated Manny's plan, but saw the logic in it. I hated it even more when Daniel and Luc took their weapons from their holsters, their body language changing to that only seen in a combat situation.

Daniel held out his handgun to Colin. "In case."

Colin blinked twice before he took the weapon with an ease developed from familiarity. The only solace I found in this situation was that I knew how much Colin hated firearms.

Luc glanced out into the hallway and looked back at us. "Daniel and I'll go first. The women follow tight behind me. Frey, right?" He didn't wait for Colin to nod. "You'll bring up the rear. Be alert and stay safe."

Daniel took position in front of Luc and waited until Luc tapped him on his shoulder. Isabelle had a firm grip on the back of Luc's trousers and stayed very close to him as we went into the hallway. Roxy's body language loudly communicated her fear, but she stayed a step behind Isabelle.

I couldn't be that close to them. I needed at least fifty centimetres between me and Roxy, but was comfortable with Colin's arm around me. I was not as comforted by the gun in his other hand. The red emergency exit lights flashed along the hallway, casting everything in a light that did nothing to ease my mind.

The last two rooms on this floor were empty. We were moving away from the anxious shouts of the doctors and nurses as they continued their lifesaving care. It felt as if my heart was beating in my ears as we rushed to the end of the hallway. We stopped at the last door. Daniel tried to open it, but the door didn't budge. He dropped to his knees and looked at the lock. He glanced at Luc. "I can't pick this."

Luc turned to Roxy. "Is there liquid nitrogen on this floor?"

"Um, yes." Roxy pointed at one of the empty rooms. "It's in there. We use it for removing malignant skin lesions."

"Let's get it."

"I'll go with you." Daniel got up and lifted his weapon as they approached the room. He held out his other hand to stop Roxy from entering the room. He went into the room and came back a few seconds later, nodding for Roxy to follow him. A minute later they came out, Roxy carrying a small silver canister.

Luc took it from her and aimed it at the door lock. He sprayed the liquid onto and into the lock until I was sure the canister was empty. He stood back and Daniel was there with a fire extinguisher. He aimed it at the lock and hit it with a force that made me take a step back. The lock shattered and the door swung open.

Daniel stepped into the stairwell, grunted and disappeared. Luc took one step, Isabelle right behind him. As Luc's leg lifted to take another step, his body tensed and a loud bang came from the stairwell. Luc fell to the ground, pulling Isabelle down with him.

"Luc!" She pulled her hand from his belt and turned him over. "No! No. Luc!"

A man stepped into the hallway and grabbed Roxy's wild curls. She screamed and fought hard to escape the firm grip on her hair. He pulled her tight against his chest and pressed a large weapon against her head. The moment the barrel of the gun pushed against her temple, she ceased her frantic fighting and stilled. The man moved out of the shadows and kicked Luc's gun away from him. It slid across the smooth hospital floor into the room Roxy and Daniel had just been in.

I couldn't believe this was happening. Not again.

I didn't want a life where I was facing violence on such a frequent basis. Analysing data, finding criminal activity from the safety of my viewing room was one thing. Looking at the barrel of an assault rifle aimed at an innocent woman and wondering if Daniel was still alive was something completely different.

"Put it down or she dies." The man shifted around and I saw the tattoo on his arm. Darkness crept closer, inviting me to disappear in its warm safety, but I resisted. I took a deep breath, looked up at his face and saw his light hair, the freckles on his nose. Claude. He shook Roxy, her curls flying around. "Put it down now or she gets it."

I didn't understand what he wanted until Colin slowly leaned forward and put the gun Daniel had given him on the floor.

"Kick it away from you." Claude nodded when Colin did as he asked. He looked at Isabelle as she was pressing her hand against a bleeding wound on Luc's shoulder. "Madame President. Get up. Get up!"

Isabelle looked at Claude, anger twisting her mouth. She must have seen the cold brutality on Claude's face and slowly got up. She wiped both hands on her white overcoat, staining it with Luc's blood. A shudder shook my body. I tried to dissociate myself from what was happening, but couldn't. I wasn't even able to call up one of my favourite Mozart compositions to calm my mind.

Claude kept his hold tight on Roxy and pointed his weapon at Isabelle's face. "Anyone moves and Madame President's brains will be all over these walls." Claude's smile was genuine when he looked at me. "Genevieve Lenard. It's a pleasure to meet you. I've heard so many good things about you."

I didn't know if I should respond or what I should say, so I kept quiet. He winked at me and released Roxy. "Don't go anywhere, curls. I'll shoot the president's pretty wife if you even think of running."

His hand disappeared for a second and came back holding another weapon, trained on the back of Roxy's head. He looked at me, then at Colin. "Where are the others? I know the old man and that giant are also here."

Colin hesitated and Claude pushed the gun harder against Roxy's skull. Her eyes widened, fear flooding her face. Colin put both hands up. "Okay, okay. They're in a room behind us."

"Let's go visit them." He tilted his head and narrowed his eyes. "You better not be playing me, pretty boy. I've been waiting a long time to kill the president's wife. You'll just make it happen much faster. But not before I finish what I started when I hacked your car. I was annoyed that I wasn't able to eliminate you and Genevieve from interfering with my plans then. I'll do it now if you're playing me."

Colin raised his hands even further. "No games. They're in the room and there's another man with them."

I wondered why Colin would tell Claude Serge was in the room with Manny and Vinnie. And why he would leave out Francine's name.

"Well then. Move along." Claude pushed his guns against Roxy and Isabelle. "You go first and we'll follow."

I didn't want to turn my back on that man, but Colin left me no choice. He pulled me against his side and pushed me towards the large room. Even though his muscles were tense, his facial expression concerned, he was not as alarmed as I would've expected in this situation.

The eighteen metres back to the room felt like a ten-kilometre hike. Every step was excruciating, knowing that we were bringing danger to Manny, Vinnie and Francine. I reached into my mind for ideas how to stop this, but faced only blankness. Combat situations like this were not my forte. I didn't know what to do and that feeling was most bewildering.

We reached the room and I entered it with a reluctance bordering on paralysing terror. Manny looked up from where he was sitting at the desk and frowned. "Doc? What are you doing here?"

"I'm sorry, Manny." I felt responsible for not stopping Claude.

"What the hell?" Manny jumped up from his seat, his weapon drawn. Serge and Vinnie reacted as well, drawing their weapons and training them on Claude as he pushed Isabelle and Roxy into the room in front of him.

"Well, hello, everyone." Claude stopped two feet into the room. "Before you heroes get any ideas with those guns, just ask yourself if you want to risk these two women's lives."

"Who are you?" Serge glanced from Claude to Roxy to Isabelle and back. "What do you want?"

Claude ignored Serge's demands. He was standing with his back to the door, the emergency exit light throwing his face into shadow. It made it hard to read his facial expressions. But his cold tone was unmistakeable. "If you want these two lovely ladies to live another minute, I suggest you slowly put your weapons on the floor and kick them over to me. Now!"

His loud order startled Roxy and she blinked a few times while taking shuddering breaths. Isabelle was clenching her teeth, her posture stiff as if she was controlling her emotions at a great cost. Serge was the first to react to Claude's order. He raised both hands and held his handgun lightly between two fingers. Manny glared at him and did the same. Both men lowered their weapons to the floor, keeping their movements slow and non-threatening.

It was only then that I realised Francine and her laptop weren't in the room with us. Panic settled around my throat like a noose and I struggled to breathe. Where was my best friend? My attention hadn't been on the room when we'd made our way to the stairwell, so it was possible that she'd gone somewhere else. I immediately dismissed that idea. Manny and Vinnie would never have let her go anywhere alone.

I took a moment to assess the situation and realised that Vinnie, Manny and Serge had placed themselves in such a way that Claude would not have a view of the washroom door. Could she be in there? Relief at that prospect warred with the dismay at the unhygienic environment into which she had taken her computer. I would have to ask her to disinfect that laptop if she ever wanted me to touch it again.

I shook my head to remove this irrational thought and looked at Vinnie. This was the situation I had dreaded from the moment I'd learned the role Claude and Emad had played in my friend's life. The pallor of Vinnie's face, his tightly pressed lips and flared nostrils were only a few of the nonverbal cues communicating his internal struggle. He was showing the restraint that I had wondered about, but it was not easy for him. The pure hatred and rage radiating from his body language left no doubt as to his feelings towards Claude.

"You too." Claude looked at Vinnie and pushed the gun against Roxy's skull. "Drop your weapon now or she goes!"

Vinnie's face paled even more and he slowly followed Manny and Serge's examples. Unlike the other men's movements, Vinnie's were stiff almost to the point of being clumsy. He kicked his handgun across the floor until it stopped a metre in front of Roxy's feet. He straightened and glared at Claude.

"Hey." Claude narrowed his eyes and stared at Vinnie. Then his eyebrows rose and again his smile was genuine. "Hey, I know you! You were supposed to die."

Vinnie's *masseter* muscles bulged on the sides of his jaw and his lips completely disappeared. The paleness of his face didn't come from fear, it was from a fury that I didn't know how much longer he could leash. Still, he didn't respond.

"Yeah." Claude nodded happily. "Yeah, I remember. You had that kid in your bed and she got her number punched. It was supposed to be you. Emad had a hard time finding your crib. I didn't have such a hard time putting that bomb under your bed. Expected you to buy it. Yeah. I never did a kid before that. Or after for that matter." He paused to think. "But I would again if I had to."

Vinnie didn't take his eyes off Claude. "Her name was Becks."

"Oh." He shrugged. "I don't care. Now I want all the men to get on your knees. Including you, pretty boy." He looked at Colin. "On your knees, cross your legs behind you and put both hands on your head. Only Genevieve gets to watch this while standing."

Manny gave Vinnie a warning look before both of them

went onto their knees. Colin breathed loudly through his nose as he lowered himself to the floor. He held his body still, communicating harmlessness with his body language. He was convincing.

"You're not going to get out of this alive." Serge was still standing, his posture defiant. "You're not getting away with this."

Claude tilted his head to one side and looked at Serge as if he was a curious specimen. The slight increase in his shoulder muscle tension was the only warning I got before he moved the gun from behind Roxy's head and shot Serge in his thigh.

Serge fell to the floor with a loud grunt, gritting his teeth. His gun slid away from him, out of reach. He rolled to his side and grabbed his thigh with both hands. Claude returned the gun to Roxy's head, looked at me and shrugged. "I don't like him."

Roxy was looking at Serge's wound with an intensity becoming a doctor reacting to an emergency situation. Three seconds later, her body language relaxed marginally. She must have determined that Serge had not been critically wounded.

Claude's confidence and the calm manner with which he'd shot Serge intrigued me. A man without much empathy for others, but feeling wronged by so many people was easily diagnosed as a psychopath. It interested me that Gallo, Claude and Emad—three men with similar psychological profiles—had combined forces to bring about a plan as convoluted as this.

I kept my focus on studying Claude's behaviour, analysing

it. Manny's worried glances towards Vinnie and Colin also gave my mind a plethora of information to process. If I didn't analyse everything happening at the moment, I would give in to the darkness that was now permanently on the outer borders of my vision.

Manny turned his head slightly to hide his left ear from Claude's line of sight. Vinnie had done the same. It would be logical to deduce that Vinnie was trying to prevent Claude from seeing his GIPN earpiece. Could it be that Manny also had one?

Vinnie remained unmoving, but once in a while Manny's blinking would increase. I hated not knowing what was being communicated to them, but I needed to keep Claude's attention focused on me if the GIPN team was nearby and the bomb squad could gain access to the building.

I took a step forward and ignored Colin's grunt. "What do you want?"

Claude gave Serge one last look of disgust and turned his attention to me. "Gallo told me that you see the truth behind everything we do and say. He told me that I shouldn't try to trick you. So I'll tell you the truth." He pushed the gun so hard against the back of Isabelle's head that her neck bent forward at an awkward angle. "Killing Madame President is a little bonus I'm giving myself. The real payoff is showing the world what a lying swine her husband is."

He eased the pressure against Isabelle's head and she slowly straightened, the corners of her mouth turned down, her lips in a thin line. Claude smiled. "I also want to show the world what a laughable hypocrite my father is and how gullible the UN and a long list of governments have been to believe his crap." He tilted his head. "And of course, I want to kill you."

"Me or all of us?"

"Just you. I get paid for two things. To transport shit from one country to another and to kill people. What? You didn't know that? It's true. I discovered that pleasure when some moron tried to stop me moving fifty kilograms of heroin." His expression softened at the memory. I was horrified to see the truth in everything he said. He sighed with contentment. "You know what fascinates me even more? How avidly my victims listen when I tell them why they're going to die."

"You've had a conversation like this with everyone you've killed." And he most likely had enjoyed watching his victims' fear grow as he tortured them psychologically.

Claude glanced up and left, recalling a memory. "Yeah. Yeah, I have."

"Are you going to tell me why you're going to kill me?"

"Of course." His tone implied I'd been simple-minded to ask that question. "It's a tribute to Gallo. You see, he's the reason all this fell into place. He contacted Emad for transport to Europe after we did the diamond deal with him. That's when Emad decided to have a deeper look into Gallo. Most times I shout at Emad when he doesn't leave the computer and internet stuff to me, but this time I didn't mind when his search into Gallo triggered some alarm.

"Fradkov was looking for Gallo and Emad's search had sent Fradkov our way to find out why we were looking into Gallo. At first, Gallo threatened us with slow deaths, but when the plan started coming together, he was also happy to reunite with his old pal." He looked around the room, his eyes lingering on Vinnie before he returned his attention to me. "I think that I'll also finish what I started with scarface over there. And knowing myself, I'll just do everyone then. I'm like that. I like to do a thorough job."

"Is this all Gallo's planning?" I wondered how far I could push Claude.

"It's our plan." This time his smile held nostalgia. "Gallo is a visionary. Everything he predicted has happened. He planned for everything. Even his contingency plans have contingency plans. He and Fradkov really are amazing. Gallo might've pissed Fradkov off with veering off plan when he hacked that Sartre guy's car."

"Gallo hacked that car?" I didn't believe it. Gallo had been in Rousseau & Rousseau during that event.

"Not himself, no. I did that. I didn't mind setting it up when Gallo asked me to do this. I love technology. Such fun." He laughed. "Fradkov was so pissed! The only reason he didn't kill Gallo sooner was... well, the plan we had, but also Gallo gave him two old paintings. I don't get it, but Fradkov immediately forgave Gallo when he saw those paintings. They're shit-ugly things, but hey, I'm not going to judge."

"If your plan is to kill me, why haven't you killed me yet?" I held up my hand to stop him from answering. "And if your plan is to expose President Godard and your father for whatever crimes you believe they have committed, why haven't you done it yet?"

The one-second hesitation was telling. "How do you know I'm not busy doing it right now?"

"You're not." I made sure my smile was condescending. "You were part of Gallo's plan. You just didn't see it. You were too busy enjoying the hunt, enjoying instilling fear and anticipating this moment. Tell me, what was Gallo's great plan for exposing the president?"

"I gathered all the intel. It will be sent to all the news outlets together with a document detailing all the immoral deals, agreements and trades Godard has made in the last four years. He and all the other western leaders need to be held responsible for their colonial paternalism, their ridiculous belief that France is the only nation that truly understands being civilised. I've got enough evidence to put an end to their attitude of entitlement and superiority. WikiLeaks will look like a tabloid compared to this."

Again, Manny's blinking increased. First, his muscle tension decreased, then he rolled his shoulders, his body ready to act at any moment. Vinnie's reaction mirrored Manny's, but was more subtle. His underlying anger masked most other nonverbal cues. I didn't know what was happening and it increased my distress exponentially. I forced my mind back to Claude.

"Who is going to send all that information? You?" I looked around the room. "I don't see your computer. I don't see you sending these so-called documents. You have considerable IT skills. Did you double-check what Gallo was doing? Or did he successfully manipulate you into believing that he was going take care of everything?"

"Nobody manipulated me!" He shook one of the guns at me. "*You* are trying to, but you're not going to succeed. Gallo and I both worked on those documents. I wrote the code to encrypt the files and he set it up to send everything an hour from now."

I schooled my face into disbelief. "I don't believe you. Gallo would not have trusted anyone else to encrypt sensitive files. He would've done it all himself."

Claude inhaled deeply, then held his breath and tilted his head. "Are you fucking with me, Genevieve? Are you trying to make me angry?"

"No. I'm trying to understand why you are talking to me. Why you are not acting." Realisation came to me. "You want to witness the explosion."

"Gallo was right again. You really are smart."

"And it appears he was not that smart." I took a step to the left to prevent Claude from seeing Vinnie trying to communicate with Roxy. I wondered if she understood his pointed eye movements. "Gallo's in a coma with only a few hours to live, which means he cannot bring your plan to fruition. Your brother is in police custody. That leaves you and this inane conversation. Do you see a way out of this room? Out of this building? Surely you know how many armed and trained people would be here today."

"Ah, but that's part of the plan. Emad is no longer in custody and he has all the leftover polonium-210. My brother is untouchable." His smug smile turned into triumph when a loud explosion rocked the hallway.

Then everything happened at once.

Roxy dropped to the floor and in one motion grabbed Vinnie's pistol, twisted and fired continuously. My hands flew to my ears to block the loud blast of each shot as it entered Claude's torso. Vinnie yelled and dove towards Roxy.

Manny ran to Isabelle and tackled her to the floor, placing his body over hers.

Daniel and another team member stormed in, their assault rifles at the ready as they swept the room. I couldn't move. My hands were pressed tightly over my ears, but the chaotic yelling still reached my overstimulated senses.

"Clear!" Daniel kicked both weapons away from Claude's body. "All clear."

"The leaders?" Manny asked.

"Being escorted to safety as we speak." Daniel moved his assault rifle to hang down his back. "The bomb squad has disabled the bomb."

I stared at the holes in Claude's light blue shirt and the red stain growing until it spilled over onto the floor. Darkness closed in on me and I tried to push back. I needed to know everyone was unharmed. Manny got up and helped Isabelle to stand. Fear was undisguised on her face and increased when her eyes found mine.

"What the fuck did you do?" Vinnie grabbed Roxy by her shoulders and shook her. "I signalled you to drop! Not to kill that motherfucker! You weren't supposed to do that! He was mine!"

Roxy looked at Claude for a long time, her expression changing from horror to guilt to determination. She turned to Vinnie, tears pooling in her eyes. "I'm sorry."

Vinnie shook her again. "Don't say that. Don't you ever be sorry. Do you hear me?"

"Jenny?" Colin touched my forearm and I jerked away. Most times his warm touch calmed me. My mind had received far too much stimulation. Anything else was going to send me into the shutdown I was trying to avoid. He didn't touch my arm again, but stood close to me, making sure not to crowd me. "We're all okay. See?"

The washroom door opened and Francine stood there, her laptop tucked under her arm, looking around the room with concern. Her shoulders lowered with relief when she looked me up and down and her eyes connected with Manny's. "Now you can call me queen of all interwebs with a porcelain throne."

She was safe. Everyone was safe.

Somehow it was the sound of the toilet flushing that was too much for me. I sank down onto the unsanitary hospital floor and let the darkness take me.

Chapter TWENTY-THREE

"That bloody Privott!" Manny stormed into my apartment, his face red. Francine walked in behind him, her face a comic attempt to suppress laughter. Colin frowned when Manny shoved a bottle of red wine at him. "Take this. I swear that man is going out of his way to piss me off."

"What happened?" Colin looked at the label on the bottle and lifted one eyebrow. "Supermarket wine? You couldn't go cheaper, Millard?"

"Bugger off, Frey." Manny walked to the sitting area and nodded a greeting at Phillip. "What was your impression of Privott?"

"I thought he was courteous and professional." Phillip had arrived with Nikki an hour ago. He'd insisted on accompanying her to the hospital to be tested for polonium-210 poisoning.

I was glad Phillip had been there to support Nikki, since it had taken me an hour and twenty-two minutes to come out of my shutdown. Apparently, I had allowed Colin to carry me to the safety of the GIPN operational truck where I'd spent that time curled into myself on one of the chairs.

The rest of the afternoon and early evening had been taken up with ensuring that the leaders were indeed safe and Gallo had no other contingency plans to take revenge on me or anyone else.

I had been relieved to learn that the loud explosion hadn't been another bomb, but a flash grenade GIPN had used as a distraction. When Daniel had entered the stairwell, Claude had hit him hard over the head. Daniel had tumbled down the stairs and had two broken ribs to show for it, but was not seriously injured. When he'd regained consciousness, he'd heard our discussion on his earpiece and had decided to find a way to get his team inside the hospital.

My suspicion that Manny had also had a GIPN earpiece was confirmed, but I was surprised to learn that Daniel had given Colin one as well. If it weren't for my concerns about hygiene, I might insist on having one if ever we were in a similar situation. The lack of information had exacerbated my panic. I was just relieved that Daniel had been able to hear what was happening in the room and had been able to make the right decision by gaining access into the hospital for his team.

He'd just reached the exit when Francine had sent him an SMS that she'd been able to open the doors. Three GIPN teams had entered the hospital. Daniel's team had come to our rescue, the other two had gone straight to the lower level. As soon as they'd secured the leaders, the bomb squad had moved in to disable what had turned out to be a simple bomb. Vinnie had speculated that Claude had not been as prepared for the earlier meeting as he had implied.

The Italian president and the German chancellor had first been secured at a different location and then returned to Roxy's hospital for expert treatment. They had both tested positive for polonium-210 poisoning. The chancellor was not as sick as the Italian president. Roxy had told Francine she didn't know if the Italian president was going to make it. I worried about the effect it would have on world politics.

When I'd spoken to Isabelle, she'd mentioned the pressure on her husband to explain why he'd insisted on having as little as possible security at the hospital. His reasoning that it would've attracted attention and possible enemy action wasn't being accepted. Nor the fact that they'd arranged for her visit at the hospital as an excuse to take extra security measures. There was a lot of animosity coming from the other countries, especially Germany and Italy.

On top of that, Claude had succeeded in sending damning evidence to numerous media outlets about President Godard. Isabelle had told me that her husband's staff had already proven thirty percent of the claims to be false, but the damage was done. She'd sounded tired and extremely concerned about her husband and their future as leaders.

Daniel had also told us that Luc, Serge and Émile's associate Bruno were going to make full recoveries. I would inquire about Bruno's health again when Vinnie, Colin and I had brunch with Émile next weekend.

Manny's grunt brought me back to the present. "Courteous? Privott must be nice to you because you wear smart suits."

Phillip laughed. "Or maybe it's because I'm courteous to him."

"I don't have time to make nice when I'm on a deadline." Manny sat down and looked around. "Where's Nikki?"

"Powdering her nose."

"She's vomiting." I'd seen how pale she was when she'd entered the apartment.

"We don't usually share that with everyone." Phillip's smile softened his rebuke. "It might be true, but it might also be embarrassing for the other person."

"Who's embarrassed?" Nikki walked into the room and sat down next to Phillip, curling her legs under her.

I was relieved to see colour on her cheeks. "Phillip suggested that I might embarrass you by telling others that you were in your washroom vomiting."

She shrugged. "Nah, I'm not embarrassed. Just desperate for this morning sickness that doesn't really come in the mornings to stop."

"How're you feeling, Nix?" Francine sat down next to Manny and put her hand on his thigh.

"When I'm not tossing my cookies, I'm feeling like always. Except my boobies hurt."

Manny jumped up. "No! You don't say things like that in front of me. I don't need to know that."

Francine leaned forward and slapped her palm against Nikki's in a high five. For the first time since the hospital I relaxed. I couldn't stop the small smile lifting the corners of my mouth when I saw Manny's embarrassment. "Nikki told you about her breasts because she knew she would get that reaction from you."

"Bloody hell, missy." Manny leaned away from me. "You're making it worse."

"Oh, no, Jen-girl. You're making it better." Vinnie was stirring a stew that he'd promised would only take another five minutes before we could eat. I was hungry.

A knock on my front door stopped all banter. Manny took his handgun from his hip holster and walked to the door. Vinnie was already halfway there, lifting the back of his t-shirt and drawing his weapon. Manny reached the door first and looked through the peephole. His head jerked back and he opened the door. "Who invited you?"

"You are such a grumpy Smurf. Manny, the grumpy Smurf. Or is it grouchy? It is! You're Manny, the Grouchy Smurf." Roxy looked past Manny into my apartment and waved at Vinnie. "Hi! I brought cake."

"Let her in, old man." Vinnie pushed Manny away from the door and waved Roxy in. "Dinner is almost ready."

She exhaled in an exaggerated gesture of relief as she walked towards the kitchen. "Oh, good. I thought I was late."

Vinnie followed her and looked at his watch. "You *are* late."

"Stop harassing the woman." Francine got up and walked to the kitchen. "Ignore them, Roxy. Put the cake on the counter. Red or white?"

"Red, please." Roxy placed a large cake tin on the counter and turned around. Her eyes widened when she noticed everyone else. "How rude of me. Hi, everyone. I'm Roxy."

"You're Roxy?" Nikki jumped up and rushed to the kitchen, her hand stretched out. "I'm Nikki."

"You're the pregnant fairy!" Roxy pushed Nikki's hand out of the way and pulled her into a hug. "Congratulations."

"Um. Thank you." Nikki returned the hug, then stepped back. She inspected Roxy from her boot-cut jeans to her flowy, colourful top and stopped at her hair. She reached for a curl. "Oh, my God. I love, love, love your hair."

Roxy gave a most unfeminine snort-laugh and accepted a glass of red wine from Francine. "Glad you do. There's no taming this mop."

"It does look very unkempt." My comment did not have a positive outcome. Nikki turned to me and widened her eyes in some kind of warning. Francine tried to hide a shocked laugh by pretending it was a cough and Vinnie glared at me. I studied Roxy's expression. "You're not offended. Why is everyone else cautioning me? Did I err in commenting on the state of your hair?"

When Roxy laughed, her head tilted back, her cheeks lifted until her eyes were almost closed and the light, happy sound of it affected everyone. All frowns were replaced by smiles. Roxy stepped towards me. "Hi, Genevieve. I was hoping to see you again at the hospital, but things got really crazy. I'm glad to see you're okay. Oh, and about my hair? Nothing you say about this craziness on my head will offend me. Except if you want me to change it. I've grown to like this craziness."

I thought about this and nodded after a few seconds. "I can accept that."

"Doctor Ferreira." Phillip stepped closer and took Roxy's hand in his. "It's truly a pleasure. I'm Phillip Rousseau."

Roxy shook his hand warmly. "Please call me Roxy. The whole doctor thing is so ridiculously formal. Especially when I have good news."

"Ooh, I love good news." Francine's eyes were wide. "Spill."

"I put a rush on your tests." She looked at Nikki. "All your tests. Then had them double-checked. You're all clear. No radiation poisoning."

It felt as if a heavy weight lifted from my chest, even more so when I saw the relief on Nikki's face.

"I still want to know who invited you." Manny glanced at the cake tin, Vinnie, then back at Roxy. There was no animosity in his expression, just curiosity.

"I did." Vinnie took the pot from the stovetop and walked to the dining room table.

"No, I did." Francine slapped Vinnie's shoulder when he slapped her hand away from lifting the lid of the pot.

"As did I." Colin winked at me and sat down on his usual chair at the table. "Shall we?"

"Where do I sit?" Roxy waited until I pointed at the chair between Vinnie and Phillip, then sat down and wiggled in her chair. "You guys have no idea how cool it was to get so many invitations."

I sat down next to Colin and leaned towards him. "Should I also have invited her?"

"I think she got plenty of invites, love." Colin kissed my cheek and reached for the large salad bowl. It took five minutes for everyone to fill their plates with baked potatoes, stew and salad.

I tried hard, but when everyone started eating, I could no longer wait. "Manny, why were you so angry with Privott?"

Manny glanced at Roxy, narrowed his eyes for a second, then looked at me. "Did you know that Doctor Roxanne Ferreira has high-level clearance and that she's been working with the police, with the DGSE and Interpol on numerous cases?"

"I didn't know that."

Roxy shrugged and cut a potato in half. "That's what

happens when you choose to specialise in things that can be used as weapons."

"Huh. That means we can talk about secret stuff when you're around." Vinnie heaped stew on his fork and lifted it to his mouth. "Doesn't mean we trust you though."

"Vinnie!" Nikki elbowed him in his side. "That's rude."

"But true, Nikki." Manny stared at Roxy. "You ever break a confidence and I'll make sure you are completely discredited."

Roxy didn't look intimidated. She smiled at Manny, then turned to me and whispered loudly, "Nobody knows what happened to my youngest brother's blankie after he threw my Barbie in the toilet. And nobody will ever know. This wild-haired chick knows how to keep secrets."

I didn't know what to make of her outrageous story, except to analyse it the best I knew how. "She's being truthful."

Everyone laughed.

Manny pulled the pot with the stew closer. "Now that's settled, I'll tell you how I almost asked supermodel to digitally wipe Privott's bank account clean."

"You were going to ask me that?" Francine's eyebrows rose high on her forehead. "That's so illegal. And so sexy."

Manny ignored her. "I'm pissed off that Privott didn't tell us the moment he found out where the meeting was going to be held. If he had told us that earlier, you would've made the connection. Isabelle Godard told you that she was going to be in a hospital this weekend and you would immediately have put it all together. I'm meeting with the president, Privott and Chris Gosselin, the head of the GSPR, responsible for the president's safety, on Monday to deal with this. We could've stopped the leak before two leaders got poisoned and all of them were locked in a room with a bomb."

"What leak?" I didn't understand what was leaking.

"That means an insider was sharing the information, love." Colin winked at me.

"It also means that it's an insider who betrayed the trust given to him, Doc." Manny shook his head. "Privott mobilised a team very fast to get all the coffee and water delivered to Délicieux et Rapide, that catering place. They ran tests and couldn't find any radiation in the coffee or water. Nothing."

"But?" It was clear in his expression.

"They found it in the water on the buffet table. Those bottles were the same brand that the delivery truck was supposed to have delivered to the catering company."

"And the bastard who put the bottles on the table turned out to be a German bodyguard." Francine sighed. "He managed to get those bottles from the catering company into the very secure VIP conference room. I found him, even though it was too little, too late. He's the same person on the third recording who gave Claude the blueprints of the hospital. I found footage of the handoff between him and Claude. They were stupid enough to do it close to a jewellery store. The internal security cameras were fortunately strong enough to give us a really good look at both their faces. I then traced the payments this idiot got to one of the new accounts we found on Gallo's computer."

Guilt was clear on her features as she talked about belatedly finding the man. "He was one of the chancellor's bodyguards. It turns out that he's furious about the influx of immigrants and the dangers they pose to his beloved Germany. I checked some of his internet history and saw visits to neo-Nazi websites. Why it didn't raise red flags within the chancellor's security, I don't know."

"So it was Gallo who paid him, not the Vernet brothers." Colin's eyes narrowed. "He betrayed his country and possibly killed his chancellor because he doesn't like immigrants?"

"That and for money." Francine shrugged. "I looked at his finances. With the mountain of debt he'd had before he got his payment, money would make as much sense as his sick political beliefs."

"At least Gallo will no longer be empowering other criminals," Roxy said.

When Daniel had told me that Gallo had died shortly after the flash grenade had gone off, I had felt nothing but relief. But the far-reaching aftermath of his actions was going to change European politics. I wondered if Germany would still be as hostile towards President Godard when it came to light that it had been one of their own bodyguards who was responsible for the polonium-210 poisoning.

Something Gallo had said on his video bothered me. "How did Gallo and Fradkov know each other?"

"I'm not sure, Doc." Manny shrugged. "But I can imagine that their paths crossed when Fradkov was in Brazil. Just before he went to the US to study, he spent eighteen months in Rio de Janeiro. It's not impossible that they met there."

"I have a question." Roxy held her hand up as if she was in a classroom. She lowered her hand when everyone turned to her. "Why couldn't anyone else phone out from the conference room? Only that one man's phone worked."

"That's easy to answer." Some of the guilt left Francine's features. "Privott had two phones. One for emails and all other internet activity. The Bluetooth is also activated on that phone. The phone that he was able to use is his private phone for his family and closest friends. It's only for calls and SMSs. He disabled the internet and Bluetooth functions. Claude somehow managed to hack and block all phones that were connected to the internet or Bluetooth."

"But our phones worked," Roxy said.

"Because he limited it to the lower level. My guess is that with the security details unconscious and the presidents unable to phone anyone else, no one would be alerted to a problem. If the whole hospital suddenly couldn't use their phones, it would've made people take notice."

"Hmm." Roxy looked at Francine's phone and tablet lying next to her plate. "I'm thinking I might want to go back to paper letters. Or maybe smoke signals."

"Where is Emad?" When I had asked Daniel, he'd told me he would find out and let me know. He never had.

It became quiet around the table. Vinnie lost some of the colour in his face and his hands tightened around his utensils. Manny put his knife and fork down and rubbed both hands over his face before he turned to Vinnie. "He's in the wind."

"What the fuck, old man!" Vinnie's nostrils flared, his jaw working as if he was trying to stop the rage erupting from his lips. "He was in GIPN custody. What the fuck happened?"

"The DGSE happened." Manny looked just as angry as Vinnie. "Their bloody lawyer went to the GIPN offices and since the spy agency outranks the GIPN, they had to let Emad go. That would still have been bad enough, but then Emad slipped his DGSE tail."

Colin touched my forearm. "Someone from the DGSE was following Emad and he found a way to get away from them."

I nodded. "Have the DGSE found him on any of the city surveillance cameras? Airports, stations?"

"No." Manny shook his head.

"What about his father?" I wondered how Alain Vernet was handling the death of his oldest and only biological son.

"Alain has tendered his resignation, citing family obligations." Manny picked his utensils up again. "From what Privott says, the guy is out of his mind with guilt and grief."

Nikki pointed at my face in a manner I realised I usually did. "When your eyes get all squinty like that, you're worried about something."

Roxy leaned closer and stared at my face. "Good to know."

"Doc?"

I leaned away from Roxy and considered my words. "Claude said that Emad has more polonium-210. Apart from a few photos, we've not seen Fradkov even though we know he played a pivotal role in planning everything."

"And Émile said that Reiss told him it was a man with a Russian accent who told him to go to the warehouse." Vinnie glanced at Roxy. "We were sent into a trap that turned out to be a bomb."

"A Russian accent?" Colin asked. "Could it have been Fradkov?"

"That's what I'm thinking, dude. We didn't really have anyone else in this case with a Russian accent."

I didn't think the Russian president would phone Reiss to send Émile's people into a building with a bomb, so I didn't say anything.

"When did you speak to that criminal?" Manny scowled.

"He phoned when he heard about the hospital."

"Bloody hell!" Manny put his knife and fork down. "What did he hear? We've been keeping a very tight leash on the media about this. Everyone agreed that it would do nobody any good if the extent of this is made public."

Vinnie shrugged. "He didn't hear much except that there was a lot of activity around the hospital. He figured he would phone and find out if it had anything to do with why his people were blown up."

"Nobody was blown up." Not that I knew of.

"Sorry, Jen-girl. You're right." Vinnie speared a potato with his fork. "We need to find Emad and Fradkov before someone really gets blown up."

"I agree." Manny leaned back in his chair. "We haven't seen the end of Emad and Fradkov."

I was glad Manny had said the words I was loath to verbalise. "We need to put all our energy into finding Emad."

"There's a warrant out for his arrest and all agencies are on alert."

"They won't find him." Vinnie put his knife and fork down. "He's a fucking spy. He's trained to be invisible."

"But you'll find him, big punk." Nikki leaned against Vinnie and put her head on his shoulder. "All of you. This is the best team in the world."

"And this is the best stew I've ever had." Roxy pointed at the pot and waved it towards her. "More. I want more."

Some of the anger left Vinnie's eyes when he saw Roxy's genuine enthusiasm and impatience when Manny took too long to pass the pot to her. The rest of our dinner was interrupted only once when Nikki had to rush to the washroom. When she came back, she pushed her half-empty plate away and only had a glass of water.

I worried about her. Nikki was one of the most optimistic and caring people I'd ever met. She was also very sensitive. I didn't know what she was going to decide about her pregnancy and feared that I was ill-equipped to support whichever decision she made.

The last few days had presented no opportunities to think about the future, but I planned to fill my personal library with books on this topic. I needed to understand the many schools of thought on this matter so I could come to my own conclusions.

I wondered what conclusions Nikki would come to.

After dinner, Roxy presented her homemade cheesecake as if it were a Michelin-starred dish. She pretended to be offended when everyone laughed and teased her about the awful shape of the confection. Even I was surprised at the delicate taste of it and the perfect balance of sweetness and its smooth texture.

I watched Vinnie as he joked with Roxy and she shared her attention and affection freely with everyone. Despite her hair, I liked her. The last few days had been hard on Vinnie and a warm feeling flooded my chest every time he chuckled at Roxy's frequent inappropriate and irreverent comments.

I held onto that positive feeling to dispel the oppressive concern about Ivan Fradkov's plans for international political chaos and Emad Vernet dealing with the loss of his brother and the loss of his cover. I shuddered to think what the future might bring when those two men decided to take action.

Roxy found my music collection and decided that African tribal music would be perfect to show her uncoordinated dancing skills. She got Nikki to join her, but wasn't successful in getting Francine to pretend they were dancing around a fire in the jungle. Again, I focused on the laughter and the positive energy of this moment. I didn't know how long it would last.

~ ~ ~ ~ ~

Be first to find out when Genevieve's next adventure will be published.
Sign up for the newsletter at
http://estelleryan.com/contact.html

~~~~

Look at the paintings from this book
and read more about car hacking, Vecellio and polonium-210 at:
http://estelleryan.com/the-vecellio-connection.html

Other books in the Genevieve Lenard Series:

Book 1: The Gauguin Connection

Book 2: The Dante Connection

Book 3: The Braque Connection

Book 4: The Flinck Connection

Book 5: The Courbet Connection

Book 6: The Pucelle Connection

Book 7: The Léger Connection

Book 8: The Morisot Connection

Book 9: The Vecellio Connection

and more…

~ ~ ~ ~ ~

Please visit me on my Facebook Page to become part of the
process as I'm writing Genevieve's next adventure.
and
Explore my website to find out more about me and
Genevieve.